I HOPE TO
HAUNT YOU
Eternally

Also by Elisabeth Roberts Craft

A Spy for Hannibal

In the Court of the Queen

The Ambassador's Daughter

I Hope to Haunt You Eternally

A NOVEL

Elisabeth Roberts Craft

Bartleby Press
Washington • Baltimore

Bartleby Press

P.O. Box 858
Savage, MD 20763
1-800-953-9929
www.BartlebythePublisher.com

Library of Congress Cataloging-in-Publication Data

Craft, Elisabeth Roberts, 1918-2010
I hope to haunt you eternally : a novel / Elisabeth Roberts Craft.
p. cm.
ISBN 978-0-910155-79-3
1. Retired women--Fiction. 2. Law reporters--Fiction. 3. Chemical engineers--Fiction. 4. Engineers in government--Fiction. 5. Human experimentation in medicine--Fiction. 6. Washington (D.C.)--Fiction. I. Title.
PS3553.R213H67 2012
813'.54--dc22

2012030151

Printed in the United States of America

Prologue

A year ago, I bought a one-bedroom condo on the twelfth floor of a high rise. The smartest thing I ever did. Night after night, I holed up inside. My automobile was ensconced in its own little indoor parking space, no longer subject to weather conditions or difficult-to-find street parking.

My neighbors were pleasant enough when I met them in the corridor or on the elevator. Riding up and down, I got used to the faces of people getting off and on from other floors a well as my own. Many were elderly, but a few toddlers navigated between falls in the lobby area. The names escaped me, but we chatted amiably on nothing or everything. I just saw the working crowd, middle aged and young, early or late, rushing in or out, or at the mail boxes. A couple of the older women asked me if I wanted to join their bridge group. I thanked them, but had to admit that I didn't play bridge. Actually, I kept myself busy with volunteer work anyway.

Before too long, I became aware of an attractive young

woman, maybe middle twenties, going in and out of an apartment at the end of my corridor. Had she just moved in? I couldn't recall ever seeing her before. She had long blonde hair and a sweet smile. Intrigued, I began to watch her comings and goings, her friends and a nice looking, tall, dark-haired man. Somehow the idea of a boyfriend pleased me.

I met her in the laundry room one Saturday morning. She introduced herself as Eleanor. We compared notes on apartments, the number of rooms, and how long we had lived in the building—nothing special. I found her intelligent and pleasant. Then, for a stretch, I didn't run into her and forgot about her in my own busy spring activity.

Late one afternoon on a clear, sunny day, I stopped at a sidewalk café for some coffee. It had been a long day. I was tired. I sipped the hot coffee slowly, sighed with content and leaned back against the chair.

"Hi," a chipper young voice came from right behind me.

I turned my head around and met the sparkling blue eyes of my young corridor acquaintance. "Hello, "I said, smiling up at her. "What a nice surprise."

"May I sit with you?"

"By all means. Please do." I pulled my cup and pastry plate closer together and thought about her while she went into the shop and returned with a Coke, plus some kind of dip and chips.

As she sat down, she said, "I go to school across the street and needed a break before going into a speed class."

My mind gave a start. Speed class! What kind of school is that? "Really? What are you studying? I thought you told me you worked in an office," I added, puzzled.

"I do—to earn some money. But I study at the Court Reporting School across the street in the evening."

I almost fell off the chair, but managed to control myself before calmly saying, "How far along are you on speed? Have you passed the 125 words-per-minute test yet?"

She cast down her eyes and grinned. They were shining when she raised them to look at me.

I laughed and shook my head in amazement. "Eleanor, you'll never believe this. I did free-lance court reporting from 1957 until I retired in 1983. And that was over twenty-five years ago."

"You did?" she almost yelled, as she leaned towards me.

I kept shaking my head. "I'm having trouble believing this." Again, I laughed.

She laughed too. We sat there grinning at each other. Finally, she picked up the Coke straw, sipped, and looked at me. "Perhaps you could advise me. What speed do I need to be competent? What speed did you have?"

"162 words per minute."

She stared at me, an amazed expression on her face.

"Well, tell me what you plan to do. Will you go into the government court system, or start out on your own with one of the agencies?"

"Did you work for the government?"

"No, I worked out of an agency, but I also had clients of my own. I'll tell you right now that's harder than court work."

"Meaning?"

"In courts, you can stop the speaker if you don't catch what was said. Particularly with a sworn witness where every word is important. You can't do that in free-lance reporting, and it can get rough. Also the hours are much longer. You need a lot of stamina." I hesitated, fiddling with my coffee cup. "I understand court reporting today is much different than when I was in the business. Do you use the stenotype machine or a mask covering your mouth to record every word on a disk?"

"The stenotype."

"Good girl." I smiled, pleased. "I hated how the mask caused reporters to be plugged into the wall... My machine was metal, 8x12 inches more or less, with a tray that pulled out to receive the tape as I worked. The metal stand snapped onto the bottom of it, making the whole thing heavy." I stopped and looked at her.

She laughed. "It really is different. Mine is a sturdy plastic about half the size of the one you used and totally computerized. It not only records what I write, but takes down what the speaker says at the same time and sends the writing to the typewriter."

My mouth dropped open. "That's a totally different kind of reporting! Somehow that it cuts the need for a good vocabulary."

"I hate to admit that, but it's true. There are some people in my class who have barely graduated from high school. I don't know how some of them will manage."

"I'm appalled. That totally cuts out the professionalism of the older method of reporting."

"I heard one of the teachers say that the old type of reporter doesn't exist anymore." She lowered her eyes embarrassed.

"Please forgive me," I said, touching one of her hands that lay on the table. "That was very rude."

At that moment, a noise began to emanate from her

large purse. Eleanor deftly reached in, retrieved a phone, glanced at me and began typing on the small screen. I had been totally forgotten.

Suddenly, she became conscious of my annoyed look. "Oh, I'm sorry," she said, sheepishly putting the phone away. "I turned it off."

I nodded. "As I was about to say, forget the professionalism; it's a totally different kind of work in which I have no knowledge and can't advise you. From what you say, maybe it's all nine to five now. In that case, it wouldn't matter if you joined the government or wanted to freelance. You would have time to do other things, which I couldn't do when we were really busy." I smiled at her. "You'll have a much easier life."

"I want kids and would like to spend a lot of time with them. So I should probably look into applying for the court system. That might be better."

"I think, under the circumstances, you are making a wise decision."

"How did you manage? Did your husband object? Did you have children?"

"Actually I never married."

"But," she said as she played with her straw, "why? Forgive me for saying this, but you must have turned heads—I saw a few when you walked in."

"Oh it's probably because I'm such an old dinosaur. Have you ever been in love?" I said in an almost maternal way.

"Many times," said the young lady as she lit up a cigarette.

"Oh my," I pulled back my head and blinked at her.

She laughed. "I'm just kidding. I tried dating but

then I met Mark. I went to grade school with him. We bumped into one another on an elevator. I hadn't seen him for years."

For a second, her eyes shining, she looked into space. "You know it must have been made in Heaven the way we fell in love. We've been together for two years now." She smiled sheepishly, not knowing how I would take that.

"I know exactly what you mean." I checked my freshly manicured nails before taking a sip of coffee.

"So there *was* someone special. Tell me."

"I was in love, once. Seriously," I added. "But it's too involved to waste your time listening to me."

"I've got time," she pleaded. "Especially if there's mystery and suspense. And a little dirt, too."

"I don't know about that." Her enthusiasm was catching, but I wasn't sure how much to tell her. "Where to start...?"

"Start at the beginning," Eleanor said matter-of-factly.

I pushed the coffee cup aside and smiled. "Good idea."

One

1958

"I wonder if you'd have a drink with me?"

I looked up from the spreading tiny wooden jigsaw puzzle on the table before me. My immediate perception was of bulk—large, sturdy bulk—maybe six feet tall, yet somehow loose jointed—in an immaculate tan corded suit. His long face ended in a square, dimpled chin. Electric blue eyes behind thick lenses looked at me, and the shadow of a smile hovered on his sensitive face. In one arm, he carried a ridged paper sack, the bulge the size of a whiskey bottle.

Really attractive, probably married, just looking for an evening's companionship or considerably more than that. I didn't care. Mentally, I shrugged. Every night the same thing. I was fed up with being left totally alone all week while my clients, those doctors and their wives, partied. And just a drink invitation meant that I wouldn't have to struggle with an eager male at my bedroom door.

Without hesitation, I said, "I'd be glad to."

"I was afraid you'd say no." He quietly let out his breath. "I saw you go into the Casino alone for lunch. As this hotel isn't exactly the place for singles, I was going to speak to you then, but after I got through the buffet line, I couldn't find you."

As he talked, I rose. So he was alone, too—not one of the convention crowd. I wondered why he had come since he thought it wasn't a place for singles. And if he really were single that might put a different light on things.

Together, we walked across the empty game room with its puzzles and cards laid on shining, dust free, tables and entered the bar. That lovely room held discretely placed small tables and plush chairs organized for the hotel guests, transporting their own liquor, to have alcoholic drinks in the dry state of Virginia.

He led me to a tiny round table in front of a sheltered corner love seat upholstered in flowered chintz.

"We can sit together here."

The waiter relieved him of his bottle and, in the space of a few minutes, brought us the indicated mixed drinks. We settled down and sipped. Wow! He supplied good whiskey. I sipped again and heard him say his name was Henry Martz, or Hank as he was known to his friends.

"Arabella Robbins."

"Arabella. That's a lovely old-fashioned name."

"Obviously, my mother liked it." I laughed. "What do you do?"

"I'm a chemical engineer and work for the government in Washington."

"Which means you're a rising executive?" With his slicked back salt and pepper hair, I decided he could be forty.

"No. I stick to chemical engineering."

I watched him sideways from under my eyelashes, a little smile in the corners of my mouth.

"Don't look at me like that. I'll forget what I'm saying."

I lowered my eyes and brushed a crumb from the peanuts on the table off my skirt. In raising them, I noted the dimple in his chin and tingled at the strong character indication in that square, manly chin. Meeting his eyes, I said, "I live in New York City. I'm a free-lance court reporter."

"Good Lord, you must be bright."

Fluttering my eyelids, flustered, I pretended I hadn't heard. "I'm down here to take verbatim notes of the Orthopedic Surgeons' Annual Meeting."

"That confirms it."

In my embarrassment, I ducked my head and gently laughed.

"Do you use that little machine?"

"The stenotype? Yes."

"I'm fascinated whenever I see somebody operating it. How does it work?" he said, jiggling his fingers as if playing the machine.

That comment surprised me. He must watch murder mysteries on T.V.

"It's syllabic. The machine has left and right banks of consonants with the vowels in the middle below, operated by the thumbs. As all the keys can be hit at once, you just punch in syllables." I hesitated, wanting to elaborate, making it clearer. "For instance, the word 'dog.' You hit the letter D with the left hand, the O with the right thumb, and the G with the right hand, all at once. 'Dog' comes out on the paper tape."

"Amazing." Hank shook his head. "And how fast do you operate it?"

"Well, to do the kind of reporting I do, I need to have a base of 250 words a minute."

He let out a low whistle.

Shifting my position a little so I didn't have to twist my neck to look at him, I said, "If you think this is no place for singles, why do you come?"

"Twice a year, I drive down to take the sulfur baths and play some golf. I have a back problem, nothing much, but one of the masseurs here at The Homestead knows just what to do for it. So I get his expert treatment every day and spend the rest of the time trying to perfect my lousy golf."

I decided he was single. Maybe divorced, but single. My spine did a little dance.

"What's your handicap?"

"What's my handicap? You sound like a professional." His eyes crinkled, sending a shiver through me.

"Goodness no. I don't even know how to hold a club. A number of my friends play. I listen to them."

He told me that he grew up in New Jersey and went to Rutgers University; that he took a job with DuPont right out of college. DuPont right out of college! He must be bright, and I liked bright men.

Our eyes met. I wanted to lean over and kiss him. His supple, sensual mouth was too close. Forcibly turning my head, I noticed the bar had emptied. "Where did everybody go?" I exclaimed in amazement.

"I can't believe how fast the time passes when it's spent in such pleasant company," Hank said. "How about having dinner with me?"

Good, I thought. Some of those doctors will see me come in with this attractive man and know I wasn't sitting around waiting for them to entertain me. I wanted to get up and do a jig. Instead, I said, "Shall I meet you by the dining room door at seven-thirty?"

"I'll be on one of those couches near the door."

I skipped upstairs on winged feet. In my room, I had a terrible time deciding which of the three formal dinner gowns I had brought with me I should wear. Thank goodness Mrs. Henderson had told me that I would need formal dinner clothes when she assigned me to The Homestead meeting. Which of them would Hank like best? The Kelly green dress always looked good on me and gave me a lift. With my auburn hair, Kelly green was one of my best colors. I ran my hands over the other two dresses. The cut of the dusty rose gown probably looked the best of the three. It made me look taller than my five feet four inches, slim and elegant. But the pale lavender sang of spring, of shy softness, of promise, and the taffeta slip added a faint rustle to my movements.

I looked at the ceiling, waiting for some mystical enlightenment to enter my blank mind. As nothing did, I decided to wear the lavender gown. I guess that was a good choice because Hank jumped from the sofa when he saw me, and his eyes swept over the dress. "You look smashing," he said.

Putting his hand under my elbow, he guided me to his assigned table in the dining room. As we passed it, I looked at the empty little table I usually occupied and wondered if my waiter had been told that I would not be dining there tonight. After we ordered, he suggested we dance. The five-piece orchestra that played smaltzy music in the lounge during tea had now shifted to the dining room. The musicians had set up their instruments against the wall behind the minuscule square of flooring set aside for dancing. Dining tables, elegantly set with white linen and crystal, surrounded the polished wooden square.

As we stepped onto the dance floor, Hank's left hand found the small of my back, his right hand took mine, and we twirled. "Wow," I purred. "The perfect partner." Obviously, he loved to dance, too. He held me close, led masterfully, and kept exact time to the music. What absolute joy. I melted into his arms, and our steps moved in unison.

His waiter must have signaled to him because suddenly, he said, "Our soup has arrived." The hand on my back slipped to my elbow.

We cautiously maneuvered through the dancing couples on the floor and sat down to a steaming bowl of creamed spinach soup. I always thought soup had to be hot when eaten. This soup was hot and perfect. The minute the waiter removed our empty plates, we danced. When the entree was brought out, Hank received the signal that the hot lamb and vegetables had arrived. We danced again before dessert was served and afterwards as well.

Never had I met such a man, a man whose very touch sent me into orbit. I loved the feel of his body as he held me close, giggled at the funny little things he whispered in my ear. After dinner, he taught me to play backgammon. At first, he beat me badly, but I gained on him. In the end, even though he won, I had a fighting chance.

"I better quit while I'm ahead," he said finally.

"And I better say good night or I'll never be able to cope with those doctors tomorrow."

"Will you meet me at the clubhouse for lunch?"

"I can't come until they break. So far, it has been twelve-thirty."

"Whatever time, I'll wait. I'll be sitting on one of those chairs lining the gravel walkway."

At my door, he leaned over and lightly brushed my cheek with his lips.

"Until tomorrow," he said, and hurried away.

As I fitted the key into the lock, I watched him walk down the corridor, a gorgeous male who seemed to like me.

I undressed slowly, floating back and forth to the closet, back and forth to the bathroom, back and forth to the dresser, my feet tripping on the stuff of clouds. In my total existence, I couldn't think of ever having had such a delightful evening. What was it about him that mesmerized me? He's like catnip, I finally decided. I picked up the bedside alarm, studied it, and automatically engaged the mechanism. One o'clock, and I had to be up by seven with my wits about me to contend with those doctors. Yet, I continued to fuss with my clothes, rearrange the pile of fluffy white bathroom towels, stand still in the middle of the floor and relive the evening.

Two

In the morning, I seated myself in the auditorium's front row, right under the podium on the foot-high stage. I tried to listen as intently as before, as I usually did. But remarks in Hank's voice constantly interrupted the speaker's comments, making me work harder to catch up. His face appeared when I looked at the statistical slides, sending me into panic that I wouldn't remember. Forcefully staring at the slide, I concentrated on the first column of figures. Hank's face faded. Relief flooded through me as I worked in my normal rhythm.

On the dot of twelve-thirty, the doctors reached the end of the speeches, the end of the questions, the end of the morning. I ripped the few notes from my stenotype machine, snapped the tray shut, and placed it against the upturned front row seat next to mine.

While I was pushing the notes into the manila envelope I kept handy, I heard the organizational secretary call from mid-aisle. "Do you have a minute? Let's go through the program so I know which manuscripts are still outstanding."

Drat. Why does he have to do that now?

"Okay." I pouted, and reached into my pocketbook for the program. I knew my face showed my annoyance, but also knew that he couldn't see my face as he came down the aisle from the rear of the room. Quickly, I checked the program in my hand. "Only a few of speeches haven't been handed to me yet," I said as he reached my side.

Page by page, he went through the inked notes on my program and made notes on his. Then he skimmed through his program a second time, slipped it into the breast pocket of his jacket, and said, "I'd like you to report the whole session this afternoon."

"All right," I said, glad I was to be working rather than sitting idly while some doctor read a scientific paper, then have to jump in when they asked questions at the end. I tucked my program deep into my purse.

"I guess that's it, then. I'll take these manuscripts."

"Thanks," I said. "See you at two o'clock," and practically ran up the aisle in my eagerness to see Hank.

I walked rapidly along the gravel path between the hotel and the Casino, where lunch was already being served. I was so busy looking at each seated man on the chairs along the walkway that I stood in front of Hank and stared at him before I realized who he was. Wearing a blue, short-sleeved sports shirt open at the neck, and gray slacks, he sat relaxed, his legs crossed. Seeing me, he instantly rose.

"How lovely you look in that Chinese red dress," he said. "It goes with your auburn hair and chestnut eyes."

"You have a perfect eye for color," I said, feeling my face flush. Abruptly, I changed the subject. "How was your golf game?"

"Undistinguished. All I could think about was you," He drew my arm through his, and we walked the remainder of the gravel path to the Casino.

During lunch, he said, "Are you really going to leave this afternoon?"

"Yes. The six o'clock train. I should be through around 3:30."

"Why don't you stay over until tomorrow? I'll drive you back to Washington. You can take the train to New York from there."

"I can't. I'm obligated to get back and start producing the transcript." No more was said on the subject. He didn't mention seeing me again when he left me at the auditorium entrance at a quarter of two. That sent me into a tizzy at the start of the session. Shape up, I told myself. Don't blow it—not now when the hard part's over! Other thoughts surfaced. Will I see him again? Should I call him? Would he be in his room or playing golf? What should I do? Pay attention. Pay attention. The refrain overpowered. Pay attention.

I saw him lounging by the door when I walked out of the auditorium. I beamed

"Let's deposit your stuff," he said, as he took the stenotype case from me, "and walk around town. I'll show you the horses in the stables. There are some beauties."

Walking down the steps behind the low, white spa building, serviced by the underground thermal aquifers, I turned to look at Hank's profile. An internal voice said, "This is the man I'm going to marry." Stunned for the moment, I missed my footing and stumbled.

"Woops!" With a fast, masterly reflex, he caught me. "Gives me a chance to get my arms around you."

To cover my confusion, and to give myself a moment to think about what had happened, I asked him to repeat what he'd been saying.

Smiling at me, as he held my elbow to steady me, he repeated.

We talked, looking at the horses, the brown, the black, the piebald. We talked, sauntered through the main street of the town, looked in all the store windows, then, along its extension with the lovely old white clapboard houses set back on clipped green lawns, and talked some more. Somewhere along the way, he took my hand. We talked mainly about ourselves, what we did, our interests, my work. He wanted to know how I happened to chose court reporting for a profession.

"One of those serendipitous things." I shrugged. "Another woman and I were acting as secretaries at a conference. At the lunch break, the court reporter came out to the lobby and entertained us with stories of traveling to the West Coast and Europe to work. I cried, 'That's for me,' thinking only about the travel." I blushed and looked at Hank.

He laughed.

"I cornered the reporter the minute the meeting ended, and we spent the evening in the hotel bar talking about court reporting. As a result, Charlie—Charlie Stevens—nursed me though the basic course and through the high speeds. Once I mastered that, he recommended me to Mrs. Henderson who owns the agency where we both work." I stopped talking for a minute to consider my background. "It's really amazing. I graduated from Columbia University with degrees in ancient history and fine arts and ended up as a freelance court reporter. It's a different place, different people, different subjects and different vocabulary every day. I love it," I said with emphasis. "Though I worry about every transcript—sure I'll be complained about. Charlie tells me it will be five years before I feel competent."

"Have you been complained about?"

"No. Not so far."

He smiled at me. "You won't be." I asked him about his work. He skirted the subject, repeating that it was top secret. He did say that he traveled a lot and that he lived at the Manger-Annapolis Hotel in Washington. The name didn't mean much to me. But living in a hotel? He must really travel a lot. Then I quickly backtracked. Why should I think that strange? After all, I lived at the Midston House, a residential hotel on Madison Avenue and Thirty-Eighth Street, a short walk down Park Avenue to my office on Thirty-Second Street. Heck. He had a point. He didn't have to make the bed or do any housekeeping.

Hand in hand, we were standing before the window of a sporting goods shop when Hank said, "If I send for some tickets and come to New York, will you have dinner with me and go to the theater?"

"Of course. Did you think I wouldn't?"

"After some of the things that I have said about the top secrecy of my work, I wondered."

"I'll see you whenever you can get to New York."

"I'm glad you said that, Arabella. I could manage to be a frequent visitor."

For a few seconds, I stood looking at him. How did he manage that? Did he come up regularly on business or use a lot of overtime?

He shot out an arm in a sudden motion to look at his wristwatch. "We better get back so you can check out."

After I paid my bill at the desk, he said, "Come up to my room with me for a second before we go to the station."

That surprised me. Why? We didn't have a lot of time.

In his room, I glanced around. The single bed against the wall, the pale green décor, heavy brocade draperies, exactly the same as the room I had occupied.

He walked over to the desk and picked up a package. With it in his hand, he returned to me. "I bought you something," he said, handing me the package.

Overwhelmed. I looked at the long, thin, narrow package then looked at him.

He smiled. "Open it."

First glancing at him, I quickly tore off the wrapping paper. The box certainly looked like a jewelry box. Slowly, I lifted the cover. A gold colored bracelet and earrings of white enamel leaves and turquoise stones lay nestled in the white satin box interior. I caught my breath at their beauty.

"These are gorgeous," I stammered. Lifting the bracelet up, I asked him to fasten it around my wrist. "It really is exquisite," I said, slowly moving my arm so we could admire the bracelet.

Hank laughed softly. "Come along, we better send the porter for your things and go to the station."

The station lights were on when we reached the waiting train. Few people had arrived yet. Pullman porters bustled along the platform, shouting to other porters, directing the baggage. Porters arriving with piles of luggage that they thrust down and hurried off for more.

The overnight train, a spur that would be hitched onto another train at a major junction, glowed pleasantly. Hank and I stood close together. We didn't say much. I felt myself getting teary, not wanting to leave him. That flash across my mind at the back of the spa telling me that I would marry this man haunted me. I knew that I had found the perfect husband for me. I wanted to remain at Hot Springs and talk and talk the way we had been doing. I felt certain that he was as caught up with the sense of our belonging to each other as I was.

When the time came to board, his hand went to my waist and swept me willingly into the secure haven of his arms. I raised my face. I could see the emotion in his eyes. Then his lips found mine. All sense left me except for that wonderful, passionate kiss.

When he finally released me, I had to use every last ounce of my willpower to step onto the train without looking back at him. In my sleeping compartment, I drew the partially read paperback from my purse, opened it, and laid it on my lap, only to ignore it. My mind swirled around Hank. One kiss and I was ready to crawl after him on my hands and knees. I couldn't even put words to my feeling other than being completely obsessed with this man.

There had been other men in my life, men I really liked, men who wanted to marry me. My mind reviewed them. Somehow, though, I enjoyed their company, liked going to dinner with them, to the theater, and dancing, I had never been able to imagine living with any of them for the rest of my life. Strange. How strange. Two had been physicians—all the others had been professional men. All eligible. I hadn't married any of them.

Hank was different though. The attraction had been so instant, so all-consuming. Love? I didn't know yet. I differentiated between love and pure physical attraction.

The train started to move, and slowly picked up speed. I sat motionless, thinking about Hank. When the porter came to turn down my bed, I got up. Try to keep your head, I admonished myself. You have to. He said he'd come to New York. When? How could I possibly wait?

I was so caught up in thinking about Hank that I didn't bother to look out the window. The next time I saw him, he told me that he had thrown stones at the window until he was afraid it would break.

Three

Still walking on air Monday morning, I reached the large sunny room of our tenth-floor office at Number Two Park Avenue. Eight typewriter desks were lined up, four against each side of the room. I carefully stacked the week's notes by date on my desk, the second on the right, glanced at Charlie Steven's desk behind mine and noted that neither Marian Gruber nor Elaine Hicks had come in yet. Their uncluttered desks, across the room from Charlie's and mine, looked unused. I turned and headed for Mrs. Henderson's small office down the hall. Sitting in her swivel chair, going through papers, she looked up when I rapped on her door.

"Well, from the expression on your face, Arabella, the trip was successful," she said. "Come in and tell me about it." She settled back in her swivel chair, patted the wave in her short white hair, adjusted her glasses and motioned me to sit in the straight-backed chair.

As I seated myself, she said, "You had no trouble with vocabulary?"

"No. The organizational secretary gave me a bunch of abstracts. I had time in the evenings to check through them for the vocabulary I needed. I only had to report the fifteen minutes of questions and answers after each paper until the wrap up of the whole meeting on the last afternoon. The secretary, Mr. Woodward, asked me to report that."

"So I gather that you enjoyed yourself?"

I lowered my eyes, not sure what they might show. "Yes, I did after the first three days."

"What do you mean by that?"

"Well, the doctors and their wives gathered each evening for noisy chatter over cocktails and dining and ignored me. In fact, other than Mr. Woodward who said 'Good morning,' each day, nobody spoke to me." I shrugged my shoulders. "The last night, I was asked to have a drink and go to dinner." I hoped she would assume the invitation came from some of the doctors. I didn't want her to ask detailed questions.

"Very good. I'll give you today and tomorrow to type. The end of the week is busy. I have scheduled you on Wednesday for the morning meeting at a large Wall Street brokerage house." She turned to the papers on her desk.

Relieved that she had stuck mainly to the business part of the trip in her conversation, I stood up, took a quick look at Mrs. Henderson in her black designer suit and hurried to my own desk.

Just before noon, Charlie buzzed in after his morning hearing.

"Hi, Arabella." He grinned at me and held up an inch-deep pack of notes. "That's all I got the entire morning." He tossed the notes on his desk. "How was your trip?"

"I didn't get any volume either, maybe only twenty pages for the whole morning, instead of one hundred—if I'd taken down everything. So I guess from Mrs. Henderson's standpoint the meeting wasn't a great success. But I had no trouble with the content."

"Good girl." He sat down. "So what's the place like? Did you meet any interesting people?"

Trying to stay clear of any comment that would lead to a discussion of Hank, I gave him a detailed rundown of the hotel, the dark green carpet along the entire length of the great pillared hall, the scrumptious comfort of the rooms, the fluffy bath towels, the elegance of the dining room service and the delicious food, plus the reason for the few pages I got. I left it there.

Happily, before Charlie could ask questions, Mrs. Henderson summoned him. I watched him walk to the front of the room, his tall, athletic figure and curly black hair, and fretted about his next move. I pointedly concentrated on my typing when he came back.

"She gave me a hearing for this afternoon," he said, "to make up for this morning."

I nodded, and continued typing.

He didn't move from the side of my desk. I looked up, wide-eyed innocence. His blue eyes bore into me, a hard, quizzical look, and he went to his own desk without saying anything more. That unnerved me. Damn his hide. He's getting serious, and he's suspicious. Somehow, I've communicated that something special happened. He'll mull it over and react.

Two days later, at six P.M., the desk clerk at the Midston House handed me a letter. A letter! I scowled. I didn't get mail at the Midston House. I looked at the envelope and saw "The Homestead" in the upper left-hand corner. My heart leapt. While I didn't recognize the handwriting, the letter could only be, must be, from Hank. The postmark showed the date of May 21st.

In an excited twitter, I rushed to the elevator. On the seventh floor, my hand trembled so that I had trouble getting the key into the lock of my room door. At last. I dropped my handbag on the bed and sat down by the window on the desk chair. Sticking the tip of my tongue out of the corner of my mouth in concentration, I carefully opened the letter and glanced down at the signature: "Till then, Henry." Only then did I let out my breath. But, my, he was being formal with his signature. During our time together, I had called him Hank. I knew his name was Henry. I liked that name. It was also my father's name.

He wrote: *Dear Little Keg of Dynamite:*

How funny. That sounded as if I had bowled him over, too. I hugged myself. Our involvement seemed to be instantly mutual. Somehow, I found it hard to believe. Things like that just didn't happen to me.

I turned back to the text of the letter.

I spent this morning looking for bones. Thought if I found some I might entice you into coming back.

So he remembered our conversation in the bar that first night when we had talked about my interest in archaeology.

As predicted, today is sunny and warm. The pool is delightful and the countryside is beautiful. However, it could be a lot more enjoyable, but let's face it, Martz doesn't have it.

Martz has it, all right. That remark is just a comment.

Hope you had a good trip back. Hope I get to see you again.

You will see lots of me if I have any say in the matter. *Hope I haunt you eternally.*

What an odd thing to say, yet how meaningful. I thought about that phrase a long time and was almost afraid to think about what it might be telling me.

Thanks again. You are a very lovely person, sweet, too.

Till then, Henry.

Tears of happiness flooded my eyes as I gently placed his letter back in the envelope and carefully laid it in the desk drawer.

To my surprise, I received another letter from The Homestead dated May 23rd. It carried the same signature. That letter read:

Dear Dyna: If you have no objection, from this day on, I'll call you Dyna, for obvious reasons.

I wasn't sure I wanted to be called Dyna. But that would probably wear off.

Now that you're back in New York, The Homestead is far removed from your mind and probably so is the clown that went with it.

Clown, baloney. He should know that, that so-called clown has ruled my thoughts ever since we met.

But anyway, I'll never forget.

One tidbit of news that I think you may enjoy. Remember the evening at dinner, we heard the big crash. It sounded like a waiter dropped a tray of food. What really happened I find out now is as follows.

This dowager was flouncing in, making a sort of grand entry, head held high, nose in the air and she ran smack into a tray of food in a stand and she went ass-over-head into the tray of food, she and the food all over the floor.

I'm leaving tomorrow, will arrange for the tickets, and you should have them some day next week. Might even get bold and call you.

Do. Please do get bold. I'd love to pick up the phone and hear your voice on the other end.

Till then, Henry

The letter, slowly and exceedingly carefully, joined the first one in the desk drawer.

On May 28th, an envelope containing two tickets arrived from the theater. What bliss. Another whole evening with him for dinner and to see *The Music Man* on Wednesday, June 3rd.

Hank called at nine Friday evening. "Did you receive the tickets?"

"Yes. They came on Tuesday."

"Will you have dinner with me?"

"Yes. I'd love that."

"I'll meet you at five in the lobby of your office building."

Concentration the next day turned into a big problem. And I had to type. I had to finish the brokerage house transcript. But I couldn't think of anything except Hank. Twice, I noticed that I had typed the same sentence over again. After the second time, I got up and walked out of the office. Glancing at the clock over the elevator doors, I noticed that it was twenty minutes after two. A giant gong clanged in my head with ascending notes. Spring came all over again as my mind sang, I love him, I love him, I love him. Warmth, contentment, and belonging, swirled through and around me.

Suddenly shy, afraid that someone would see me, I walked casually into the nearby washroom and looked at myself in the mirror. My face shone. I peeked at my shoulder blades to see if I had sprouted wings. This wonderful thing, this thing that authors of romance novels talked about, that young women yearned for, had happened to me just out of the blue. I knew it was forever.

Fortunately, my assignment the morning of June 3rd involved a speech by Henry Cabot Lodge. One hour had been specified. Even if he talked the whole hour, I could finish typing his lecture by five o'clock. He was always charming in manner, reasonably slow in his speech, precise, and used good grammar. Anyway, I had to finish. The transcript had to be delivered in the morning.

As I ripped the last page from the typewriter, I looked at my watch. Twenty-five minutes after four o'clock. I dropped the page on top of the pile on my desk, straightened the pages and took the transcript to Joel, the office boy, in the room next to Mrs. Henderson's. Only then did I go to the lavatory to wash my hands, comb my hair, and repair my makeup. Happiness flooded my soul.

At the desk behind me, Charlie had been madly typing all day. When I returned from the washroom, he said, "I'm almost through, Arabella. Why don't we go across the street to the Vanderbilt Hotel and have a drink?"

"Not tonight, Charlie. I'm going to the theater."

He shrugged, said, "Another time," and went on typing. But his body language and the suggestion of a drink upset me. He should have sensed from my actions that I had something else to do. Otherwise, I would have hung around and not fussed with my looks. Actually, I realized, he probably did understand and was trying to find out where I was going and with whom.

I got the distinct impression that he thought another

man had entered my life. How come? I hadn't said one word that might give him ideas. Well, so what? I didn't care. I was too much involved with Hank to worry about him.

I left the office at five on the dot. Standing in the lobby, waiting for the elevator, I checked in my purse for the theater tickets, which were just where I had put them. With a soundless, amused sniff, I snapped the purse shut, realizing that I must have checked on the tickets at least fifty times during the day. What a state I was in. And all over a wonderful man.

As I stepped off the elevator, I saw Hank standing near the front door.

Seeing me, he stretched out his arm to look at his watch. What did that mean? I wasn't late.

"You're three minutes late. I was beginning to wonder if I were being stood up."

My lord. I caught my breath. Three minutes! I bet he's been hurt in the past and is very sensitive, swept through my mind. I better watch myself in our appointments, though working as I do I'm used to being early.

Quickly I said, "Hank, I will never stand you up. But if I'm ever caught in a meeting, there's no way I can let you know. There's nothing you can do except wait."

"That's important. Thanks for telling me, Arabella."

After putting the tickets that I handed him in the breast pocket of his jacket, he tucked my arm in his and we left the building.

Walking slowly to the corner of Broadway after the theater, Hank hailed a cab.

"Midston House—Madison Avenue and 38th Street," he told the driver as I climbed in.

"Is dinner a week from Sunday evening okay?" he said as the cab pulled up in front of the Midston House.

"Lovely. I'll have trouble waiting."

Hank smiled

He opened the cab door, helped me out and paid the driver. Slowly, we walked towards the entrance.

"Then, I'll be gone for five days."

"Where?"

"I can't tell you, Arabella. You know my job is top secret."

"Yes, you did mention it that last afternoon at The Homestead."

"You just have to get used to my coming and going."

"I'll try." I ducked my head then smiled up at him.

He pulled me close, and wild kisses erupted. In time, I pushed open the door, waved to him and walked unsteadily to the elevator.

From Wednesday through Friday, I worked. We all worked. Mrs. Henderson assigned me to two luncheon speeches, one at the Pierre Hotel, the other at the Roosevelt Hotel.

On Friday morning, I reached the office by nine, wanting to type a little before leaving for a short deposition at eleven o'clock. Buttoning her dark gray designer suit jacket, Mrs. Henderson rushed out of her office.

"Thank goodness you are reasonably early, Arabella. We have an emergency. Somebody forgot to call in an important business meeting at the Yale Club. They have to adjourn by 11:30 to greet guests at a cocktail party. Go up there immediately. I'll get the first reporter who comes in next to take your deposition."

Irritated, I scrambled my equipment and extra note pads together and ran from the office. As I hit the elevator button, I heard Mrs. Henderson yell, "Take a cab."

In the cab, I thought about her. She had been sitting in her office with her jacket unbuttoned. I grinned to myself in amusement. I had never seen her with one hair out of place. The phone call about the emergency hearing must have really taken her by surprise. And if I weren't mistaken, that was an Adrian suit she had on. A well-known Hollywood fashion designer, his stuff was easy to spot.

The cab stopped in front of the Yale Club. I slipped into the meeting room as quietly as I could, set up my equipment at the back of the long room and walked to the front, past all the rows of occupied chairs. I kept my eyes down because everybody turned to look at me. I found an empty seat in the front row of chairs, right under the podium, which was set on a foot-high platform.

A tall, blond young man dressed in a black business suit stood at the podium reading. From what I could gather, he was laying out the objectives of the meeting and what he wanted to learn from the audience. He signaled that he would give me his script later.

After that, the meeting turned into a jumble, everybody trying to talk at once. I threw my hands up, making sure they were high enough for the chairman to see. He understood, nodded, and banged the gavel.

"If you want a decent transcript, one that lays out what you have said, you have to talk one at a time. And say your name," he added. "You'll have to speak up, too, so the court reporter can hear those of you in the back."

He emphasized that he intended to keep order and

valiantly tried to do so. When the meeting broke up, he handed me the pages he had read and asked me to deliver the transcript by nine o'clock the next morning, Saturday. "What a pistol," I muttered. "If I have to stay late tonight, I have to stay late. But I don't want to."

In my snit, I slammed my stuff together and went back to the office.

Charlie sat typing when I got back. I held up my notes, made a face at him and flung them down. He rolled his eyes up towards the ceiling.

I obtained some cheese crackers from the vending machine off the lobby and set to work.

Transcribing my ragged notes slowed me down. I had to spend too much time figuring out what the speaker was trying to say. At 6:15, I threw the last page on top of the pile of completed pages and flung myself back in the chair, my arms dangled at my sides.

Charlie stopped typing. "Okay, Arabella, we're going across the street to the bar. We'll get you relaxed before I take you to dinner."

I was willing to take a bet on the fact that he had stalled his typing to wait for me to finish. I fumed. Yet, I didn't have the strength to say no. I knew that cocktails and dinner would be as traumatic as the meeting I had just been through. I felt sure that Charlie had figured out that I had a new man and intended to pop the question before his rival did. How he knew was beyond me. Deep inside myself, I talked to him, "It won't do you any good, Charlie. You wouldn't be happy with me. I'm fond of you, but that isn't love. You need a clinging woman who would adore you and wait on you hand and foot. I'm not that kind of woman." But how could I say that to him?

Sitting at a round table in the bar, we ended up having three drinks each before I became desperate for food. "Charlie, I have to have something to eat. All this liquor is going to my head." Charlie ordered hamburgers and french fries right there in the bar. And then he proposed.

I told him I thought him a fine man, that I was fond of him, but that I didn't love him and couldn't marry him. I added that being married to me would only make him unhappy.

He countered that I wasn't playing fair, that I was seeing another man instead of being faithful to him.

Even though I had suspected that he'd guessed, I was flabbergasted. Two dates with Hank, and he sensed it. Suddenly, I realized what else he had said. The comment riled me.

"What do you mean by I'm not being faithful to you? We have no binding understanding, no understanding at all. We have never discussed the subject." My temper was rising. "You have no right to say that."

"I have every right. You haven't seen another man since I met you two years—no, going on three years—ago."

"That doesn't mean I'm being faithful. All it means is that I haven't met anybody I liked all that well. Anyhow," I said, warming up to the subject, "I have seen other men that you never knew about." Charlie glared at me then hailed the waiter and ordered another round of drinks. I said, "I don't want another drink."

The drinks came anyway and didn't help. Charlie became morose and argumentative. I ignored my drink, withdrawing into silence, feeling helpless yet angry at his behavior. He guzzled his drink.

Finally, unable to take more of his slobbering accusations, I stood up. "Charlie. I said that I wouldn't marry you and I don't want to hear anything more on the subject. I'm going home."

I flounced out of the bar, stormed up Park Avenue, angrily arguing with myself over the things Charlie had said. At 38th Street, I crossed to Madison Avenue, and walked into the Midston House. If I had been able to slam the door, I would have done it.

Four

Charlie didn't show up for work on Monday, nor did he come in on Tuesday. I worked at the Roosevelt Hotel all day both Wednesday and Thursday so I didn't see him. Friday morning, I went directly to the building on Wall Street where I was assigned to report a luncheon meeting. I wanted time to look over the setup, the podium and where I would be sitting, and, if possible, to get a list of names. Mrs. Henderson had told me that the luncheon would be very elegant with long, drawn-out speeches. I would have to eat as best I could in between sentences.

I returned to the office at 3:30, my mind full of that luncheon. I had been able to eat in a drawn-out manner and savored every morsel of the elaborate, excellent food. But what really got to me was that all the middle-aged, experienced waiters served while wearing white gloves.

Without seeing either Mrs. Henderson or Charlie, I stacked the notes in the desk drawer, laid the stenotype case on the desk, out of the way of the cleaning people, walked swiftly up Park Avenue to 38th Street and turned left to the Midston House. As soon as I had cleaned up and changed my clothes, I hopped onto the subway, headed for Long Island City and the garage where I left my silver and gray three-year old 1955 Chevrolet during the week. Maybe I could reach my parents' home on the north shore of Long Island before the rush hour got too far underway.

Tomorrow, I'd sit on the side porch of our house and write letters for Hank. He had five days of work, five days when he would be out of touch with me. From the small things he did say about his work, I thought it must be something like Star Wars. Anyway, I intended to write him five letters, one for each day he was gone. I'd get back to the Midston House early in the afternoon on Sunday, leaving ample time to copy my letters nicely and put them in envelopes marked with the days of the week before Hank arrived at four.

Sitting at my desk in the Midston House on Sunday afternoon, I constantly looked at the clock, wishing the phone would ring and announce Hank's presence. When it finally did ring, I jumped.

"You have a guest in the lobby," the desk clerk said when I answered the phone.

I quickly checked my hair and makeup in the mirror and hurried to the elevator. As I stepped off the lift in the lobby, I saw him standing just to the left, smiling.

"Yellow and white colors tonight," he said and kissed me. "You look beautiful."

We took a cab to a seafood restaurant that made good sole stuffed with crabmeat. Later, we walked south along

Broadway, turned left at 42nd Street and followed 42nd Street across town to Madison Avenue. At Madison Avenue, we again had to turn south until we reached the Midston House on the corner of 38th Street.

"Would you like to come up to our roof?" I asked. "I can't invite you to my room. Men are not allowed on the seventh floor."

"Then I'll never be able to picture you in the room where you live," he said as he held the door for me.

"I wrote you some letters, one for every day you'll be gone." I let out a little giggle. "I left them in my room."

"You wonderful creature. However, I'll admit that I will read them all at once."

"Oh, pooh." I shook my shoulders playfully and frowned while I smiled at him.

The elevator carried us to the roof. "Isn't it gorgeous?" I said as the city in all its sparkling illuminated glory lay spread out before us.

"It is. And so are you." Hank drew me into his arms. As my cheek slid against his, I whispered into his ear, "I love you."

An ecstatic sound escaped him, and his arms tightened. Later, as we descended in the elevator, I got off on the seventh floor. He went ahead to wait for me in the lobby.

When I reached him, I extended the large manila envelope I carried. "The letters are all in this envelope. I didn't want you to lose one."

"Fat chance," he said, taking the envelope from me. "I'll call you in about a week."

In my room afterwards, I realized that he hadn't said he loved me. I mulled it over. I thought he did. I stood in the middle of the room and ran through his actions, his eyes on me, his attentiveness, and whispered, "I know he does."

Dressed in her lovely Chanel suit and obviously upset, Mrs. Henderson caught me the minute I walked into the office on Monday morning. "Come into my office," she snapped.

I wondered what I had done to cause the abrupt summons. I followed her into her office and stood in front of her desk.

She sat down and fussed with some papers on her desk. Feeling a little worried as well as disturbed, I stood there and silently watched her. Then, as I continued to wait, I started to glance around the small, square room. On the top shelf of the bookcase behind her, a blue and gold rococo clock with pink putti ticked loudly. The clock seemed out of place in the off-white Spartan room. Moving from the clock, I started to read the book titles: a college dictionary, Roget's Thesaurus, Who's Who in America, a shelf of reference books. The rest of the bookcase contained stacks of papers and transcripts.

"What have you done to Charlie Stevens?"

Her abrupt attack startled me and instantly brought my attention back to her.

"What have I done to Charlie?" I repeated, taken aback. "I haven't done anything to him. Why?"

"He went to Florida on an assignment last Monday. He came back on Wednesday, but didn't show up here. Finally, late Thursday, I reached him. He was very drunk. He said, 'I quit. I'm never coming back.' I was flabbergasted. Friday afternoon, I sent Joel around to get Charlie's notes. He finally got the management to let him in. He found Charlie comatose on the sofa. The place was a mess and stank. Charlie's stenotype and the notes were on the table. Joel brought me the notes." She leaned back in her chair. "What do you know about this?"

What she had said shocked me. I caught the edge of the desk and my mouth dropped open. I had to wait until I grasped its full meaning of what she'd said before I could speak.

"I can tell you what happened a week ago last Friday night. That's all." I stood in front of her, my head turned slightly to the left, my eyes down, trying to think. I admitted to myself that I had probably brought this on. But his reaction to being rejected really upset me. It was worse than I'd expected. Poor Charlie. He was my friend. I was truly fond of him.

"Well?"

"He'd asked me, or rather he commanded me, to go over to the Vanderbilt for a drink after we finished typing Friday night. We had three drinks each before I demanded food. While we ate right there, he asked me to marry him. I tried to be kind, but turned him down. He became loud and abusive. I got up and walked to my hotel, leaving him there."

"Poor Charlie," she whispered sadly. In silence, her long, perfectly manicured hands toyed with her letter opener. "Though, I don't blame you. If you didn't want to marry him, I guess you had to tell him so." She paused. "Is it definite? No chance?"

"Absolutely definite. I'm in love with somebody else. I'm sure Charlie guessed that before he asked me to marry him and was forcing the issue."

Mrs. Henderson threw down the letter opener. "I've had him taken to the hospital to dry out, then we'll see what we can do about it. He's a good reporter. I don't want to lose him."

I was really disturbed, remorseful that I had hurt Charlie, yet I had to do it. How could I have been kinder? How could I have prevented this? In a total quandary, I sat down at my typewriter.

I slaved all week, taking on an extra heavy load to make up for Charlie. Friday morning, I went back to the brokerage house where I had reported their early spring meeting. This time, the chairman had requested me. That knowledge really raised my confidence level on my ability. I had just started to feel a bit more secure about the transcripts I produced.

The meeting broke promptly at noon, and I returned to the office by twelve-thirty. Poking my head into Mrs. Henderson's office, I said, "I'm back, but I'm leaving now to drive to Long Island for the weekend."

"See you Monday."

Sunday morning, I moped around the house, much to the annoyance of my father. Why didn't Hank call? Had he forgotten me? Was our affair over? At eleven o'clock, the phone rang. I sprinted across the dining room to the kitchen counter where the phone lay in its cradle.

"Hello!"

"Hi, Arabella." His voice came through loud and clear.

"You're back."

"Boy, is it ever good to hear your voice. I haven't forgotten what you told me."

I laughed softly. "I'm glad." After a second, I said, "How did you like my letters?"

"I kept them under my pillow. All those guys worried about what their wives were doing. I didn't. It was a nice feeling."

Did he think of me as his wife? What paradise. I would sure like to be.

Later in the conversation, he said, "I'm going to take a few days off. How about driving out to the Hamptons that afternoon?"

"I'll do my best to keep Mrs. Henderson from assigning me next Friday afternoon."

"Can we take your car?"

"Of course."

"I'll meet you at two o'clock in the Midston House lobby."

When I left my parents' home Sunday night, I took with me my bathing suit, two beach towels and the three summer dresses that I kept at home. I put them in a plastic coverall and asked the garage man to hang them in his office until next weekend.

First thing Monday morning, I stopped by Mrs. Henderson's office. "Oh, Mrs. Henderson," I begged, "please, please, try to keep me off the book next Friday afternoon. I've had a lovely invitation for the weekend."

She laughed. "Believe me, I will try, Arabella. I'll work it out anyway I can so that you are free by noon on Friday."

Bubbling happily on Friday morning, I sat down at my office desk around 7:30 A.M. Mrs. Henderson had managed to leave me totally off the book so I expected to finish a lot of typing.

At twelve-thirty, I poked my head into her office. "I'm through typing, Mrs. Henderson. And I do thank you for leaving me free today."

She raised her head to smile at me. "Have a good time."

Hank picked me up at the Midston House on the dot of two o'clock. We walked up to Grand Central Station and took the subway to Long Island City where I housed my car. At the garage, we collected my clothes from the manager, laid them on the back seat, stowed his suitcase in the trunk along with mine, and headed for South Hampton. The drive out restored my soul after the hectic week. Hank, too, seemed to leave his work behind. He lounged in the seat next to me and sat sideways as we talked. The only trouble was that he looked at me, and I had to look at the road. I'd much rather have looked at him. The drive turned into pure joy despite the traffic.

He had reserved two rooms in an attractive mustard-colored bed and breakfast place recommended by one of his colleagues. After settling into my pretty room with its chintz curtains and a double bed, in which I thought should have a certain person joining me, I hurried down the stairs to the living room. Already there, Hank was talking to the middle-aged couple who owned the house. We said farewell, climbed into my car, drove to the large hotel also recommended by his colleague and headed for the bar.

Seated on bar stools facing Peconic Bay, sunlight and blue water met our vision whichever way we looked. In absolute delight, I laughed. "The whole side of the building is glass. How marvelous."

Hank agreed.

He chose a charming seafood restaurant for dinner.

By dessert time, the usual week's end tiredness plus depression hit me. I knew I was sagging and also knew I better shape up. I tried to laugh and sparkle. Finally, in desperation, afraid I would go to pieces right at the dinner table, I excused myself and went to the rest room where I had a little cry to get the ill humor out of my system.

The real problem, I realized, wasn't too much work and being tired, but that Hank had never said he loved me, even though I had told him that I loved him. Why? I thought he did. He seemed to. He was so thoughtful, so attentive, yes, so caring in his dealings with me.

"You have to pull yourself together," I muttered, "go back and be cheerful." I tossed the used Kleenex into the trash receptacle, carefully powdered my nose, put a drop of Murine in each eye to clear them, added lipstick, and presented a smiling face to Hank. I exclaimed over the rich, creamy, multi-layered cake and rolled my eyes.

To my surprise, instead of leaving the restaurant when we finished the last bite of cake and after dinner coffee, Hank led me out into the garden behind. Leaning against a low stone wall, he drew me towards him. "So you want to be a Martz?"

At first, I stared at him in surprise. Was that a proposal, just bang out of the blue, no lead into it with "I love you?" I gulped and said, "Yes," nodding repeatedly.

"I love you, too. I have from the beginning. But I didn't want to tell you just yet."

At last, he had said what I so desperately wanted to hear. Tears flooded my eyes. I cried softly. "I cry both when I'm sad and when I'm happy," I told him, smiling through my tears.

We stood there in the garden close together, talking

about the future. Hank explained that his job was dangerous, that he had been trying to get transferred, which he had wanted to do before he asked me to marry him.

"Unsuccessfully, so far," he added.

Again, I asked about what he did, but as before, he said he couldn't tell me. He did say that he had turned my name into the Secret Service and that I had been cleared. All that astonished me and made me review out loud some of my activity. Hank laughed at me. "They wouldn't go into that."

By the end of the weekend, life had taken on a whole new meaning for us. We belonged to each other. I knew that when he could rearrange his work, we would get married. I asked him about working myself, and he said, "I assumed you would want to."

Leisurely, on Sunday afternoon, we drove back to Long Island City.

"How beautiful this eastern end of Long Island is," Hank said, "with all these lovely little towns and the clapboard houses."

"And the bright flowers everywhere, the vibrant colors." My vision seemed to have improved when my relationship to Hank settled. Everything had a bright glow.

While looking at one old mustard-colored home with its large veranda, Hank said, "Someday, we'll stand on the front porch of our own home."

Hearing the longing in his voice, I gave him a radiant smile. I had a hard job keeping my attention on the road.

Five

During the phone call on Wednesday night the first week of August, Hank suggested we meet in Philadelphia on Friday afternoon.

"Great," I said. "I'm dying to see you."

Hank chuckled. "That goes for me, too."

I could hear him fuss with some papers.

"I have the train schedule before me. Can you make the two o'clock train out of New York on Friday afternoon?"

"I will be on that train, no matter what happens. Even if I have to quit," I added, laughing.

"I wouldn't go that far."

I overslept on Friday. Lying in bed in the dim light, I tried to focus on the half-closed blinds. Motion behind them catapulted me out of bed. Rain, pouring rain, a steady downpour that beat against the pavement in shattering white light.

"Drat," I exclaimed aloud. "I hope this doesn't keep up all day." Yanking the belt of my robe tight, I flip-flopped in fluffy scuffs to the bathroom. One glance at my watch, lying on the shelf above the sink, elicited a groan. Eight-thirty. I had meant to be at the office by eight. A lot of typing had to be finished before noon. At least Mrs. Henderson, being a good trooper, had left me off the assignment book.

If I left the office at noon, I would have plenty of time to eat a sandwich and make the two o'clock train. I'd treat myself to a taxi for the short distance from the Midston House to Pennsylvania Station.

In spite of my hurry, I carefully dressed, choosing a soft, cream-colored cotton that made my skin took tanned. Then, after some consideration before the mirror, I added a Kelly green silk scarf, fastening it at the shoulder with a jeweled pin.

Under my fingers, the typewriter clacked evenly and fast all morning. At eleven forty-five, I pulled the last page of the transcript I had to finish from the typewriter. I breathed a deep sigh of happiness. Laying the sheet of paper on top of the others, I picked up the whole pile, tapped it on the desk to straighten the pages, rose and walked into collating.

"Oh my goodness," I said, staring at the bright sunlight coming in through the window glass. "What a nice surprise." With my back to the window and totally engrossed in typing, I hadn't noticed the sun. "The weekend will be perfect."

Not seeing Joel in the room, I laid the transcript on his desk, the pink order sheet on top, and went back to my desk, where I fondled the notes in the drawer. Oh, heck, it was too late to start anything else now. I slammed the drawer shut. That pack of notes could wait.

Exactly at noon, I left the building. Instead of turning up Park Avenue towards Thirty-Eighth Street. I walked across Thirty-Second Street and turned up Madison Avenue in order to buy a sandwich at the small burger and sandwich shop I frequented. I'd eat the sandwich in my room while I finished packing.

Twenty minutes after one by my watch, the taxicab driver dropped me at Penn Station. I purchased a round-trip ticket for Philadelphia and boarded the two o'clock train. I walked along the aisle of the reasonably full coach until I found a window seat on the left-hand side. After stowing my suitcase in the overhead rack, I sat down and looked at my watch. Seven minutes until departure time. Once the train started, I would see Hank in an hour and a half.

An hour and a half later, I spotted him waiting at the top of the escalator leading from the train platform to the main station. I could feel my face light up to match the joy in his.

We taxied to the Belmont Hotel. As the cab drew up in front, he said, "I ordered a suite."

"Oh, my goodness," I said, startled. So, we had a suite, not single rooms. My conservative family upbringing raised its head. I contemplated it, shrugged, and pushed it down. I didn't care. I was as interested as he was.

Hank registered. The bellhop picked up our luggage and led us upstairs.

The room we entered had the usual sofa and chairs around a coffee table, wall to wall carpeting in a dark cream color, and soft brown-colored paint on the walls. I thought the room pretty, but wasn't sure we needed a suite.

As soon as we were alone, Hank said, "If you don't want me sleeping in the same room with you, I can sleep here on the sofa." He pointed to the sofa.

It crossed my mind that, that particular sofa wasn't long enough for him. I said, "Why don't we just go in there when the time comes," pointing to the bedroom door, "and go to bed?" I started towards the bedroom. "I'm going to unpack before we go out."

Sunday morning, we had a leisurely breakfast before spending a lovely day, even visiting the zoo and eating in Hank's favorite German restaurant. All too soon, we returned to Thirtieth Street Station. While standing together on the train platform, Hank said, "I'll be gone about ten days. I'll call you when I get back and come up to New York for dinner."

"I'll miss you."

He took my chin between his thumb and index finger and tilted my face up. "How did I ever deserve you?"

"That's just what I think about you."

The New York train pulled slowly to a stop.

He held me close. "Ten days, more or less," he said, turned and left me. From the car vestibule, I watched him walk towards the escalator before hunting a seat in the moving train.

I counted the days until Hank finally called on Tuesday night, saying he would be in New York the next day, Wednesday. "Five o'clock in the Vanderbilt lobby?"

"As far as I know, that's fine."

At three o'clock Wednesday afternoon, Mrs. Henderson approached me at my desk.

"Marian," she said, turning to Marian Gruber, "come over here by Arabella."

Marian rose slowly and walked across the room, her face and movement wary.

"I just received a long distance call from Washington, D.C. They are having a rush meeting here in the Pennsylvania Hotel at four o'clock. They want two reporters. The transcript has to be on the train tonight for morning delivery in Washington. I'm sending the two of you."

"I have a dinner date. I can't go," burst from me.

"You must go. I have nobody else to send."

I looked across the room at Elaine, busily typing.

"No, Arabella, Elaine cannot do this hearing. It takes a more experienced reporter. You have to go." She spoke with a finality that I couldn't counter.

I turned towards Marian. She looked crestfallen.

"I'll call my husband." Marian went to the receptionist's desk, picked up the phone and dialed.

"I'll give you the particulars," Mrs. Henderson said to me and headed for her office. Seconds later, she returned, an official order slip in her hand.

I hadn't moved. I felt the corners of my mouth draw down, and I sat glumly, disheartened. I couldn't even contact Hank. The train from Washington took three and a half hours. He had probably already left the Manger-Annapolis Hotel. I sulked.

She observed me, laid the directions on my desk and walked away.

I could hear Marian talking to her husband, almost weeping in her apologies for having to work late. I had never had much to say to Marian. I thought her a rather mousy and uninteresting person.

The minute Marian hung up, Mrs. Henderson appeared in her doorway. "I suggest," she said in Marian's direction, "that you both take and split up your notes." Her glance swept over me, and she backed into her office.

In the Hotel Pennsylvania, we discovered that the huge meeting room, lined with rows of straight-backed, bargain-basement chairs, already had a number of people milling around. An immaculately dressed woman in black told us to sit unobtrusively in the back of the room.

Glancing around, I noted the raised podium and microphones placed strategically—one in front of the podium and three others distributed along a wide central aisle. I turned to the woman in the black silk linen suit. "Sitting in the rear of the room the way you suggest, we would have everybody's back to us and not be able to hear well."

"There are microphones," the woman said pointedly.

"I need to see faces to lip read," I said. "If you want a good transcript, it is necessary to see as well as hear."

"Well, where do you want to sit?" She drew her lips together in annoyance.

"It would be best for us to sit at the end of the platform, one on each side. That way, we could see everybody."

"All right. Do as you want. There will be a presentation on some changes in FDA rules. Then the people in the audience will have a chance to make comments and ask questions. Each speaker will have to go to a microphone and identify himself before speaking."

Marian and I set up our stenotypes and were standing together looking over the audience when the chairman walked up to us.

"I have a prepared presentation," he said, "but I intend to ad-lib, so please take down everything. And I think we are ready to begin." He jumped onto the two-foot high platform, grabbed the gavel lying on the podium, and banged it on the wooden block.

He spoke well, made his points slowly, and opened the meeting for questions. Even though he made the speakers go to the microphone and identify themselves, I had trouble understanding some of the mush-mouthed southerners. I hoped Marian understood the ones I didn't.

We worked continuously, with breathers only when speakers changed, until 5:30. I frantically threw my machine in the carrying case, packed up the stand and notes, and said, "Let's go," to Marian.

"Right."

We grabbed a cab back to the office. I dropped my stenotype on the desk, handed my notes to Marian, and said, "I'll be back after dinner."

The clock in the hall indicated six o'clock when I stepped onto the elevator. I flew across the street, into the Vanderbilt lobby, and saw Hank sprawled in an overstuffed chair. He saw me and rose. In my hurry to reach him, I almost ran into him. He kissed me then reached for his lightweight coat.

"Let's go into the bar."

"I'm so sorry you had to wait an hour."

He shrugged. "It was longer than that. I came early, hoping you would, too."

"Oh, darling." I clung to his arm.

"It doesn't matter now." Smiling, he looked down at me. "You need this lovely brown dress and jacket tonight. For August, it's chilly." As we walked across the lobby, Hank pointed to a woman who had accosted him. I glanced at her, and she looked at me, but I was too concerned about the office and having to type later to pay attention to the girl. Frowning unhappily, I said, "I have to go back to the office after dinner. What a miserable afternoon. I couldn't get out of it. Ever since Charlie checked himself out of the hospital and disappeared, we're short-staffed."

"Never mind, honey. These emergencies happen. We'll eat quickly, then I'll bring you back here."

"Don't make it too quick. I'd rather be with you."

He smiled at me. "That goes for both of us."

I thought, this man has the most wonderful disposition. He's so understanding and thoughtful. How can he be so in love with somebody like me?

We didn't rush having dinner, but we didn't dawdle either. Then Hank took me back to my office building. At the entrance, he said, "I'm about due for my September stay at The Homestead. Why don't you fly down for the weekend?"

"What a wonderful idea." On tiptoe, I reached for his mouth and hustled to the elevator.

I found Marian typing. A note and an envelope on my desk told me that I would have to place the transcript inside the envelope, seal it, take it to Pennsylvania Station and have it put on the overnight train to Washington. I picked up the envelope and read the address. Someplace on Fourth Street and Independence Avenue in Washington. It meant nothing to me.

Marian's typewriter stopped. "It's going well. Mrs. Henderson split the notes."

I placed my share of the notes in the long, narrow transcription box, draped the beginning fold over the upright arm, settled the start of the paper tape to refold in the holding box and propped Marian's notes on a book next to the box before starting to type.

Marian finished, laid her part of the transcript on top of my desk and departed. I plugged on, trying not to think of Hank and The Homestead. At eleven-thirty, I took a cab to Penn Station and deposited the carefully addressed envelope containing the completed transcript with the trainman at the overnight delivery counter.

Six

The plane rolled to a stop at Roanoke Airport on Friday evening. From my window seat, I could see Hank, dressed in tan slacks and a dark jacket over a blue plaid sports shirt, waiting at the fence. I melted within myself at the sight of him, thinking, 'and he's mine.' When the line of passengers getting off started to move, I got up, picked up my pocketbook and joined the queue.

"I'm parked nearby," he said after kissing me. "We'll get your luggage and head out."

Though we waited and waited, my luggage didn't come. The airline crew apologized vociferously. They would bring it to the hotel as soon as the first plane arrived in the morning.

"In the morning?" I cried. "I need it tonight!"

"I'm sorry, Madam. Your flight was the last flight of the day."

Upset, I couldn't resist saying, "Being sorry doesn't help," and turned away.

As we left the building, I said, "You're stuck with

me in this dress for a formal dinner, darling." I drew my brows together.

"Never mind, sweetheart." He caught my arm and squeezed it against his body. "I'll take you any way you are." He opened the car door for me. I scrambled in and scooted across the seat to be near him. He gave me a hug. We drove slowly crossing the mountains so we could enjoy the view. I laid my arm across his shoulders. We didn't talk much during the ride, just lived the happiness we felt in being together.

Before dinner, I took great care in freshening my makeup. Fortunately, I had a nice-looking yellow linen suit and a flowered silk blouse on.

The next day I was relieved. I found my suitcase waiting on the luggage rack in my room when I returned mid-morning. The gnawing worry in the back of my mind sailed off to find better accommodations.

"At least, I can get dressed up tonight," I told Hank.

"You'll blow them away," he grinned.

"Wait until you see," I countered.

Before going down to dinner, I surveyed myself in the mirror. The pale cream chiffon over the fitted silk print in soft greens and oranges did look nice.

"Wow," was all Hank could say when I opened the bedroom door for him. "What a gorgeous dress. I'd like to eat you up, but that would mess up the dress." He kissed me repeatedly. "Let's get out of here before I throw you on your back."

"Oh my," I said primly and smirked.

He laughed.

As we sat down at our table in the dining room, Hank said, "Every head in the room is turning."

I flashed an amused smile at him.

During dinner, we danced. "All the women are green with envy," he whispered.

"Because you're so handsome."

"Touché." We both chuckled.

After dinner, we sat on the sofa and talked. He asked me what I thought of the old couple sitting across from us.

"He's probably with the convention that's here, and she's enjoying the luxury."

"I think they're just married because his wedding ring looks so new." I stared at the ring. Good grief, he was observant. It looked neither old or new to me, just gold.

Later when we were alone, he said, "Do you want me to wear a wedding ring?"

I looked down before saying, "I think that's up to you. It wouldn't make any difference to our marriage one way or the other. Would you like to wear one?"

"I don't know." He bounced on the seat, stuck his left hand straight out, and looked at it. "I'll have to think about it. But I want you to wear one."

I ducked my head and smiled in pure joy.

Sunday morning, we wandered around the extensive grounds, jumping from rock to rock in the little stream that bubbled its way along among the trees, and took pictures of each other. Walking through the grassy meadow, Hank a few steps ahead of me, for some reason beyond me, I said, "I can't have any babies."

He turned to me and said, "That's okay. We can adopt a little girl about eighteen."

That cracked me up. He had the most wonderful sense of humor.

As usual, parting brought trauma. He held me tight. I

bemoaned the fact that I had to work the next day. Hank didn't seem able to let me go.

"I'm going to be gone for a while," he said. "I don't know when I'll get back."

"Darling, darling," I moaned.

There came a point when I had either to get on the plane or be left behind.

As an afterthought, he hurriedly said, "Why don't you call my sister? She'd like that."

So, he has discussed me with his sister. Actually, I'm not surprised. I'm glad.

"I will." I quickly wrote down the number he gave me and boarded the little two-engine propeller plane. As the plane took off, I mused. If I had ever doubted him, thinking he might be using me as a plaything outside of a marriage, giving me his sister's phone number put an end to that. He would be afraid she might babble. But I had to admit, I had never given that another thought since our meeting in Hot Springs. Still thinking about his sister, then adding his family, I suddenly thought his parents must be dead.

On Tuesday, a letter dated September 28 came. He started, "My Doll." I threw my arms around my ribs and squeezed myself in delight. An attorney I once knew liked to call his wife 'My Doll,' and I had always liked that.

You left The Homestead an hour ago and already it seems like a month has passed.

"It always seems like an eternity to me, too, in my longing to be with you," I whispered.

I write this because there are a few things you should know.

l. The two old folks that sat across from us by the fireplace Saturday night. You guessed they were here on a convention. I guessed they were retired or just married because of the new look of his wedding ring. The facts are they are here from Boston celebrating their forty-eighth wedding anniversary.

2. You really "wowed" them with your outfit on Saturday night. The Haymans, the Townes, and two old gals I didn't even see in the dining room all told me how perfectly stunning you looked. See why I'm proud?

Much to my amusement, he had ended the sentence by drawing a long question mark in heavy black ink. "Remember, Hank." I smiled softly to myself. He had signed the letter "Hank." But of course, we were engaged now, so this was a little different than his first two letters. Even though he felt about me the way I felt about him, he had been formal.

Below, in parentheses, he wrote, "Thanks again, dear."

I folded the letter. Yes, I had already figured out that he liked me to look elegant. And with my interest in clothes, he had no worries on that score. I had also noticed that he was always perfectly groomed himself. I shivered. He would look gorgeous in a tuxedo—"tails," as they were called.

Carefully, I stowed the letter in the desk drawer along with the others.

Seven

Work. I'll work hard and try not to fret about not seeing Hank for a while.

As if reading my thoughts, Mrs. Henderson unexpectedly sent me to a briefing for the media by the chairman of one of New York State's agricultural committees. Elaine accompanied me.

"Both of you take and divide the notes," she said. "This is a series of briefings. It ran one and a half hours last week, and it's fast delivery. You have to type there."

I gulped and gave Elaine a sidelong look. Her work was an unknown quantity to me. It could be a rough afternoon.

At the Agricultural Committee's offices, Elaine and I chose seats side by side in the front row of the fifth floor briefing room. We then went to check on the typewriters that were set up in a small room on the second floor. Satisfied that the typewriters were where they were supposed to be and worked, we returned to the briefing room, unpacked our equipment, filled the trays with paper, and sat down.

Elaine started stabbing at her stenotype with long,

bony fingers. I watched her. She used three times the necessary motion, expending untold extra amounts of energy, tensely and wildly striking the keys. The paper shot out in jerks from the uneven stroking. The machine itself clattered with each key depression, not a clatter that needed oil; the whole thing seemed disjointed.

"Do you always warm up like that?" I asked.

"Yes. Don't you warm up?" Elaine sounded surprised.

"Not really."

She stared at me. "How can you be so casual? This whole business makes me jittery."

Silently I watched her hands, mesmerized by the uneven finger action.

After a bit, she said, "I hope this doesn't last long."

"I don't know what more the chairman's going to say today. There hasn't been much new in the paper."

Elaine glowered, but maintained her uneven stabs at the machine. I wondered if the constant jangle of her machine would be distracting. However, when the chairman started to talk, I was so busy with his speech, my mind cut out Elaine.

As I surmised, he didn't have much more to say. The briefing only lasted thirty minutes.

Spreading my hands on my machine, I looked at Elaine. She sighed and let down, her face tightened, her shoulders sagged.

"How'd you do?" I said.

"I guess I got it. Let's go to the second floor and divide the notes."

On the second floor, her long brown hair falling over her face, Elaine hunched her skinny frame over the desk to fiddle with the notes.

"Do you want the beginning or the end, Elaine?"

"I'll take the end if it doesn't matter to you." She flipped over the paper folds in jumpy fashion. "I can't understand why the chairman wants two reporters. He could get instant transcription with typists."

"That's his business, if he wants to pay for it." Without meaning to, I sounded brusque. "Shall we divide this where the woman asked about pork bellies? That should be half."

Elaine pulled out the typing chair. "Yes. I just passed that." She sat down and carefully tore her notes at the designated spot. Standing up, she walked across the small room and handed the front half to me.

I settled the first fold of my own notes over the upright panel of the transcribing box I had brought with me and propped the first fold of Elaine's notes on a book for easy reference.

Seconds later, a member of the staff hovered around until each of us had finished the page in the typewriter, snatched what was completed and rushed off, only to repeat the maneuver in five minutes. When he left the last time, I wormed the chair back and hooked one foot over the metal support, relieved at the position change. "How many pages did you type, Elaine?"

"Nine and fifteen lines on the tenth."

"Perfect. I had ten plus the title page."

Relieved, the pressure off, we picked up our gear and headed for the office. We found Mrs. Henderson talking to the receptionist.

"Come into my office, Arabella, and give me your totals."

Standing in front of her desk, I said, "Twenty-one pages total."

Mrs. Henderson searched among her papers for a scrap of blank paper. "How did Elaine do?"

"She's a bundle of nerves, raw nerves. Granted, it takes a long time even after you have the speed to feel competent, but she seems to fall apart."

"She knows the system," said Mrs. Henderson. "Perhaps she would be better off typing other people's notes. It wouldn't be so hard on her. And we have plenty of work for typists who can read the notes of the reporters."

"I feel badly," I said, "as if I had undermined her."

"Don't. The handwriting has been on the wall. I just asked to make sure you had the same reaction as the other reporters she has worked with." She picked up a piece of paper. "Here's your assignment for tomorrow."

Walking back to my desk, I couldn't help looking at Elaine contentedly typing. Feeling guilty, I laid the assignment slip on the typewriter and fussily straightened the pages of the half-finished transcript on my desk.

Finally, my mental upset over, I sat down and looked at my assignment—a New York City government hearing on urban renewal that might last all day. Hummm. If they had a strong chairman who controlled the speakers, it could be an interesting day. If not, it could be rough to say the least. I crammed the sheet into my pocketbook and started to type.

The next morning, in the large auditorium lighted by multiple chandeliers, I walked down a side aisle towards the front row of movie-theater style seats and looked at the long table on the stage with committee members' name cards and five chairs. On my way, I spotted a typist's chair partway up the main aisle. Before I could retrieve it, the gray-haired chairman appeared at the edge of the stage.

He beckoned to me and said, "Come into the committee room for a minute," and started towards the door at the rear of the platform. I climbed the four steps to the stage and followed him into the panel's room. All five members of the committee on urban renewal had already assembled. Two of them sat in folding chairs, another stood looking out the window, and a fourth was washing his hands at the sink. I thought the wall phone next to the sink looked out of place.

"We have information," the chairman said, "that a so-called liberation group is going to try to break up the meeting today. Why this didn't occur yesterday while the landlords were having their say rather than today with the tenants is beyond me, but there you are. There's nothing to be alarmed about. I simply wanted to alert you."

Back on the auditorium floor, I set up my stenotype so it formed the third corner of a triangle with the left-hand staircase up to the platform and the standing mike on the auditorium floor below the chairman's seat. Then, I retrieved the typist's chair from the middle of the center aisle. I had left room for the speakers to walk in front of me, but was nearby when they presented their testimony at the mike. Only when my equipment had been organized to suit me did I carefully look over the audience. Nobody looked like a troublemaker. They all looked scrubbed and carefully dressed, many in work clothes, some in suits and ties, the women in simple dresses or business suits with hats and gloves.

Seconds before ten o'clock, Mr. Brody led the members of his panel onto the stage and waited for the woman and three men to seat themselves. He then sat down behind his large name card and gaveled the meeting to order at exactly ten o'clock. He explained that he would call ten names and ask them to occupy the front row of seats near the staircase, thus eliminating time consumed while they went to the microphone from all over the room. When that ten had spoken, he would call another ten. Each speaker was allotted three minutes.

He tapped a small box on the table with his right hand. "At two minutes, a tiny yellow light in this box will blink," he said. "A red light will start blinking at three minutes."

The formalities over, he called ten names. Instead of sitting in the seats, the speakers lined up at the foot of the platform staircase. Everything ran like clockwork. The tenants didn't try to run over their time, and they kept their mouths off the microphone, for which I gave quiet thanks. I always shuddered when somebody mouthed the microphone. The closeness shattered the sound and made hearing difficult.

After the mid-morning break, I again carefully looked over the line of waiting people. I found it impossible to determine which one might be a rabble-rouser. Some were rumpled and dirty now, true, but those speaking earlier had looked the same. They had said their piece and gone back to their seats.

The last of the current ten, a clean-cut, bearded man, walked to the microphone and started reading his statement so slowly, with a slight accent, that I gave him less than full attention. My eyes went over the audience again. Suddenly, the speaker left the microphone and started shouting at the audience from the center aisle. In astonishment, my hands automatically rose from the machine and remained stationary above the keyboard.

Mr. Brody banged the gavel and yelled, "Stop. That's enough. I'll call the next ten." Bang, bang, bang, the rapid, continuous, clap of the gavel, wood on wood, reverberated across the room. "Stop! Next witness. Mr. Hanson."

The man kept right on shouting. I had turned to look at the panel when I saw a man walk up to the opposite staircase. His attitude said, "Interfere with my friend and suffer the consequences." For just an instant, fear swept over me. He looked threatening. The panel conferred, rose like one person and rushed through the door behind them.

My intention had been to run up the stairs on my side and follow them, but by the time I collected my belongings, a burly man with half-closed eyelids had taken a menacing position at the bottom. Another short twinge of fear swept through me. What would Hank do under similar circumstances? I sat back in the chair and watched the audience. Nobody paid any attention to me. Some were falling all over themselves, trying to get out. Others hovered in the middle of the room to see what would happen next. Those in front were howling and shaking their fists in the air.

When someone yelled "Mace," the watchers ran for the doors. The man standing at the foot of the stairs near me melted into the crowd. I grabbed my stenotype, prepared to dash for the stage door when the shouter turned and walked straight towards me. I held my breath, albeit aware that my presence was unmarked by him. Though my eyes were starting to sting, I didn't dare rub them. Then, without warning, I coughed.

Swiftly, I glanced at the ex-speaker. Had he noticed me? Would he strike me? Nervous, I resumed my seat.

Movement at the rear of the auditorium caught my peripheral vision. Men in blue, the New York City Police, three and four deep, blocked every rear entrance. Down the aisles they came in a solid phalanx that spread out around the stage. Deliberately, with a crouched, springy stance, one policeman padded, stealthily, sure-footed, to the base of each staircase.

As the officers closed in, their quarry kept backing up. When he got close to me, I stood up and, putting all my strength into the thrust, pushed him. The assault from the rear threw him off balance, and he fell against the waiting police.

Scooping up my machine, I ran up the stairs towards the stage door. I didn't know I could be so assertive. Hank would be proud of me. I'd tell him all about it as soon as I saw him. When two of the policemen reached me, to escort me out of the building, I was bathing my burning eyes at the sink.

Mrs. Henderson clucked when I told her what had happened. "You got a good half-day's work and not much else. Is that it?"

"Yes."

"Then I'll assign you to a committee meeting tomorrow. It shouldn't last more than half a day."

Eight

On Wednesday morning, in the large, plain, typical government hearing room, I had just organized my equipment in front of the corner chair next to the chairman's seat at the head of the long table when a slender woman wearing a circular red skirt and black sweater entered. She pushed a baby in a stroller. The woman purposefully wheeled the stroller the length of the room, its tiny occupant slumped over in sound sleep, and stopped in back of the third chair down the table from me. I shrugged. The chairman could redirect the woman when he came.

Seeing her unwrap the baby and retrieve the utility bag, I became apprehensive. Did she belong in this room? She deliberately laid the baby on one of the chairs pushed against the wall and parked the stroller in front of the next chair. Everything arranged to suit herself, she picked up the baby and sat down on the chair next to me. Stock-still, I watched.

She hummed softly and cradled the sleeping baby,

her shoulder-length straight brown hair mixing with the baby's thick, dark tuft. Dressed in yellow, the infant appeared to be very young.

I scowled. Mother and baby had settled too close to me for comfort. The humming could easily destroy my concentration. Being sensitive to anything that might create unnecessary, unwanted noise, I also wondered what would happen when the baby woke up.

Deftly angling a large name card from a side pocket of her purse, the woman placed it on the table in front of her. I read: "Mrs. Collins," printed in large black letters.

Immediately, I bent forward and leafed through the papers I had collected from the hall table until I found the name list. Mrs. Collins from Louisiana, one of two consumer representatives, the list informed me. Mrs. Mason, the other consumer representative, came from Connecticut.

Participants began to drift in and out. A smiling, elderly man gracefully bent above Mrs. Collins and offered a pinky to the tiny gripped fist. "Is it a girl?" he asked.

"A boy," came the huffy answer.

"That's the way to win friends," the man said and turned away.

I unconsciously nodded. That certainly wasn't making herself agreeable.

At nine-thirty, a dark-complected individual with spectacles, a prominent nose, and black hair, walked rapidly around the table. He set his card down at the chairman's spot—Mr. Rothstein, chairman. A plumpish woman in a speckled gray suit hurried to the empty chair across from Mrs. Collins, then flinched at sight of the baby.

Slowly, she retrieved her name card from the briefcase she carried and set it on the table. I read the bold black letters—Mrs. Mason.

Mr. Rothstein tapped his water glass. "We have a lot to do today. I think we'll get started. We are dealing with canned food."

From then on, I worked tensely, trying to ignore the baby and keep up with the discussion at the other end of the table.

Well into the discussion, Dr. Keith said, "I don't think minute detail in nutrition labeling is necessary on cans. Putting the amounts of riboflavin and acid or vitamins on the can just adds expense."

"Consumers want all the information they can get." Mrs. Collin's hurled words shrieked argument. "We have a right to know what's in that can."

The stenotype notes on the objection came out jumbled hash, but I figured I could read them.

Dr. Keith made a cold, erudite, factual response before adding, "I don't think people read it anyway or—"

"Yes, we do." Mrs. Collins spoke emphatically.

"—understand the meaning. Particularly if the can is small, the label is illegible with all that added material—"

"Then make the can bigger. Consumers want this information," said Mrs. Collins. "It doesn't have to inflate the price, either. But I'll talk about that later." Her voice crescendoed to the last two words. Defiance blared above the slumbering baby.

Dr. Keith's quiet voice started again. I leaned forward to catch the sounds more easily. Without warning, the baby threw up his arms and whimpered, distracting me. For a moment, he subsided then yelled, flailing his arms at the same time. His mother, forgetting everything else, began to jounce him. When he didn't stop, she put him over her shoulder and patted his back, crooning low. The baby kept right on yelling.

I scowled and edged forward on the chair, tilting my head more than usual towards the speaker while trying to signal the chairman that I couldn't hear what Dr. Keith and the man next to him were saying. He wouldn't look my way. His eyes fastened on the table, his face growing redder and redder. It wasn't until the tension became unbearable that he looked straight down the middle of the table and said in an unnecessarily loud voice, "We will take a five-minute recess."

Instantly, he reached my side. "This is very awkward. Perhaps she'll get the baby quieted down during the recess."

"Can't you ask her to take him outside when he disturbs people?"

"Not very well. She has specifically been asked to participate."

Once the baby had stopped yelling, Mr. Rothstein tapped his water glass. "I think we'll go on to the subject of printing dates on food products. Dr. Morgan is going to open the discussion."

"Our group came to a number of different conclusions that involve bumper crops, storage guidelines, as well as actual dating," Dr. Morgan stated, passing a stack of sample papers down each side of the table.

"The pack date should be mandatory," interrupted Mrs. Collins.

"Please. I haven't even brought the subject up yet," said Dr. Morgan.

"Well, you brought up dating. You people always say putting a time date on would be more expensive when you put a code date on now."

"It would be more expensive. It's always more expensive to add something."

I swiveled on my chair to watch Mrs. Collins' lips. For a split second, I stopped working then had to rush to catch up. Mrs. Collins sat quietly breast feeding her infant while carrying on as if she were haranguing the crowd in London's Hyde Park. "You could make the code date understandable. That wouldn't cost more."

Two of the men looked steadily at their papers. One watched Mrs. Collins. The rest attempted to carry on. For a short time, the discussion became a forced and tumbled debate, adding nothing of substance, only returning to its normal pattern as the men at the opposite end of the table forgot Mrs. Collins.

I had no reason to look at her. But I turned instinctively when that individual broke in again to discover that the black sweater had slid up to act as a muffler around her throat. No other clothing showed between the muffler and the waistband of her red skirt.

As though chiseled in marble, my hands posed over the stenotype, waiting. No sound came. I heard nothing to write down. Finally, Dr. Morgan said matter of factly, "I'll put down a suggestion Dr. Keith made during the recess as another recommendation. It's a good point."

"What is it?" asked a man whose name card I couldn't see.

In haste, the men interrupted one another so I didn't hear any response to the question. But the momentum had gone. Soon afterwards, the chairman called the lunch break.

When I returned from lunch, I noticed a large glass of water resting close to the edge of the table on the other side of Mrs. Collins. I turned, intending to walk around the chair and push the glass back, but Mr. Rothstein hustled into the room and came right up to me.

"Can you stay later tonight?" His sharp question caused me to pull back as if I had been caught at the cookie jar. "We're not going to finish by the time indicated in the agenda, and we have to finish."

"I'm at your service, whatever you want to do," I said.

Mrs. Collins came back late. She wheeled the stroller around the table, seemingly trying to make as much racket as possible. The baby waved his arms, his large black eyes fixing each person he passed. After unstrapping him, his mother sat down, holding him against her abdomen so he could look at the people while she pointedly sifted through her papers.

The group had already launched into the third topic. Mr. Anderson, next to Mrs. Mason and opposite me, said, "I think that's all I have to say. With the smaller cans, space is a big problem. In order to get everything on it, the print literally becomes illegible."

"Thank you, Bill." Mr. Rothstein turned to Mrs. Collins. "Our last discussants are Dr. Henry and Mrs. Collins."

"I'll hold the baby while you give the report." Dr. Henry stood up and held out his arms. "I'm used to holding my grandchildren."

"Oh, no. You give the report." Mrs. Collins pulled a full baby's bottle from the utility pouch on the floor at her feet and settled back in the chair.

"We had a question of adding a pack date to the information on the can," Dr. Henry started. "Putting a pack date on discriminates against some of the older cans when there is no difference in the quality of the food. You have the same situation with bakery products. Fast-frozen dough is just as fresh when thawed as dough made that day, yet a pack date will make it unsalable."

"The consumer ought to get a price reduction advantage in a year when there is a bumper crop," Mrs. Collins broke in.

"Are you going to raise the price commensurably in bad crop years?" asked Dr. Morgan. An easy-going talented man, his usual slow and well-thought through speech became crisp, replete with annoyance. He brooked no interruption, though she tried. "You can't do that. Your comments are unilateral. Besides, you're changing the subject."

A lioness defending her cub, Mrs. Collins poured forth a compendium of consumers' right to know basic information.

Mrs. Mason cringed in her embarrassment.

Dr. Henry took up the argument. Lucid and articulate, he explained that only the fresh market was subject to fluctuation in price because of crop supply. Everyone was absorbed, listening, when Mrs. Collins screamed. My hands stopped in midair. The participants stopped all motion and looking highly amused, watched. I relaxed. Hands folded in my lap, I waited.

Mr. Rothstein jumped up, saying, "I'm so sorry. Let me take the baby."

"He's not wet, but I'm soaked. That whole glass of water went in my lap. Look at me." She stood up, laid the baby on the chair, pulled the saturated red wool skirt away from her body, and turned on Dr. Woods, sitting next to her. "How stupid of you to put that water glass so near the edge of the table. It's all your fault."

"It wasn't my water." He raised his hands helplessly.

Mr. Rothstein hurried to her side.

"I can't possibly sit here like this," she said, looking at him scornfully and picking at the wet fabric that clung to her thighs. "You'll have to adjourn the meeting until I can get to the hotel, change and come back."

"I can't do that," he said apologetically, but firmly. "I realize you had planned to stay over in Washington, but others have planes to catch. As the meeting was only scheduled for one day, we must finish before people have to leave."

That stated, he said, "What can we do to help you? Shall I have someone drive you to your hotel?"

"In which case," she raged, "you needn't wait for me. I'll miss too much to bother to return." She grabbed the baby and stormed out, leaving Mr. Rothstein to drop the overweight utility bag in the stroller and follow her.

"Please continue," he said. "I'll be right back."

To my joy, the talk continued pleasantly without interruption. Questions were asked one at a time in a quiet manner. But the time without a break, in intense concentration, took its toll on me.

By six-thirty, drained and aching, I crouched down in my chair and remained that way until all the participants had left the room. Finally standing up, I unhooked my stenotype from the stand.

Mr. Rothstein returned and abruptly said, "You put that glass of water on the table."

I almost dropped my machine, just managing to get it on top of the pile of papers I had collected. "I did not." My emphatic tone and offended attitude apparently challenged him.

"I saw you backing away."

"No, I wasn't backing away. I had started around the chair to push the glass back. Someone had placed it too precariously."

"Oh." Mr. Rothstein looked thoughtful. "I hope I get no repercussions from this. I would hate to have to poll the committee."

I simply raised an eyebrow. I didn't care whether he received any repercussions or not. I just wanted to go home and lie in a hot bath to sooth my aching muscles. "Is there a phone I could use, please? I need to call my office."

"Yes. Follow me." He led me across the hall to his secretary's office and showed me the phone.

"Thank you." I picked up the phone and dialed the office.

"I'm exhausted," I told Mrs. Henderson when she answered the phone. "I'm going home. See you in the morning."

"I've left you off the book, but come see me when you get here in the morning. There are some things I want to discuss with you."

Nine

Reaching my room at the Midston House, I simply flopped on the bed, so tired I could hardly think of Hank. True, I had made up my mind to work hard to forget my longing for him, but this tiredness changed my disposition, made me irritable. I hadn't even been home to see my folks in a couple of weeks. I had worked day and night. The book never evened out. As no new reporter had been hired to replace Charlie, I was carrying some of his normal load as well as my own.

Charlie! Mrs. Henderson had found out that he went to California. My mind wandered around, thinking of Charlie and the office at the same time, making a muddle that I couldn't straighten out. Something kept bothering me. I turned in the bed, trying to brush it away. Slowly surfacing from sleep, I became aware of a bell insistently ringing. I fluttered my eyes and yawned. Suddenly, my eyes flew wide, and I jumped off the bed. The telephone. I rushed to the desk and grabbed the phone.

"Hello?"

"Well, it took you long enough to answer," came the amused voice that I loved.

"At last." I sat down on the desk chair.

"It's been a long time, too long. I missed you every minute."

"Same here."

"Were you sleeping?"

"I guess so. I lay down and then the phone rang. But where are you? When will I see you?"

"I'm in Washington. We just got back. I'll come up one night next week if that's okay with you."

"Mother asked me to invite you to dinner. Can we do that next week?"

"Yes. I would like that. What night?"

"I'll call her when we finish talking and ask her."

"I'll call back at 9:30."

"Okay."

I sat down on the desk chair at nine twenty and pulled the phone from the back corner of the desk closer to me. This time, I would answer it on the first ring. The bell had scarcely stopped ringing when I said, "Hello."

He laughed. "You weren't sleeping this time."

I sent him an amused sniff. "Mother is delighted. She suggested Thursday next week."

"Great. That's possibly the best day for me. Where shall I meet you?"

"How about 5:00 o'clock at the information booth, Grand Central Station?"

"The information booth?" He sounded so uncertain that I realized he didn't know that famous meeting place.

"Will I be able to find you?"

"You will. It's big and round in the middle of the station and will be surrounded by people meeting other people."

In the morning, after I put my purse in the desk drawer, I went to Mrs. Henderson's office.

"Sit down, Arabella," she said abruptly.

That didn't sound like her usual friendly self. Immediately, my worry mechanism started working. I sat down and reviewed all the meetings I had recently attended and had, had no trouble that I knew of. And, I had worked very satisfactorily with Marian Gruber.

Mrs. Henderson's smooth, cool, voice instantly focused my attention.

"I have just received an order from the Gynecological Society asking for you"—she pointed at me—"to report their annual meeting."

My eyes flew open.

"More and more, I'm getting requests for you. It's nice to know that clients like our agency's work, but I don't want you getting ideas about setting up your own agency and taking all these clients with you. If you try that, I will do something unpleasant."

In shock, I stared at her. "That idea never entered my head," I stammered.

"Well, let's keep it that way." She turned back to the work on her desk.

Slow step after slow step, I walked back to my own desk. Upset, confused, I sat down and thought. Her remarks bewildered me. In the first place, even to think of setting up my own agency terrified me. I still considered myself too new at the game. And in the second place, it would never have crossed my mind. Too naïve, I guess. But her threat made me wary and changed our relationship.

I'd mull it over, think about it, but not do anything. Time would take care of it because as soon as I married Hank, I'd probably move to Washington so I better not let this bother me. Heaving a sigh and pulling my shoulders back, I started to type. I'd see him exactly one week from today.

To my surprise as I walked into the Midston House the following Wednesday evening, the desk clerk handed me a letter. The envelope had no return address, but held a Washington postmark, and I recognized Hank's handwriting. Wondering if he had to cancel the dinner party, I hurried upstairs, sat down on the bed in my room, and ripped open the envelope. Quickly, I devoured the short note.

My Dear Arabella: Attached, my lovely creature, you will find the answer to my dreams and prayers. You see, everything comes to him who waits.

There's someone down here, remember? Till then, Hank.

Stapled to the sheet of paper was a cartoon—two researchers in a laboratory. One held what looked like a huge egg. The caption said, "At last! A pill that will cure everything!"

Hum. "Everything comes to him who waits." I didn't get the point. Was he referring to his back troubles? A pill to cure his back? Or was he referring to his unsuccessful attempts to transfer out of his present job so we could get married? I realized that he didn't want to stay in that job with these constant absences and the possibility of real danger. That was a lovely thought, but not the point.

What was wrong with him? Why was he surrounded with all this secrecy?

I gave up. I couldn't make sense of any of it.

When I entered Grand Central Station Thursday evening, I saw Hank standing in the outer ring of people, nobody in front of him. 'How like him,' I thought.

Seeing me, he waved. I reached him, raising happy eyes to his. One arm went round my waist, and he kissed me. Then hand in hand, we headed for the subway. In Long Island City, we picked up my car and drove to Little Neck.

"My sister Helen and her two boys will be home," I commented at one point.

"I think you said they were six and ten, right?"

"Yes. And my father has Parkinson's disease. I think I told you that, too."

"I remember." After a short silence, he said, "Can we stop someplace where I can buy some candy?"

"There's a candy shop in our town, that sells excellent candy. John—the owner—makes all his candy."

In the candy shop, Hank bought a box of creams for my parents and a small box of solid chocolates for each of the boys.

Back in the car, he said, "Let's pull off the road for a few minutes. I haven't been able to properly kiss you."

On a quiet, tree-shaded street, away from the streetlights, we lost ourselves for almost ten minutes before driving on.

"Here's where we live." I parked in front of the gray-shingled house with green shutters set back 75 feet on top of a slight grade. Lights blinked through the trees on the lawn.

Opening the door, I led Hank into the central hall, the living room on one side, the dining room on the other, and the staircase to the second floor directly ahead. Mother had set the round dining table beautifully. I dropped my purse on the antique chair there in the hall and called, "We're here."

Mother hurried from the kitchen. Dad rose from his living room chair. After greetings all around, Hank presented his gift of candy to my parents just as the two boys came hurtling down the stairs, eager to see this man I had brought home with me.

"A whole box of candy for me!" said young Tim, his brown eyes wide and an ecstatic expression on his face as he took the box offered by Hank.

"And one for your brother, too," Hank said, handing the other box to Walt.

"Thank you," he said, grinning happily.

Then I went to the kitchen to help Mother and Hank went into the living room to talk to Dad.

"Is there time to mix Hank a drink?" I asked Mother.

"Yes."

Carrying the cocktail in one of my beautiful Swedish crystal glasses, I reached the living room. Hank sat on the black horsehair sofa, Dad across from him in the old wing chair in its faded, chintz slipcover.

"I hope you like the glass," I said as I handed him the martini, "because someday, the whole set of them will be yours." Our eyes met, and I returned to the kitchen.

Before we sat down to dinner, I noticed Tim, intent and serious, quietly disappear upstairs with his box of candy. Helen came down with him when he returned without his candy.

At the table, Hank sat on Mother's right, the six-year old next to him then I came before Dad at the head of the table. On the other side, Helen sat next to dad with ten-year old Walt on Mother's left.

Mother had made Thanksgiving dinner as long as November had already arrived. She passed serving dishes to Hank who then passed them to Tim. Each time, Hank said, "Would you like some of this, Sonny?"

Finally, my young nephew announced, "I'm not Sonny; I'm Tim."

"Excuse me," said Hank, laughing. We all laughed. The warm, happy feeling lasted the entire evening as my family gathered to themselves the man I loved.

All too soon, Hank said he thought we should go back to New York. I agreed. Neither of us wanted to leave. Young Tim said an enthusiastic goodbye to his new friend, some of Walt's chocolate all over his face.

"Darling," Hank said as we parted in front of the Midston House, "I don't know what's going to happen next. Just remember I love you dearly. Keep your mind on that and don't lose heart."

The intense, controlled emotion in his voice appalled me. "You're serious. You mean it. Is something going to happen? You make me think something drastic might happen, devastating, ending everything."

I was upset, working myself into a lather. I didn't know anything about his job. I couldn't put two and two together. My lips trembled.

"Darling, darling, don't." He pulled me tight. "Nothing, absolutely nothing, could happen, and we would be back within ten days. On the other hand, if there is a problem, it could be weeks. I'm not going to lose you—ever."

He kissed me and stroked my hair. I heaved a sigh and clung to him.

"No matter how long, just remember what I say. I love you." He pulled my chin up so he could look into my eyes and, I guess, gauge my acceptance of what he said.

I nodded.

He kissed me again and walked towards the corner. Momentarily, I watched him before going in.

I spent a restless night, worrying about his work. Did chemical engineers face untold danger, top secret danger? It must be something very important to our government, maybe even to our security, but the secrecy distressed me. Over and over, I kept repeating his last words. "Just remember what I say. I love you."

Ten

December passed. January passed. Each week, I phoned Hank's sister Debbie. The first time I called, I said, "Debbie?" and received the usual disinterested answer to an unknown voice, "Yes."

"Arabella Robbins."

"Oh, Arabella." Her tone changed to warm friendliness. She made me feel accepted. Obviously, Hank had told her of our relationship. Almost immediately, our conversation lapsed into one between warm-hearted family members. Now, when we talked we were on solid ground.

Listening to Debbie kept my spirits up. It seemed as if I had an intermediary between Hank and me, as if I had contact with him through his sister, though I didn't think Debbie actually did have any more contact than I did.

The first week of February, during my chat with Debbie, I burst out anxiously, "Where is he?"

Debbie stumbled. I sensed her withdrawal. After we hung up, I paced the floor. All my suspicions aroused.

Did Debbie know something I didn't? Was Hank seeing somebody else? I pulled myself up short, shaking my head. I didn't believe that.

Though I hadn't thought about it since he asked me to marry him, I suddenly realized that he wouldn't have let me talk with Debbie if he were married or had another woman. My mind was free of it all.

I worked. I suffered sleepless nights. Mrs. Henderson spoke to me about how worn out I looked. "Not just tired, but you've lost weight, Arabella. What's the matter?"

"I don't know," I lied. Somehow, I couldn't tell her about Hank and my worry.

She stood looking at me. I kept typing. Finally, she turned on her heel and went back to her office.

With my family, I forthrightly told them my fear. They could do nothing more than support me.

Not really caring, I got off the bed about 9:30 one night when the phone rang. A strange male voice said, "Miss Robbins?"

Instantly alert, I said, "Yes."

"You know Henry Martz?"

My throat closed up. I could hardly get "yes" out.

"There has been an accident. He's hospitalized. When he can, he'll contact you."

The man hung up. I sat on the bed, tears streaming down my face. Relief flooded through me that I finally know the problem. But more worry rapidly followed relief. What had happened? How bad was it? What hospital was he in? Where? If I went there, would I be allowed to see him? In spite of my worry, sleep came that night.

The same man called back the next night and gave me an address where I could write to Hank. Before I started to write, I studied the peculiar address in Pinehurst, North Carolina. The only thing I knew about Pinehurst was that one of Mother's friends wintered there. She was a golf addict so I assumed Pinehurst was a rather classy resort. In which case, what was a special, maybe government, hospital doing there? My assumption anyway. I did check the office atlas to see where it was located in the state. Actually a lovely area, which I expected from what I knew of mother's friend.

On February 22, Mother telephoned the Midston House. A letter postmarked February 20, 1959, Pinehurst, North Carolina, addressed to my parents' home had come. Mother thought it must be from Hank. The minute I walked in the front door Friday night, she said, "I put the letter on the dresser in your room."

I didn't even take my coat off before racing upstairs. Sitting on the edge of my bird's eye maple double bed, I opened his letter and read.

My Dear Arabella: Received your most welcome letter. I know you are upset. But honey, brush everything from your mind for a while. I have a feeling it will all work out.

My God, I hoped so. And, yes, I was upset. However, at least we had made contact. I knew from general guesswork what had happened.

I'm getting there (they say) but please don't be concerned.

Don't be concerned? Of course I was concerned. My mind was totally wrapped around Hank Martz and his medical progress. Nobody else.

I'm not all alone in this mess.

I didn't care how many others were with him. Hank Martz and only Hank Martz concerned me.

Honey, please don't contact Sis.

All right. I wouldn't call her again, even though I wanted to. What was so serious about his job that I couldn't even talk to his sister? Was he afraid she would let the cat out of the bag if he told her? Which means that he really trusted me not to talk about his work. That thought pulled me to a stop. Whatever my feelings had been about calling Debbie, chatting with her in a personal relationship was a big help to me, which I hated to give up. However, I had a lifelong responsibility.

I looked at the phone longingly, smiling because she was so much fun. But, obviously Hank chose to contact me, his wife, over his sister. I couldn't let him down.

There are too many ramifications if you do. Uncle Sam's SS boys keep me abreast of my folks, their health, etc. When I get to talk with you face-to-face, I'll explain.

That surprised me. Ramifications? What ramifications? Somehow, that indicated to me that she hadn't been told. Did the government keep his condition a secret from his family? Had they been told the possibilities when he took the job and thus, silence now? The silence told me a lot about what Debbie might know. In that case, if I called, she probably would clam up the way she had that day I called her, asking where he was. My decision was made. I would not call.

And that last comment sounded hopeful. He must be improving and either expected to come to me or arrange for me to visit him. I hoped it was the former, for a good long stay. Anyway, my decision was made.

I'll be gone from here in a day or so.

I wondered where he was going.

So my dear, don't write to me again until I can give you another address.

Your letter cannot be forwarded at this time (Maybe later).

Obviously, the doctors were moving him from place to place. I stared out the window, running that through my mind. What was the point? It couldn't be for professional medical availability, or special equipment. He would naturally be where that was. I could think of nothing.

Take care of yourself and remember there's someone down here who loves you.

"There's also someone up here who loves you, too," I whispered. Through the wet blur in my eyes, I could hardly see the last three words.

Till then, Hank.

For some time after reading the letter, I sat there on my bed and thought of Pinehurst, North Carolina. Not exactly the Washington area. And if he were leaving there in a day or two, there was no point in my trying to go there. Even if I went, where would I find him? Go from hospital to hospital, care place to care place, and ask for him? "Good grief," I gulped and again stared out the window.

Suppose he hadn't told me that night in South Hampton that he loved me and asked me to marry him? I wouldn't even consider trying to see him. I wouldn't have dared. I would have just folded my tent.

I set my jaw. Now I had a right to try to see him, to go to him wherever he was being held. I sucked in a deep breath. "Oh, Hank," I murmured, "I'm so glad you told me that you loved me even though you didn't want to."

I blinked. I now knew what he had meant when he said he hadn't wanted to tell me. He knew he faced this, whatever it was. Knowing makes all the difference in the world now. It has given me unspeakable peace against the emptiness of never knowing. As far as I was concerned, he was my lord and master. I wanted it that way.

He would be head of household. I wanted him to be assertive and take care of me, though not totally. Not like my friend who didn't know how to pay the telephone bill when her husband died. I made good money and intended to spend some as I wished without his permission. Too many women were still controlled by their husbands. I don't think I could put up with that. And I had already let him know that I intended to continue my career, though I knew I needed to cut back on all this night work and getting myself exhausted. That wouldn't be fair to Hank. I'm sure we could work it all out compatibly.

He was considerate and understanding of my wishes, such as that time I asked about continuing to work. I didn't think he had any financial difficulty.

My mind turned back to what I would do with my money after we were married. Squinting and shaking my head, I decided I wouldn't give it to him. I might offer to share expenses, but I think he would just laugh at me and tell me to keep it. Also, I had the impression that he would never complain about the money I spent. And what else? I couldn't think. There were so many things about marriage that we hadn't discussed, except that I knew he wanted a house. I preferred apartments, but if he wanted a house, we would buy a house. I had an easy-going disposition, and he had already shown me that he was reasonable. We should have no trouble.

Well, I shook myself, enough of this. He needs to get well before we face these questions.

And where was he being sent? I couldn't even guess. One of the well-known hospitals around Washington made sense to me. Anyway, Washington was his home base so that would probably be the pivotal point.

When I stood up, I took off my coat and flung it across the bed. Slowly, I walked downstairs and into the living room. Mother sat in the wing chair reading, Dad in his favorite low, green velvet chair. He put down the newspaper and looked at me, while mother put down her book.

"He says he's coming along, but there is no way I can contact him for now. I've thought it over, and I have decided to move to Washington. Somehow, I think it might be easier for me to see him if I were in Washington."

"Does he say what the problem is?" asked mother.

"No, but I have a feeling that he received a massive dose of radiation. And that's a guess on my part. I really have nothing to base it on, just a few comments he has made about men who preceded him. And he came back on a train from the south. I've read about a machine at Duke University, I guess it was, that's involved with radiation."

I glanced at each of them. "You understand that I'm just putting bits of information together. All I have is these snippets of conversation. So what I have told you is all guesswork."

Mother gasped, and Dad dropped his newspaper.

Monday morning at Number Two Park Avenue, I poked my head into Mrs. Henderson's office.

"May I talk to you, Mrs. Henderson?"

"Of course." She laid the papers she was holding on the desk. "Sit down, Arabella."

Once seated, I said, "I'm going to move to Washington."

Mrs. Henderson's face was like an emotionless mask.

She stared at me and then said, "I'm a bit stunned. Is this a sudden decision? Are we not keeping you busy enough?"

"Please. It's not that. I've been happy here. But, yes, it is a sudden decision. In fact, I decided Saturday afternoon when I was home with my parents. I received a letter from my fiancé. He has been in a bad accident and is hospitalized. He lives in Washington. I want to be there so I can see him at every possible moment."

Having talked nonstop and rapidly, I stopped and gulped.

"Well, that does put a different light on things. I hate to lose you, but can't say I blame you." She picked up the letter opener and twisted it around her fingers as she thought. "I don't know people in Washington so I can't help you. However, I do know that there are lots of reporting companies and some reporters attached to government agencies as well as in Congress. If you need a recommendation for any agency, I would be glad to give you one."

"Thank you, Mrs. Henderson. You have been most generous."

"When do you plan to leave?"

"I thought I'd take the early train down Thursday and see what I can find. You know, what's available. If I can't find something I want, I'll try to get a room at the University Women's Club until I find an apartment."

I stood on the sidewalk in front of a deteriorating Washington row house on C Street, N.W., a short street which ran into Louisiana Avenue. The smell of rancid fat drifted from the carry-out in the basement level. Revolting.

My eyes swept critically up the half-flight of wrought-iron stairs to the plate glass window on the first floor. Large block letters spelled out "Colonial Reporters, Inc."

Perspiration ran down my back. The silk blouse under my jacket felt wet. Nerves, I admitted. Why had I worn this apricot-colored, lightweight wool suit under my heavy coat? All that perspiration might damage my blouse. I pulled my coat tighter around me and shivered. How I hated wind, especially cold wind.

Starting with my first interview in the late morning, the day had been a fiasco. Nobody, at least in New York, had suspected that Washington's largest agency, the well-known one, the one whose reputation set the standard, had declared bankruptcy. "There's no use negotiating," the owner said. "Everybody's looking for another place."

Unnerved and shaken, I had tramped from one agency to another. Either I had been afraid of the rundown neighborhoods or found the owners distasteful.

Well, I might as well get this over with. I took a deep breath and noisily let it out before mounting the stairs. The unattractive box-like room seen from the street contained an old, beaten-up, dark green desk and three gray filing cabinets without looking cramped.

"Hello," said the frumpy bespectacled woman who sat behind the desk. "Can I help you?"

"I'm a court reporter. I'd like to talk to somebody about joining this firm."

"Mr. Grossman is in. If you'll wait a minute, I'll tell him you're here." She rose and disappeared through a dark archway.

An open assignment book, in which listed the day's hearings and the reporters covering them, lay in plain view on the desk. That was something new. Mrs. Henderson always kept hers hidden. I edged closer, trying to read the contents, but the woman returned before I could identify any of the items. A pleasant-faced man of medium height with dark hair and a shy-looking demeanor, who had crossed the imaginary line into middle age, followed her.

"Come back to my office," he said after I had introduced myself. The way led through a short, unlit passage to a duplicate in size of the front room. Any similarity ended there. It contained so much furniture that Mr. Grossman had to step around three pieces to reach his desk.

"Sit in the leather chair," he suggested, "but be careful how you lean back. If it catches in a certain way, it starts a gentle shaking motion."

"Really!" I exclaimed. "What do you use it for?"

With a self-deprecating silly smile that enhanced his personal charm, he said, "I nap in it."

I settled into the chair deliberately carelessly, without the hoped-for result.

"So you're a court reporter," he said. "We're always on the lookout for good reporters. What's your background?"

I handed him my resumé, watched him read it, then asked questions concerning the work of his agency.

"Washington is mostly government contracts; we have a number, mostly for administrative hearings. The House and Senate Committees are patronage. They tend to be daily copy."

"Do you do any conferences?"

"Some." He thought. "I take that back. We do an occasional convention on a one-time basis, but most of the medical work at the National Institutes of Health is what you might call conferences, whether there are five people or a hundred and five. We do some depositions, and press conferences for the government department heads. When I can't cover a hearing—for example, in San Francisco with a San Francisco reporter—I send somebody from here."

"You do? I'd like that."

George Grossman studied the resume on his desk. "I gather you've had a lot of medical experience. Local reporting companies won't touch medical. I don't even try any more; I send someone. It could be anywhere in the continental United States, Hawaii, Alaska, or Puerto Rico."

Having made up my mind that I wanted to join his company, I watched his expressive face, trying to fathom his reaction to me.

"How many reporters do you have?" I asked.

He ran his hand through his thick dark brown hair. "I think I have fifteen available to call on for overflow; two in the office full time, each one with over twenty years of experience. They're on the other side of the entrance hall. We have two rooms over there comparable to these and a third added on in the rear. They work in that third room. We use the front room for processing transcripts and the middle one for storage because it doesn't have any lights."

"What are your rates?" I asked when the discussion threatened to peter out.

"We don't pay a guarantee."

"I don't know what you mean."

"Oh! Were you always on a page rate?"

"Yes."

"Some reporters come expecting to be paid a flat sum—a guarantee that they'll be given enough work to make that much money. Anything they earn over that amount, they get paid, naturally. But if there isn't work as sometimes happens, the agency ends up paying them to do nothing."

"No, I've never worked that way."

"Good. The base rate is two dollars per page of transcript produced. More for highly technical, which includes medical. Of course, if you're overloaded and dictate something, that fee comes out of your money. But that's also a set rate."

"What if a witness, for instance, doesn't show up?"

"There's an appearance fee both morning and afternoon, thirty-five dollars each. If you don't get enough pages to make that amount, you get thirty-five dollars, or if nobody shows, you get the thirty-five dollars. I pay the reporters once a month."

"That's a switch. I'm used to every two weeks."

"Would it be a hardship?"

"No. I'd manage."

"We're generally busy enough so that the reporters do very well on a yearly basis if they're willing to work. August usually falls off to nothing because the Congress is out. And, incidentally, the page rate is higher for Hill work. Thanksgiving and Christmas are slow times."

"That's a good thing. Personally, I'd hate not to spend Christmas with my family." I laughed gingerly.

He smiled back. Conversation lapsed. The air was electric. I examined a water stain on the floor. Offer, offer, offer. If mental telepathy worked, now was the time.

"Well," Mr. Grossman drawled, "I'd like you to come with me if you want."

It took some effort on my part not to appear too willing. "I'd like to."

I knew my face lit up with a cat-and-mouse smile as broad and pleased as his.

"Would you like to meet the others?" he asked. "I think both reporters are in."

"Yes, I would," I said, supplementing acceptance by a vigorous nod of my head.

We started walking through the business office. "Of course, you talked to Theresa who runs the office and does a very efficient job."

Theresa and I smiled and nodded to each other.

He led me across the hall, to the front room. Facing me, for the entire length of the wall, ran a wide built-in shelf covered with partially assembled transcripts. Reproduction equipment stood against the wall on the other side of the room. A tall, thin man with iron-gray hair and a weather-beaten face stood in front of the table-high shelf.

Mr. Grossman said, "Pete, the office boy, is out delivering transcripts right now, but this is Bill, who runs our collating section." He motioned towards the man.

"Hi," said Bill, smiling pleasantly at me.

I followed Mr. Grossman through the short dark hall, passing the door to the lavatory on one side, that of the middle room on the other. Outlines of piled-up furniture barely showed in the middle room. As we entered the back room, two men looked up.

For the rest of my life, whenever I thought of Ned McMillan, I remembered him the way I saw him that afternoon sitting at his typewriter. Light shining through the bay window behind him outlined his muscular shoulders. A cigarette dangled from the corner of his lips, its smoke curling across his fattish face and through his sandy hair.

On the opposite side of the room, Tom Banks stood

beside his desk straightening papers. With his slicked back salt and pepper hair, his gray double-breasted suit, he looked like a 1928 matinée idol. "Hello," was all he said, but somehow I knew I had a friend.

Together, the four of us discussed the best location for my desk, finally we decided on the one remaining windowless wall. Then we used a flashlight to look over the stored furniture. We chose a dark green wooden desk from the cluttered supply in the middle room, but couldn't get it through the door because of the stacked mess.

"Never mind," said Mr. Grossman. "I'll get some of the law students on the second floor to move it. When can you come?"

"I have to go back to New York tonight," I said. "Also, I have been invited to visit in Florida for a week. I think maybe the last weekend in March, I could come."

"Fine. We'll expect to see you that Monday, March 29," he said looking at a calender. "I think that's the 29th. And call me George." He smiled humbly.

I walked the short distance from my delightfully disreputable new office to Union Station. There, I found a phone booth containing a Washington directory. With one finger dialing each number, I called the University Women's Club. A woman answered the phone.

I stated my need for a room by the week, starting Sunday, March 28, until I found an apartment. After some shuffling of paper during which I heard whispering, the woman asked me some questions about myself. I told her that I had graduated from Columbia University, that I worked as a court reporter and had just taken a job with Colonial Reporting. Some more whispering took place before the woman said I could have a room. She then asked me my age.

"Thirty-four."

"We will expect you Sunday night, March 28."

Jubilant, I boarded the next train for New York City's Penn Station.

"Mrs. Henderson," I said the next morning, as I rapped on the open door of her office, "may I come in?"

"Of course, Arabella." She put down the sheaf of papers in her hand. "What luck did you have?"

"I have a job and a room for the time being at the University Women's Club, starting March 28. I'll go to the Women's Club that Sunday evening and to Colonial Reporters Monday morning. Their office—" Amused, I ducked my head and laughed. "You won't believe this. It's on the second floor of a deplorable old brownstone over a smelly, greasy take-out food place."

"How awful," said Mrs. Henderson.

"Not really. The two men make the reporters' room in the back kind of cozy."

"Well, if you think so." I caught the irony.

"I will share the back room with the two men. Just we three. Others work at home."

"What kind of work do they have?"

"It's varied. But what interested me most is that Mr. Grossman does all the work for the National Institutes of Health. So I'll get plenty of science."

"Well, it sounds as if you accomplished a great deal during your day in Washington. Finish up your typing. I'll keep you busy when you come back from Florida with stockholders' meetings until the 26th."

"Please, I would like to finish here on the Thursday before I move to spend the weekend with my folks."

"Very well." Mrs. Henderson flipped her calendar to the Thursday date and made a note.

Four weeks later, at four thirty on a rainy Sunday afternoon the last weekend of March, I pulled my car into the parking area of the University Women's Club on New Hampshire Avenue and unloaded two large suitcases.

The plump, rosy-cheeked lady who showed me to my room had seen her sixtieth birthday, I decided.

"It's the second floor back. You should be quite comfortable," said Mrs. Graham, leading me upstairs.

From a quick glance around at the pale wallpaper with tiny blue geometric figures all over it, the brass bed against the wall, an antique looking dresser, a comfortable chair and small table, I agreed. I set the suitcase I carried on the floor and went downstairs for the other.

"Five of us are having a little supper later. We would be happy to have you join us. It's a miserable night."

"Thank you. That's very kind. I would like to." I smiled at her.

At supper, we sat around the big circular dining room table. The five ladies told me all about the area, where to eat, the good restaurants, and the not so good restaurants, the churches, and where I might be able to find an apartment. The apartment building called Winthrop House nearby on Massachusetts Avenue seemed to be their favorite. Listening to them, I decided to walk along Massachusetts Avenue tomorrow after I finished at Colonial Reporters and look at the building.

Eleven

I put my stenotype in my car on Monday morning just in case George asked me to work. Driving slowly, I followed the route I had marked on my street map—left on Massachusetts Avenue, right on New Jersey, then left on C Street. The National Savings and Trust Bank had an office across a small park, and a cafeteria occupied the ground floor of a building directly across from Colonial Reporters. I had no trouble finding the office.

As I drove up, George Grossman rushed out and showed me where to park in the alley beside the building.

"I've assigned you to a short deposition this afternoon. The attorney's office has a notary public who can swear the witness. But you'll have to get your own notary seal. And we need to start getting you cleared for top-secret work."

Now, isn't that fascinating, I thought. I wonder if I'll find out what Hank does. Will the investigators recognize my name as having been turned in by Henry Martz and connect us?

We walked through the office towards the reporters'

room in the back. In passing through collating, I spoke to Bill and shook hands with Pete, the office boy. Entering our room, I noticed that the old, dark green desk we had chosen sat in the designated spot. I possessively stowed my pocket book in the top desk drawer.

George said, "I'll have Pete put up a desk lamp for you."

He called Pete.

"Yes, sir?" Pete stood in the doorway.

"Put a desk lamp on this desk," he pointed, "and bring a stenoprompter."

"Yes, sir." Pete turned away.

"What's a stenoprompter?" I said.

"A machine to help you read your notes when you're transcribing." He turned to Ned's desk. "See, he has one there with notes already in it. A whole pack of notes can fit inside. The starting end of the tape is threaded between two little metal rollers across a slanting surface up to a small rotating wheel that sends the notes into a tray hitched onto the back just below the wheel. The whole mechanism is controlled by a foot petal."

Intrigued, I looked Ned's stenoprompter over closely then watched Pete crawl under my desk to plug in the one he brought for me.

The attorney's office where I took the deposition had thick carpets on the floor and modern furniture in the reception room. His secretary took me into a small conference room where I could set up my stenotype.

"Mr. Reeves is waiting for the other attorney and the witness. They will all come in together when they're ready," she said. "I'll bring you some coffee."

"Thank you."

She went out, returned with a mug of steaming coffee and left again. I sipped the coffee in between setting up my machine and filling the tray with paper.

The witness turned out to be a young office girl who didn't know much about the case. It didn't last long.

After typing the short deposition, I returned to the University Women's Club and parked my car. Then standing on the sidewalk in front of the Club, I looked both right and left, to make sure I headed towards Massachusetts Avenue. DuPont Circle baffled me. I had driven around that circle with its paths and central fountain twice, trying to get onto New Hampshire Avenue.

Turning left off of DuPont circle, I walked along Massachusetts Avenue until I reached number 1727. Then I crossed the street to stand and observe the building.

The location appealed to me. Next door stood a great Edwardian home set back from the street. On the other side, another apartment complex filled the rest of the block to 17th Street. An embassy flag waved above me. I recrossed the street and entered the building's lobby along with some young, well dressed, men and women.

The switchboard operator/receptionist said that the manager would be with me shortly and asked me to sit down. Seated on a nubbly tan wool upholstered sofa, I looked around the lobby. Tan upholstery, tan wallpaper, tan carpet, even light wood chairs. Boring. It lacked color. Five steps led up to the building corridor that went straight back, with the elevator on the right at the top of the stairs.

A plumpish, platinum blond, woman, dressed in a dark blue suit and looking hassled, walked down the stairs and addressed me.

"Miss Robbins?"

"Yes." I stood up. "I've heard such nice reports of your building. I am interested in renting a small apartment."

"As a matter of fact, one of our efficiencies will be available the first of May. The tenant just notified me today. So you have a month to wait. Would you care to see it? It is rather small."

"Yes, thank you."

We took the elevator to the fifth floor. The room that we entered was jam-packed with furniture and boxes of books sitting around on the floor. The confusion made it hard for me to judge the actual size of the room. One large window angled on a slant. So this apartment must be located on a curve of the building, I reasoned. I walked over, or rather zig-zaged over, to the window and looked out, right down onto that huge Edwardian house. I could see furniture and a male servant walking around a table through one of the windows and wondered who lived there.

Turning to the manager, I said, "You are right; it is small. But I'll take it."

"Fine. Come down to the office with me so you can sign the required papers."

I left the building overwhelmed by how easily my living arrangements had fallen into place. And the month's wait gave me time to look at furniture. Suddenly, I felt excited and rushed back to the University Women's Club to tell the ladies.

After two weeks at Colonial, I sensed that George no longer considered me the new girl in the office. I took my load right along with the two men. The three of us worked quietly, companionably, in the add-on back room.

The full book kept us constantly coming and going. Each day, I passed the dirty, purple lavatory on the left off the corridor between the two rooms and grimaced. The sink and the commode had purple stains. Cans of gritty pink paste sat in a row like mushrooms on the sill of the small, high window. I shivered. Ned had said the room had no heat in the winter. At that time, I had asked him about the paste.

"Occasionally," he had said, "we have to type on something called cements. It has two pages of horrible purple stuff to imprint a piece of paper plus a regular carbon and an original. Everything gets covered with that purple. It even gets in your hair. The paste is to wash the purple off your hands."

I thought about that conversation each time I looked at the cans of paste and hoped I never had to use it.

Only once after settling into the office routine did I stumble. Assigned to relieve Ned at Senate Banking and Currency, I spotted him between the high, curved senatorial dais and the witness table, head tilted, dangling cigarette, smoke curling across a closed eye, his usual position. Rapid-fire questions beat against the uncowed witness, who fought back with fast, terse interjections. Ned never missed a stroke.

"Excuse me. Excuse me," I said, flustered by the disturbance I made among the intent listeners in my self-conscious tiptoe through the crowded room to the empty chair beside Ned.

He gave me a nod, the signal for me to begin, the moment the questioner changed. Like a professional, I jumped in where he left off and worked normally until he neared the exit door. Then, suddenly, without warning, the idea that I was working in a committee of the United States Senate terrified me. I was responsible for the transcript. Any mistake on my part might damage American policy in some way. I froze.

Struggling to regain my composure, I started to punch keys, any keys. The paper shot out from the roller and refolded into the holding tray, but no combinations made a word or the syllable of a word. Unrelated letters spread across the tape. I couldn't control the trembling of my hands, or the senseless stabbing of my fingers.

By tremendous mental exertion, I focused on what the Senator was saying. The letters on the paper tape evened out and again showed what was being said. Dampness erupted on my forehead, moisture on my hands. But when Ned pushed open the exit door, I knew I could manage.

George was watching Pete collate transcripts when I hurried in, accidentally slamming the door in my haste to talk to Ned. He smiled and took a step towards me, an open invitation to chat.

"I have to see Ned," I said, nervously shifting my case to the other hand. He acquiesced by a movement of his body, but his eyes burned into my back until I entered the dark corridor. I knew he sensed that something was wrong.

"I blew it; I went absolutely rigid. What am I going to do?" I wailed the second I reached Ned.

"Before or after I left the room?"

"Before."

"Let's see your notes. I was listening. We can probably reconstruct it."

"Are you allowed to do that?"

"Of course. You should always try to fix their grammar, make them look good. They don't want to see in print what they really said; they'd look like nincompoops."

"Damn," I yelped, disgusted at my own naiveté in thinking that what I put down was important, and irked at the idea of tampering with what I considered a legal document. Like a lamb, I handed him my pack of notes.

"Humm! Well, yes, you did blow it." He flipped over a fold. "This is fine. As I remember the discussion, you've only dropped a sentence. We can stick in something that gives the context. They'll edit the transcript to suit themselves anyway."

"Good lord," I stammered, "they do that, too?"

Ned ignored me. Using the end of his notes, the first bit of mine, and what was said when the notes again made sense, he wrote out a bridging sentence that I gratefully incorporated into my transcript.

I became more and more delighted with the Washington reporting scene. The variety of hearings, the constantly new vocabulary, the people I met, all excited me. But deep inside me, day and night, Hank ruled my thoughts.

Finally, on April 11th, I received a thick letter from Mother. It must contain a letter from Hank. I tore up to my back bedroom and ripped open the envelope. Out tumbled a sealed envelope addressed in the handwriting I recognized. The postmark was April 7, 1959, from Baltimore. Quickly, I read Mother's letter before carefully opening Hank's and pulled out the thin, one-page letter.

Dear Arabella,

Been here in Hopkins for two days, (on exhibition more or

less). However, it's been rough and will continue to be so for a while. If I follow the same routine as the boys before me, I should wind up in Biloxi sometime in May.

I wondered if they carried cute little nurses, anxious to get married, around with them on their travels. I winced at the thought. Hank hadn't seen me for months. He probably had contact with lovely, sympathetic young blondes ready to attend his slightest whim. In his weakness, he had undoubtedly lost all thought of me. In my mind's eye, I saw one nurse—was she blond or brunette? I couldn't tell—who he waited for each morning to bring his breakfast and give him a bath. His face lit up when she appeared.

I shuddered. You have to stop this, I told myself. He loves me; we are committed to each other, and that's that. I turned back to his letter.

As I leave here today I honestly don't know where I'm going, except at the moment it has to be a cold climate for a short period of time.

Cold now after our spring-like weather, then hot. Biloxi, Mississippi would be hot. I shrugged. All this switching around was beyond me. But as long as it helped to make him well, I didn't care.

Hope this letter finds you and yours healthy and happy. As ever, Hank.

On the bottom left edge, he had printed five words. I turned the letter upside down. For a minute, I scowled. What on earth? I thought. I couldn't make sense of it. Then I realized what he had done. As children, my sister and I had played at writing the way Leonardo Di Vinci wrote when he wanted to hide what he said. I jumped up and grabbed the hand mirror off the dresser. Looking at the writing in the mirror, the five words became legible. "About six months to go."

Six months and he would come to me. Obviously, at the moment, at least, he didn't know that I had moved to Washington, that no day passed that he wasn't on my mind, that I waited for him. I thought he would be pleased with the little apartment I had agreed to rent. It placed me nearer to his home base and would do until he was well and strong again.

The last weekend of April, I drove to Long Island to spend the two days with my parents. Mother had laid out some table linens, as well as kitchen and bath towels as starters in my new apartment.

"That's just perfect, Mother," I said, surveying the pile of linens. "The furniture people promised to deliver the twin beds I ordered on April 30th, and I can move in on May 1st. I'll place the card table and chairs you have given me at the end of the room, making that the dining area until I have enough money to buy a proper table." I gave mother a hug. "I even have a space in the alley behind the building to park my car."

I ran my hands through my hair. "The ladies at the club expressed sorrow at losing me," I said, "but I invited them all for tea as soon as I get settled."

Mother smiled.

While sitting in front of my dressing table that night, I reread Hank's letter then gently returned it to its envelope. I now had an apartment where Hank could come as soon as the government doctors released him.

"Arabella," Mother said as she walked into my bedroom, "I hate to interfere with your plan, but are you sure this move to Washington is the best thing to do? Suppose Hank never comes back?"

"Oh, no," I cried, clamping my fists into my mouth.

"My dear child, just suppose. That's all I said. No matter what you think now, you should face the possibilities. I sincerely hope he does get well, but I can't help but worry."

"I know, Mother, and I have to admit I fret about it, too. I've tried not to dwell on it. But I must say, I like the work in Washington better than in New York. I might just stay there." I fiddled with the comb on the dressing table.

Mother watched me. Finally, she said, "Well, I think you have your feet on the ground, sweetheart. Your father and I will support you in whatever you decide to do."

Tears wet my eyes. I jumped up and gave her a big hug.

Twelve

I had stowed the two antique maple chairs in my car's trunk—they fit snugly—and rested the card table over the back seat when I left Long Island. They would be all right over night in the University Women's Club House parking lot.

With the Senate Foreign Affairs Committee hearing scheduled to start at eleven, I had time to leave the card table and chairs in my freshly painted apartment before going to the office.

Moving myself from the University Women's Club simply meant transferring two stuffed suitcases from the one place to the other. If I didn't get everything accomplished Wednesday night, I'd finish Thursday night. But I intended to sleep in apartment No. 508 Wednesday night.

As I did most nights, just before getting into bed, I re-read Hank's latest letter then carefully replaced it in the large manila envelope in the top dresser drawer and thought about how I could make him comfortable in my small apartment.

I slipped into bed and pulled the cover over me. I lay there thinking about how unhappy I was at not getting frequent letters and my joy at receiving one. Why didn't he write more often? If I had a permanent address I'd write every day. Frequent letters would certainly raise my spirits. I did get depressed and worried when I didn't hear from him for these long stretches. I knew he loved me, but I had no idea what was going on. And I didn't like that.

And why couldn't I visit him? All the mystery about his problem and how he was being treated. I was at a complete loss. All I could do was love him.

I arrived at the Senate Foreign Affairs Committee room at ten forty-five in the morning. Strong lights for television blazed along two sides of the room and cameramen lounged all over in front of the dais. I stepped gingerly over the cables. A cameraman gave me a big greeting and unwillingly hitched himself off of my chair.

"What brings you people out en masse?" I asked.

"Senator Adams, the latest candidate for Vice President, and the Secretary of Energy are going to testify on the world energy crisis. They're on opposite sides of the fence." He cackled. "There should be a few sparks and more excitement than usual."

I glanced at the stack of papers the staff had left for me on the little table next to my chair. The witness list lay on top of their statements. I counted the number of witnesses. "Five witnesses after them," I said to anybody who might be listening. "Do you think the committee expects to finish before one o'clock? I'm supposed to go to another Foreign Affairs Committee hearing up on the fourth floor."

"I'll make a bet with you they quit by twelve," another cameraman interjected. "There's an important bill coming up on the floor. No senator will stay away."

One by one, the senators settled themselves into their well-upholstered armchairs behind the beautiful long, curved, solid wooden desk on its raised platform. No sooner had one sat down, barely having time to pull the chair up to the desk before a steaming cup of coffee, steam billowing into the warm room like smoke from a manhole, was placed in front of him by the Committee Clerk. I always watched this pampering, this subservient toddying appalled me.

Five minutes before eleven, Senator Adams arrived, his cherubic face scrubbed and sausage-like with his staff jostling behind him. The cameramen rushed forward, clicking their cameras and yelling, "Look to the right, Senator. Wave at the chairman. Shake hands with somebody."

Each senator wanted his picture taken with Senator Adams. They posed this way and that, the strong lights beaming down on their shining faces. On occasion, an elderly senator pressed a neatly folded linen square over his bald dome.

The Secretary of Energy walked in almost unnoticed. A staff member whisper to the chairman, who called, "Welcome, Mr. Secretary," and hastened to shake hands with him in front of the cameras.

When the chairman said, "I think we ought to begin," I looked at the clock on the rear wall. Eleven-fifteen.

"Senator, why don't you sit there at the witness table?"

Surprised, I wondered why he didn't invite the Secretary of Energy to sit at the witness table also. The Secretary and his staff quietly sat down in the front row of audience chairs that filled the rest of the room. The chairman hurried to his central position on the dais and authoritatively thumped the gavel on the wooden block. His opening statement, which he read, began with the announcement of a series of energy hearings and ended with an elaborate introduction of Senator Adams, replete with praise, smiling head gestures, and glances of expectant agreement from the other senators present. Obviously, they were of the same political party. Privately, I sneered. He looked up and said, "We have your prepared statement, Senator. You may submit it for the record or read it, as you wish."

"I will submit my statement in full. I'll summarize it then make a few comments."

"Without objection, your statement will be printed in the record at this point as if read. Proceed."

Senator Adams launched into a vitriolic political speech, castigating the Administration, its acts, its omissions, its policies, its foibles. He left nothing untouched. During the polite questioning afterwards, old Senator Montgomery came in and took a seat. At the first opportunity, the chairman turned to him and said, "Senator Montgomery, you have read Senator Adams' statement. Would you like to ask any questions at this time?"

"Thank you, Mr. Chairman." Like a turtle, he thrust his neck forward to look at the chairman. "And thank you, Senator Adams," he directed his words to the witness table, "for taking time out of your busy schedule to come here and help us on this very important question."

He picked the top statement from his pile and gave it a little shake. "I have read your statement and find it excellent." I thought, I'll bet he hasn't read one word of it. "I don't have any questions right now, but I'll listen carefully to what others have to say." He scrunched down and went to sleep.

As soon as he was asleep, one of the committee's women knelt by his side. Being discreet about what she was doing, I couldn't see, though I craned my neck. However, from past experience, I assumed that she was checking his coat pockets for notes that his staff, not trusting his memory, wrote to the committee.

This constant covering up that went on always infuriated me, but today, I was too worried about the time and busy taking notes to let it upset me.

All too soon, the orange light on the twelve mark of the wall clock flashed. Good, the Senate was in session. Now, if only one of the other lights would flash, announcing a quorum call, this session would end.

But no. The chairman droned on with questions fed to him by the attorney sitting behind him. A cameraman on his knees, intent on getting a profile view, shooting up at Senator Adams, got his head and camera right over my machine. When he rested his elbow on the stenotype, I gave him a quick kick. He crawled away, after casting an indignant glance in my direction.

The answers to the questions were long-winded and grammatically incomprehensible, but not difficult to report. One man turned his camera towards my hands. Obviously, he was bored with the proceedings. Somebody always did that when the testimony became humdrum. To my amazement, this one zoomed in for a close-up. I wondered how my father's gold signet ring would photograph.

Not much later, the chairman thanked Senator Adams,

who made a classic exit, his entourage and the whole press crew at his heels.

What had happened to the altercation with the Secretary of Energy? Why hadn't they been asked to testify together? Maybe the verbal fireworks had been the idea of the press and not that of the chairman. With consummate political grace, the chairman asked the Secretary to come forward.

Nodding and smiling, the Secretary took the still warm seat at the witness table, flanked on either side by assistants whom he introduced. After he read a shortened version of the statement he submitted, the questions were rapid and acrimonious.

On occasion, Senator Montgomery woke up and, in his quavering voice, asked a question that had little to do with the discussion. He rambled on and on before subsiding into sleep again.

I glanced at the clock when the chairman said, "Thank you, Mr. Secretary. I have no more questions." Fifteen minutes after twelve.

The press stampeded after the Secretary as they had after the Senator. They made such a racket that the chairman had to call for order before he could continue.

The third witness said he would summarize his statement, which he did in a slow, circuitous manner, page by page, while the television crew turned off the floodlights and packed up their gear.

Every few minutes, one of the senators departed, some slowly, talking in undertones to the staff members, others so quickly that I wasn't aware that they had even risen from their seats. Soon, only dosing Senator Montgomery and the chafing chairman remained. The questions were abbreviated and polite, with little meaning. The witness finished speaking at twenty to one.

I squirmed. Should I signal the Committee Clerk to call George? Four more witnesses. Just giving them short shrift could mean another hour. I started to write a note, but dropped the pencil in the middle of a word when the chairman started to speak.

"Unfortunately," he said, "I have to leave. An amendment I sponsored is coming up on the floor, and I must be there."

Not likely, I thought.

"I apologize to our other witnesses. The staff at my request has checked with them, and they have graciously agreed to submit their statements for the record. I wish I could stay. I'm sure it would be most interesting and informative."

Oh heck! What a farce.

With that, he tapped the gavel. "Hearing adjourned."

In the office, much later, I sputtered to Ned, "He invited those witnesses to testify, paid their way from all over the country with my tax dollars, then didn't let them talk."

Ned said, "But he put their statements in the record to look as if they had testified."

"And what makes me more mad is that he only invites people who are in favor of his stupid bill, then announces everybody is for it on the basis of the record when ninety-nine percent of the people may disagree. Anyone who manages to testify against his bill, he cuts off. I'll bet those senators expunge it from the record, too."

My volume rose with my ire.

Ned laughed at me. "There isn't a thing you can do about it."

"There's something I can do about that senile old Senator Montgomery. I can write an anonymous letter to his hometown newspaper."

"Do you think they'd print it?"

"Don't his constituents know how out of it he is? What good does he do them?"

"You know his staff does all the work anyway, Arabella."

"Imagine the President sending him to Europe to represent us at a conference! It's a disgrace. And the press covers up just the way they do Senator Arnold's DTs."

Noting the amusement in Ned's eyes, I said, "Well, it does rile me up."

"So I see."

I grinned and sat down before my typewriter.

Thursday morning, I arrived at the office looking rested, rosy, and pleased with myself.

"Well," said George, who stood in the collating room, "you do look like the Queen Bee this morning."

"I slept in my new apartment last night for the first time. I love it. And I meant to ask you, George, please try not to assign me next Tuesday morning. My piano is supposed to be delivered then."

"I think I can manage that. It may mean that you have a tough afternoon."

"I don't care."

"You're something, Arabella. According to you, you have hardly any furniture, but you bought a piano." He laughed and turned away.

At eight the following Tuesday, a miserable dark, rainy

morning, I sat quietly with folded hands, waiting for my piano and wondered why Hank didn't write more often. The thought of cute little nurses bothered me.

The ringing phone sent the nurses scurrying away. I jumped from the chair and grabbed it.

"Two delivery men are here," announced the switchboard operator.

The men set the piano on the floor and removed all the wrapping. "Where do you want this?"

I designated the only decent wall space left in the apartment.

Together, the men gently moved the piano over to the wall, stood back and surveyed it.

"It's a nice looking piano," one man said.

"Thank you. I think so."

They gathered up their plastic and wrapping blankets and left.

I surveyed my home. I entered through a currently empty foyer, a coat closet at the end. Turning right into the room, one bed took the first wall space. The second bed stood perpendicular to it on the opposite wall. The big window came next. The card table and the two little antique maple chairs occupied the wall at the opposite end of the room. On the right of the piano, I would enter the three-by-five kitchen. The other side of the piano gave entrance to a large dressing closet and bath. I did need a bit more furniture and some throw rugs on the shining parquet floor, but that would come. I smiled. I just knew Hank would like it. We could easily manage while he was getting well and strong. Then I'd see what he wanted to do. The apartment would be too small with a big, healthy male around.

All during the drive to the office, lightening flashed, followed by booming thunder. Rain pelted down. I didn't care. I bloomed into a happy mood, needing only Hank to share it. Luckily, George had kept me off the book so I could get caught up on my typing.

I had just checked a spelling on the word list Scotch-taped to the wall in front of me when a drop of water hit the typewriter. Raising my head, I spied a row of water drops marshaled along the ceiling. I twisted to scan the whole ceiling. At various spots near the center, water dripped steadily, wet circles on the floor enlarging through amoeba-like creep.

"The roof's leaking," I exclaimed.

Tom glanced across the ceiling. "Pete," he bellowed, "the roof's starting to leak."

In response to my quizzical expression, he said, "It always leaks when it rains like this. Our room, being an add-on, has no second story overhead, and the old tin roof needs repair."

I got up and shoved my desk along the wall to a dry spot. "Why don't the owners fix it?"

"Because the houses along this block are slated to be torn down, and they don't want to spend the money."

"When will they tear them down?"

"Who knows? It could be years." Reaching behind his desk, Tom pulled out the bulky case he kept stashed against the wall.

"That looks like a trumpet," burst from me.

"It is." Tom laid the case on his desk. At the same time, clattering metal sounded through the narrow corridor. Pete charged into the room, carrying four tin buckets and a roll of toilet paper. Tom and I stood side by side out of the drip while Pete positioned the buckets under the heaviest trickles. He then unrolled the toilet paper and placed a wad in each bucket to deaden the tremendous resonant ping of water hitting tin. Then the three of us surveyed the dripping water and the location of the buckets.

Ned, puffing and damp, bustled in, weighted down by his stenotype case and an enormous envelope of papers. Near his desk, he emitted a high-pitched angry scream and exploded.

"Why didn't somebody have the decency to move this transcript? Look at it! It's all wet." With his handkerchief, he mopped furiously at the transcript on his desk. "I've worked in some pretty crummy offices, but this one takes the cake. If it isn't soaking wet, it's a fire trap." He gave a violent shove to his desk and loomed like an evil genie in the bay behind. Flames jetted from his nostrils.

At the sight, Pete snuck out of the room. Tom, more sanguine, took his trumpet from the case and started to play. Sweet notes, sounding like Harry James, poured towards the ceiling and filled the room until the angry spark in Ned's eyes disappeared, and the tight lines around his mouth relaxed.

"Enough," cried Ned. "If this transcript is going to get finished today, I better start. I don't want to be here all night."

I readjusted the overhead desk lamp, which had listed when I moved the desk and got down on my hands and knees to reposition the foot pedal for the stenoprompter. As soon as I had gotten the hang of it, I loved the stenoprompter. What an improvement over those little transcribing boxes we had used in New York.

I reorganized the wires along the baseboard and checked the electrical outlet. Still squatted on the floor after backing out from underneath the desk, I said in Tom's direction, "This place is an electrical hazard, if nothing else, with all the wires we have running around the room."

While easing the trumpet case behind his desk, Tom said, "They make a good cushion for the trumpet." He sat down, his back to everything and everybody. Ned was already pounding away at his typewriter. I wondered why the old IBM electric machine didn't smoke, he typed so fast. I sat down, too, my back to the room.

Shortly, something made me look up. George stood in the door facing me.

"Commerce called. They want delivery Monday of that hearing you took yesterday. Can you get it out?"

I opened the desk drawer and patted the pack of notes to judge its depth, lifted it and squeezed it. Almost a full pack. "It's two o'clock now," I said, glancing at the wall clock. "A full pack lasts two hours, give or take a little, at, what, forty pages an hour. I must have almost eighty pages here. If I stop what I'm working on now, type some of this and come in tomorrow morning, I can finish before noon. My typing isn't as fast as Ned's."

"Don't worry; you're fine."

"Tomorrow's Saturday. Is anybody going to be in?"

"I don't think so. I'll have to give you the key to this side of the building and the front door. I think the students upstairs have gone off for the weekend."

George disappeared as silently as he had come.

I gave the typewriter a thump. "Honestly," I said, "it's nothing but crises around here." As nobody paid any attention to me, I pondered the two packs of notes. Both had to be done; which one I typed first didn't matter. There went my plans to read the newspaper at leisure over coffee in the morning.

With an air of resignation, I tore the notes out of the stenoprompter, put them in the drawer and threaded the Commerce notes over the stenoprompter's slanting face. Slight pressure of my foot on the pedal made the notes move across the surface until they reached the spot for easiest reading. I checked the holding box in back to make sure the paper would fold correctly and started to type. By the time George returned with the keys, I was engrossed.

"I'm going to be home tomorrow," he said. "Why don't you call when you're finished? I may come down and collate. Bill and Pete will have enough to do on Monday."

"Okay."

Imperceptibly, George faded into the dark corridor, and stillness settled over the room except for the even clacking of the typewriters and the steady drip of the rain.

At a quarter of nine the next morning, I propped my wet umbrella in the corner by the front door. If only the law students were upstairs; I didn't like being alone in the building. After relocking the door, I tested its security and nodded my head. Okay.

From the picture window where I stopped to peer out, the leaves on the trees looked soggy, they were so wet. One person on the other side of the street leaned into the pelting rain behind a man-sized black umbrella. No other brave soul faced the foul weather. Turning, I surveyed the high-ceilinged, dim rooms.

My imagination furnished them with carved wooden furniture upholstered in red velvet, gewgaws and knick-knacks in every available space. Antimacassars became pinned on chairs; table coverings and draperies fell to the heavily carpeted floor. My fantasizing left nothing out of the classic Victorian style. Taffeta and silk covered women poured tea while frock-coated men made witty conversation. Perhaps some Senator and his family had lived in this house. The area must have been fashionable when the buildings were new. I wondered how Hank would look in a frock coat, leaning towards me as I poured tea into a delicate porcelain cup and handed it to him.

Passing through the hall, I glanced into the always cold, always messy bathroom. Cans of pink cleansing cream, as usual, humped along the eye-level windowsill. Dried blobs of purple cream, purple from being rubbed over ditto-purpled skin, decorated the floor, discolored the sink, and stuck to the faucets. I made a mental note to tell Pete the sink needed suctioning out again.

Damn! Would the day ever come when we didn't have to type on ditto masters? The cleansing cream never got all the purple off my hands. Occasionally, I found purple between my toes when I undressed, and it invariably decorated my pillowcase. The stuff undoubtedly seeped into my bloodstream. Wondering what disease I could get, I scowled and passed on through the corridor to my room.

In the doorway of the workroom, I reached around and ran my hand up and down the wall until I found the light switch. "Oh, my God," burst from me as light flooded the room. Water still oozed through the split seams in the ceiling. At least an inch of water covered the floor. The large plastic sheet on Ned's desk had kept his things dry; the other two desks were out of the way of the leaks.

Yanking off my raincoat in vexation, I flung it across the typewriter. My precious typing time must now be wasted emptying buckets. The water already on the floor would have to remain there. Only when I was ready to type did I fold my raincoat over a dry chair.

Pages rolled from the typewriter in rapid succession until an odd popping noise distracted me. Turning, I saw a strange blue flame darting along the baseboards. It streaked around the room. The acrid odor of an electrical fire struck my nostrils. Could the place burn in spite of being so wet? The trumpet! The old dried-out case rested on the wires.

With one swift movement, I crossed the room splashing water as I went. The bottom of the case had caught fire. I rolled the whole thing in the water. A crackling sound made me whirl around. Loose papers in Ned's wastebasket, which had been left against the baseboard in yesterday's commotion, blazed. Any moment, the whole thing would ignite.

I had no idea that I was capable of such giant steps, but I managed to reach the wastebasket and kick it over. The contents spilled into the water before more than one or two scraps of paper burned. I ground out the charred bits with my foot.

Methodically, I checked the entire room. Nothing else had caught fire. The sour smell remained, the only evidence of the blue flame. I was scared. My hand shook uncontrollably as I retrieved the trumpet from the floor and laid it on Tom's desk. After another quick look around, gulping in panic, I hurried into the front room and called George.

"I'll be right down," he said.

Back at my desk, I placed my hands on the typewriter, looked at my notes, and removed my hands. Suppose the flame went around again and I didn't see the blue flicker. The resulting conflagration could destroy the building. With my pulse pounding in my throat, I faced the center of the room and watched the baseboards. If the building grunted, twigs hit the roof, some sound reached me from the street, I translated it into a key in the lock. Each time George didn't walk in, my strong-willed defenses toppled a little more as fear undermined them. I chewed at a hangnail, nervously fiddled with my hair, and whispered, "Oh, come, come. Please hurry."

When the sound of the key turning in the lock finally reached me, I shot from the room like the proverbial Jack-in-the-box. At sight of George, I broke into hysterical laughter. He was trying to get his still open umbrella through the door while holding a bucket and a mop in each hand.

"You go on with your work now, Arabella," he said. "I'll take care of everything."

His non-chalant attitude, as if this happened everyday, made my knees go rubbery. I lurched and grabbed the wall.

"Are you all right?" George reached my side, still holding the buckets.

"Yes. I hadn't realized how tense I was." When he didn't move, I said, "I'm okay. Really. I'll go type now."

Although I heard buckets banging, water sloshing, the mop hitting the furniture, the noise comforted me. I worked steadily until two o'clock when I drew the last page of the transcript from the typewriter.

Thirteen

As usual, I reached the office early on Monday. To my surprise, George had arrived before me. He wandered around, fussing at the table in collating, looking over the book in Theresa's office, uneasy, restless. What's with him, I wondered? Why is he in here so early?

The minute Ned, Tom, and Bill from collating arrived, George called all of us together in collating and told everybody about the electrical fire that had happened on Saturday. They all looked at me in amazement. I lowered my eyes and blushed.

"All this wiring has to be redone. I have called an electrical company. They will be here tomorrow. The three of you," he indicated Ned, Tom and me, "will have to move out. Two of you will move here," he pointed his finger at the floor, "into collating."

Ned, Tom and I surveyed the room skeptically.

"Some of this stuff will have to be pushed into the storage room. The third person will have to squeeze into the front office with Theresa."

We slid our eyes around to each other under lowered lids, not liking the idea at all.

"That will be distracting and very inconvenient," said Ned.

George countered, "What do you suggest?"

"Put some strong light on one spot in the storage room. Get the electrician to do that first." He added, "How long is this going to take?" Ned sounded as irritated and angry as only he could get.

"Probably the rest of the week. Where would you like to sit?"

"You must do something about lighting before we make any decisions." Ned's voice started to rise.

"I'll call the electricians back and see if they can come over this afternoon and take care of that point. Then you can decide."

"I have work to do now." Ned stormed back to his desk.

Somehow, the three of us weathered the five days. Tom and I decided to move to the back-end of collating. George had the electrician beam a high-powered lamp at the wall in the storage room. Ned sat facing the wall, the lamp behind him.

Friday afternoon, George buzzed around the collating room and the back room, distracting everybody. Desks had to be moved, new plugs tested, typewriters carried around. I went home. The mail contained a thick letter from Mother. "Oh, joy. A letter from Hank," I murmured.

I paced back and forth, impatiently waiting for the elevator, my heels clicking on the stone flooring.

Once in my apartment, I plunked down on the first

bed and drew the letter from the envelope dated May 20, 1959, from Clifton Forge, Virginia.

Dear Arabella: One year ago about this time and about ninety miles from here we met at the Casino in Hot Springs. In one year many things have happened (to me, for sure, l'amour).

Me, too.

Suddenly and wonderfully in those last two days of my stay in Hot Springs, on a Friday, we met. Had you just come that day or had you been there and we hadn't seen each other? Whichever way, it changed my life.

Thinking back, we spent so little time together, but every minute was wonderful.

You have probably wondered what's been happening all this time. Well, to make it short and painless, it's been one thing after another. Right now my blood count results are so low that leukemia is a foregone conclusion.

My darling, my darling. How awful.

Been getting whole blood to try to stem it. This amongst other things keeps me in a state of confusion.

In any event, brush all this from your pretty head and live a normal life. Dismiss me from your mind temporarily.

"No way. No way could I dismiss you from my mind," I almost yelled, angry at the suggestion.

Some day, I hope to catch up with you.

Hope you and yours are all in good health. Take care, Hank.

I sat still, holding Hank's letter. He sounded worse instead of better. And this business of "Dismiss me from your mind temporarily." I rolled that round and round in my head. It sounded ominous. I had no way to reach him, no address, no phone number, no way to comfort him. Feeling helpless and frustrated, I cried myself to sleep.

With the morning sun, I woke slowly and lay mulling Hank's situation, over and over in my mind. I couldn't let it go. The feeling was pure and simple, one of my sudden flashes of insight. It could be totally wrong, but some how I didn't think it was. Right from the beginning, I had felt that he had received a massive dose of radiation.

To try to satisfy my assumption, I had gone to the library and read all I could find on the subject. The first symptoms were severe nausea, vomiting, diarrhea, and anorexia. I didn't know whether he had gone through that phase; I had no way of knowing and no way to find out. And that didn't help me make a diagnosis. The same thing held for fever, electrolyte imbalance and dehydration. However, I did know that his blood count had dropped exponentially, way below normal, disastrously low, and that he was in a state of confusion. Those two symptoms agreed with what I had learned from my reading.

Feeling depressed and out of sorts, I went to Garfinckel's and shopped. That store did have wonderful sales. I pawed my way through the racks, finally deciding on a green and white cotton dress with a solid green jacket. It looked smashing on me. I did like smart clothes. The outfit would put a dent in my budget, but I didn't care.

Later, not wanting to be alone to stew, I arranged to meet some friends for dinner, then walked around in my area as long as I dared. Walking after dark in Washington was not a good idea what with the mugging and knife attacks. I watched the traffic, the other people on the sidewalk, anything to keep myself from thinking and worrying. Finally, I stopped at my apartment building, went upstairs and dropped into bed.

Work went on at a rapid pace, new places, new faces, new vocabulary every day, but I couldn't shake my depression. If only I had some way to contact Hank. But that was if, if, if! I didn't have a way. I had to face that fact. Knowing that didn't help, but work did with its constant variety.

One day, Ned returned from Senate Banking shortly after twelve. "Arabella," he said, stopping beside my desk, "Can you come across the street with me for coffee? I want to talk to you."

Surprised, I said, "Okay."

Ned had his usual sandwich bag on his desk. I had seen it. He ate his sandwich in big bites at the end of typing each page. What was up? Had I done something to displease him? Early in my association with Colonial, I had realized that Ned had a great deal to say about what went on in the office. I also soon learned that he was reputed one of the best reporters in the business.

Seated at a table for two in the midst of a chattering crowd, Ned ordered coffee and pie for both of us before saying, "Arabella, I was asked this morning if I would go to Africa with Dag Hammarskjold, the head of the United Nations, and would I get a second reporter? I'm asking you if you will go."

My chin almost reached my chest. "—I-I-I don't know. I don't know whether I could do the work. I-I—"

"Oh, come on, Arabella. Why do you think you're number two in the office?"

"I didn't know I was. I thought Tom was."

"Tom's a superb reporter. He worked the Nuremberg trials in 1945, right after the war."

"He did?" For the second time, I stopped dead, stopped chewing, stopped cutting the pie, fork in hand.

Ned laughed at my expression. "I see there's a lot you don't know. Tom drinks."

I closed my eyes and swallowed hard. Another Charlie.

"George is careful where he sends Tom. For instance, he doesn't send him to the Council meetings at NIH. And, incidentally, they will be coming up soon now, and you'll see what I mean—the pressure, the long days, the fast delivery of transcripts. Tom can't take it."

Ned finished his coffee. "So, will you go?"

"Yes."

"Good girl."

All afternoon, I thought about Africa and Dag Hammarskjold.

I heard nothing more about it for three weeks. Then, late one afternoon, as he passed my desk, Ned said to me, "I have to tell George. He'll go into a funk and won't talk to us for days."

George didn't talk to us. He sent Theresa in with messages.

Ned said, "I wish he'd stop moping around."

Ten days later, as he left the room, Ned said, "The trip is postponed."

That day, June 26, I had a phone message handed to me as I entered the Winthrop House lobby after a late Friday night in the office finishing a daily. It said:

"To Miss Robbins from Hank. 6:15 June 26. Hank." I almost screamed in my excitement. He had called. He must be better.

The "will call again" line was checked. Then under "Remarks," the switchboard operator had written, "Hotel

Willard 6 o'clock Sunday June 28." I caught the wall to keep from falling in my excitement. At last, I would see him.

At last, at last. I danced to the elevator. As I waited for it, I realized that he knew I had moved to Washington, that he knew my address and telephone number. He had said in one letter that the Secret Service boys kept him informed about his folks; they must keep him informed about me, too. Somehow the thought comforted me. His concern meant a great deal. It helped to boost my spirits during my lonely wait for him.

I slept peacefully that night.

Fourteen

As I waited for six o'clock Sunday evening, I found myself in a tizzy. How could I possibly wait? I prowled the length of the one-room apartment, rearranged small bits of brick-a-brac, checked the time. Finally, I threw up my hands and decided to leave anyway. I looked at my watch as I pushed open the back door of the Willard Hotel. Five forty-five. I shrugged. So what? I'd rather wait here than be sitting in a chair at home, watching the clock.

Joy bubbling through my being, I slowly walked along Peacock Alley, the Willard's bar, into the hotel lobby. Hank was sitting on the circular red velvet sofa in the middle of the lobby floor. He turned his head in my direction. Our eyes met. He stood up. My knees became so weak that I feared I would fall. Instead, I walked straight up to him. He folded me into his arms, moments of paradise. Loosening his grip on me, Hank said, "Let's go into Peacock Alley and talk for a bit before we go to dinner."

As we sat close together over drinks, he caught me up on what had happened to him, though he couldn't tell me much. The whole blood had worked. The leukemia had subsided. I hugged his arm and beamed up at him.

He smiled. "I'm starting to feel better, though I still have bad moments."

He said that his best friend had died in the accident. The friend's wife had been at the station when the train pulled in. "She had on a beautiful dress, just beautiful." Silence, then he said sadly, "I'll probably never see her again."

He was quiet, his fingers twisting his drink glass. I gently stroked his arm without looking at him. In a few minutes, he said, "Shall we go?"

We walked over to O'Donnall's on Eleventh Street for dinner. I smiled when Hank suggested it the sole stuffed with crab meat.

"You like it as much as I do." He gave my arm a squeeze. We both grinned.

'I better learn how to cook that,' I thought.

Hank said, "Do you remember the time we were standing on the platform in Newark, New Jersey, waiting for the local New York train? We kissed and kissed good-bye. The fact that people were standing all over the platform didn't seem to make any difference. Then, when the train stopped, we both got on."

We broke into loud guffaws. "The train platform with people coming and going made the perfect time to be kissed," I stammered, unable to control my laughter.

"Any time is the perfect time." He leaned over and pecked my cheek.

"Some difference," I sniffed.

"You just wait." His eyes sparkled as he looked down at my happy face.

Over dinner, the conversion turned to my work. Hank asked about the kind of assignments I received.

"I love the work here. It's much more interesting than New York."

"For instance?"

"Well, soon after I came, George sent me back to New York on some negotiations with the Russians that President Eisenhower had asked John McCloy to conduct.

"Really! That must have been interesting."

"Actually, it wasn't. The chief Russian spoke at a snail's pace. Everything had to be translated. He constantly conferred with his Russian colleagues behind him. Our side waited. When he talked, I had to concentrate. When I wasn't concentrating, I lost track of what he said. As far as I could tell, he didn't say anything substantive anyway."

Hank laughed. "Typical."

"What was interesting was the elegance of the legation. Gorgeous thick carpets over the whole room, very different than my understanding of Communism."

"Amazing the way people take to luxury the minute they get a chance, no matter what their ideological beliefs."

I told him about the work with the National Institutes of Health Councils that the office had just completed with all the famous doctors and Nobel Prize Winners I had met.

"Good Lord," he said. "It sounds frantic. No wonder I can never reach you."

"Oh, Hank," I said, ready for tears.

He caught my hand. "Darling, I know you're busy and seem to love it. I keep trying."

Later, on the way back to Winthrop House, he said, "I'm coming up to see your apartment so I can picture you in it."

"Our apartment," I said softly on my breath.

"Our apartment," he said as softly.

When he left me that evening, he said, "Can you meet me for breakfast at nine?"

"At my office?"

"Yes. There's a restaurant nearby that I've always frequented."

Standing behind the plate-glass window of the collating room in the morning, I watched for Hank. Suddenly, there he was, crossing the street. I hurried down the cast iron steps right into his arms.

"What a lovely kiss," I said when we drew apart, knowing full well that every staff member already in the office had front row seats to watch every move we made. I didn't care.

Smiling, he took my hand, and we walked up the street.

Two weeks after that, a letter reached Winthrop House, postmarked Baltimore, dated July 13, 1959.

Dear Arabella: Hi lass, so close and yet so far. Only here for a few hours.

As I looked at the envelope, with its Baltimore postmark, I supposed that he was at Johns Hopkins Hospital being examined.

Didn't call because it was during your working hours. Boy was it ever good to see you and hold you again, I've lived it over 1000 times. Things are happening faster than I can keep up with them.

What did that mean? For the good, I hoped. His letter sounded upbeat.

I should get to see you later in the month. (With your permission of course).

Since when did he need permission to see me?

Be interesting to hear what the folks at Federal had to say about your being kissed on the sidewalk at 9 A.M.

Nobody had said a word. But the two women who had been in the office welcomed me back with broad grins on their faces. I had ignored their expectant looks and walked straight through collating to my own desk.

Take care, and God bless you. Hank.

P.S. Hope you had a nice holiday and that you found all the folks just fine.

If Hank had lived our few hours together over a thousand times. I also savored it over and over, certain that he had reached the end of the bad times. He could only get better now. Then he would come to me forever. I couldn't wait. I worked hard, enjoying it, but counted every day that passed.

But the end of the month flew by and no word from Hank. Why? Why? Walking restlessly around the apartment evenings, I fussed with the Lenox vase on the desk, the fake rose, the makeup jars in the bathroom, and stewed. Why? The refrain ran constantly through my mind. Why? Why? Why hadn't I heard from him? Obviously, something had happened. As usual, my disposition plummeted in my helpless frustration at not being able to find out what was going on and how serious it was. By this time the euphoria I had been living in had evaporated.

Fifteen

Instead of coming in person, Hank sent a letter, which I received on August 21st. It was postmarked August 20th from Washington.

My stomach did a flip-flop. After reaching my apartment, I flung myself on the first bed, tore open the envelope, and read.

Dear Arabella: Hello my dear, tried to get in touch with you today and this evening.

Oh, God. I missed him. Internally, I collapsed. I had just been wandering around town.

Gather you are busy or you may have gone to see your folks.

Had a little setback as you have probably guessed. However, about half way out of it now. Looks like I'll make it in good fashion.

Oh! I let down, tears of joy prickling my eyes.

Hope you're just fine. You deserve to be.

Should be back shortly.

God, I love you. Hank.

I doubled over, heartbroken at not seeing him. I sat there pouting, then suddenly pounded the bed with my fists, wanting to scream in frustration. Seconds later, I said to myself, wow, imagine how badly he feels. Especially because he holds everything within himself just the way he did about the trips his work requires. His work! I didn't know exactly what he did. He didn't tell me that so he wouldn't tell me of his pain, if he had pain, his depression, his unhappiness. Our entire relationship had been pure joy, glorying in our love for each other. No other feelings entered into it, until his illness. Then I wasn't with him enough to know what his feelings were, how he showed them, if he did.

When it came right down to it, I didn't know much about his feelings, his attitudes. We had been so completely taken up in ourselves. Also, we had actually had so little time together. But I knew, and expected that he did too, that I had met the great love of my life. And that was it. I carefully folded up the letter, but grieved for him and myself all evening.

The following day, I received another letter along with all the junk mail. A quick glance informed me that I didn't recognize the strange handwriting. Okay, calm down. Sitting at my dining room card table, I opened the letter and glanced at the signature. "Irene." Irene? Who's Irene? I started to read.

Your mother suggested I write to you. I've always lived up the street from you, but being younger, we never really knew each other.

My mind whirled. Oh, I thought, that girl, the little girl with crossed blue eyes and the huge nose that put her face out of alignment.

I would like very much to come to Washington to work. I'm a fast, accurate typist, if I do say so myself. Could I be of use in a court reporting office?

I thought about that. Actually, George had mentioned the possibility of my using some typist he knew. If I dictated notes such as the long days at NIH that required three-day delivery, I could handle a lot more work. Irene needed to have a good vocabulary. When I thought about it, I didn't know anything about the girl.

I discussed it with George.

"Tell her to come down and I'll talk to her. She would be doing mostly your work. You would have to keep her busy. Ned and Tom type all their own."

I nodded.

"I don't know about putting her on the staff," he added, "unless I took on another dictating reporter."

"I'll tell her to come down with no promises."

On Tuesday afternoon two weeks later, when I returned to the office after a hectic day at the Department of Commerce, George cornered me. He said that Irene had come by the office that morning straight off the train from New York City. He set her up with some dictation at my desk, the room being empty and quiet.

From the hallway, he listened to the fast, even flow of the typewriter. "I was impressed," he said, puffing out his lower lip. "I let her type twenty minutes before taking the typed pages from her. Quickly glancing over them, I saw no mistakes."

He had then taken her into his office and told her he thought she would be an asset here as my typist. He also told her that there would be times when we weren't busy, really slow periods when nobody had much work, and asked if she could manage.

He ran his hand through his hair before saying, "Her

response to that question was the only thing I didn't like in the whole interview. She said she suspected she could find supplemental work." George pulled his head back. "I don't like the suggestion that she could go elsewhere at times. The girl knows she's damn good. I'll have to work something out. I asked her when she could come down. She has to give two-weeks notice."

George picked up Irene's resume, which lay in plain sight on his desk, looked at it, and laid it back down.

He called to Theresa to bring in the book. Immediately, she entered, carrying the book, and placed it before him. He flipped through the pages, looking at the hearings for the next few weeks.

"Where is she now?" I asked.

"She took the next train back to New York. She'll let me know just when she will arrive."

He continued to flip through the assignment book.

"September looks very busy. Long, heavy stuff. The end of September and early October, we have the NIH Councils, which as you know are three-day turnaround on heavy work. With Irene typing for you, I could use you all day."

I felt and probably looked wary. The way George said that made it sound like all day taking and all night dictating.

He noted my expression and realized what I was thinking. "It would still be half days, split morning and afternoon. But this way, you could work every day."

Irene arrived in Washington two weeks later and moved into an apartment with a girl she knew. She dropped into the office late afternoon on the Monday she arrived. George brought her around, introducing her to all of us. I looked at her sharply. Her nose still put her face out of joint, but she glowed intelligence. And I liked the way she dressed.

After she left, Tom said, "How can any woman be as ugly as that new typist?" He set his head wagging in disbelief.

Momentarily, I gaped at him then snapped, "What an awful thing to say. She's a nice girl. Get to know her, and you'll forget about her crossed blue eyes and extremely prominent nose. Besides, she can't help it. If you noticed, she dresses beautifully and keeps her blond hair neatly cut."

"Oh, oh, that must be the girl you were telling us about." Tom turned to Ned. "Ned, did you meet the typist George hired for Arabella? You had gone out of the room when he brought her in here."

"You mean the one with the— " The sentence dangled unfinished.

"You're both horrid," I cried. "You don't give her a chance."

"At least, she could get her nose bobbed," said Tom.

"As long as she's a good typist, I suppose it doesn't matter what she looks like." The subject was closed as far as Ned was concerned.

"Please, Tom, try to be especially kind to her. She's sensitive, and she wanted this job to broaden her contacts. You'll see, she's learned to dress becomingly, she's interesting and bright." I stopped for breath, only to realize that I had made up most of what I had said. I hadn't seen Irene since she was a child. I based my comments on seeing her when George brought her into our back room.

"Hold on, Arabella." Tom laughed penitently. "You don't have to give me a sales pitch. I'm not going to be rude to the girl, for pity sakes."

"Well, go the other way. Try to make her welcome." I still felt defensive.

The two men solemnly took an oath, cross-my-heart, raised hands, hope-to-die, and winked at each other before we settled down to work.

George set Irene up in the storage room with plenty of good lighting. In no time, my production picked up. For the NIH Council work, I took the dictating equipment home so I could dictate undisturbed. Each morning, Pete collected the work from the desk in the lobby of my building.

On September 20th, in the middle of the Council push, I received another letter from Hank, postmarked Stevens City, Virginia. The letter carried a date of September 14th. It read:

You folks in Washington must be in a state of who knows with that Russian Butcher in your midst.

That surprised me. I thought Washington residents were delighted with Mr. Gorbachev. Hank's sentence sounded as if he expected the opposite reaction.

Hope you had a pleasant summer. I'm sure you had a hot one. Say hello to Mother and Dad for me when you see them.

I hope to be up in Washington before the month's end or the first week in October.

Take care you lovely--

Sincerely, Hank.

I breathed a sigh of relief. Somehow, the letter had a cheerful pitch. He sounded much better. I pinched myself.

The end of September had arrived. I might be within a week of seeing him. My joy faded a bit when I thought of the pace of work until the Councils finished this October round of meetings. I'd have to get some rest from the grueling, nonstop work.

The Councils ended the second week in October. Still, I had had no word from Hank. Nights, in bed, I fretted, even shedding some tears.

George started assigning me to long mornings at Senate Banking or Commerce or one of the House Committees. Having Irene to type for me, I could handle their daily copy.

Not until October 26th did another letter come on The Homestead stationary. I looked at it, stunned. Was he there without me? The postmark read New Castle, Pennsylvania. I scowled and ripped open the envelope.

October 23, 1959.

Dear Arabella: Writing on this stationary is about as close to this place as I'm going to get (from the looks of things right now). I never did get to Washington early in October as planned. I sure would like to see you. Wonder if you ever think of me.

Ever think of him? Only all the time!

I do hope you are in good health and all your folks are the same.

I'll not promise when I expect to get down your way. But with a little luck, I may surprise you one of these days.

Take care.

As ever, Hank.

Flabbergasted, I sat on my bed. He had had another setback. What caused them? Why couldn't his doctors control them? This letter, so different from the last, sounded depressed. And I couldn't tell him, I had no way to tell him, that I thought of him constantly. Day and night, I thought of him and worried about him. He should know how much. The letter upset me. Why, suddenly, was he not doing well? I started to cry, many quiet tears coursing down my face of their own accord. I dampened Kleenex after Kleenex trying to keep the tears from wetting my blouse and then had trouble sleeping that night.

I worked. George gave me no time to do anything else. I didn't care.

The office remained busy right up to December 20th when the book just about shut down. I went to my family on Long Island. The minute I arrived, Mother handed me an envelope from Hank.

"He guessed that I would come home for Christmas," I said, "so sent this to you here." I turned the envelope over in my hand. "It looks like a Christmas card, which he mailed in New York City."

I picked up my suitcase and, carrying his card, ran upstairs to my room. I took a lovely card, sparkling with pine trees and deer from the envelope.

Dear Arabella: Been here at Cornell Medical Research Center for the past five weeks. Hoped I'd stay over the holiday, but no such luck.

How miserable. Why did those doctors have to move him just before Christmas?

Headed for Virginia today.

Hope you all have a Happy Holiday.

Hank.

I smiled down at the lovely card. Then I sat up straight as a thought crossed my mind. Had he sent a card to his sister? Did he write to her? I'd never know.

I couldn't ask her. Many times, I had wished I had her phone number. On occasion, I would have appreciated a long conversation with her. But I had automatically done what he asked me to do. No questions asked.

I rumpled my hair. She had never called me. Did Hank not give her my number or did he ask her, too, to throw it away? Somehow, I didn't think she was able to contact me anymore.

The minute I returned to my parents in the living room, I unloaded. "Why didn't those doctors let him stay at Cornell Medical over Christmas? Why did they find it necessary to drag him away on that one day from a group of people he had gotten to know? Cold weather, hot weather." My voice started to rise as I became angry over the medics' unfairness to Hank. "There isn't all that much difference between Cornell's weather in New York City and Virginia."

"There isn't anything you can do about it, so calm down," my father said.

I nodded agreement, and blinked back the tears.

January turned out to be as slow as the end of December. What work was assigned to me, I typed myself as Irene stayed in New York with her family. Tom didn't come in.

When I said something about missing Tom, Ned commented, "He's probably drying out from the New Year's binge."

I thought that it was a snide remark so I didn't answer.

Ned's wife stayed in Illinois with her mother after Christmas so Ned had to batch it, which he didn't like. One Wednesday evening, he suggested that we go over to Georgetown to a restaurant called the Rive Gauche for dinner.

"Is that a French restaurant?"

"A very nice one. Is that okay with you?"

"Yes. I could use a night out."

"We both could. It's funny; when we're busy, we don't have time to do anything else. When we're not busy, we don't have any money."

I laughed. "Isn't that the truth?"

In the restaurant, we ordered snails first, salad, delicious veal ragout, cream caramel and coffee.

Ned said, "Remember the trip to Africa with Dag Hammarschjold?"

"Yes." I leaned forward eagerly.

"Don't get your hopes up. I found out that George got in touch with the people and told them he couldn't do without me; they had to find someone else. He didn't know that I had asked you."

"How despicable," I fumed.

"He's like that. The minute he thinks one of us has something nice in the wings, he panics. He thinks he's going to lose us permanently."

"That's ridiculous."

"That's George. He's very insecure. Besides, something's going on. I feel it."

"What do you mean?"

"I can't put my finger on it, but something's in the air. Something's going to happen."

Sixteen

In his rage, Ned swore. "What a way to start the week!" He slapped a pad of stenotype paper on his desk.

That miserable, rainy afternoon, in his quiet, mousy way, George had appeared in the middle of the workroom after we three reporters had returned from our various hearings.

Instantly, Ned's typewriter stopped. Tom stood up, and I swung my chair around.

George cleared his throat. "For the past three months, I have been discussing a merger with the owners of Superb Reporters. Some minor details remain to be worked out, but because of the poor condition of the present building and the fact that it will soon be torn down along with every other building on the block, I have arranged for the immediate removal of all personnel."

He ran his hand through his hair. "Space at Superb may be temporarily limited until we can rent another room for reporters. Everyone on the permanent staff will have an equal, if not better, job. I will personally oversee the assignments of the reporters. You will carry on as you always have. There will be no favoritism." He hesitated. "Naturally, any reporter is free to leave, but I hope you will all stick with me."

Then ducking his head and giving us his shy smile, George left the room.

"I never thought it would come to a merger." Tom half sat on his desk, head lowered, eyes unfocused.

"Most of their reporters are note read. I don't want any part of that," rasped Ned.

"He meant no note reading in his comment about carry on as we always have. We won't have to get involved with note reading," said Tom.

"Don't be silly! You know there'll be coercion. What do you expect?" sneered Ned.

"What's note reading?" I asked.

"After doing what editing you feel necessary on your notes, you turn them over to a typist who types from them the way you do, but without having been to the meeting, without having heard what went on. There's no possibility of recall. You get grossly misread outlines. That's the way they operate. The whole office is geared to those typists. And I don't approve of that system at all," Ned announced adamantly.

"All because their reporter-owner doesn't want to type himself," put in Tom. "But I'll bet some boo-boos go out in his transcripts. He doesn't even look at them."

"I hear he makes the typists learn his method of writing, but makes the other reporters change their writing style to suit the typists," said Ned.

"You're kidding." I caught myself as my chair started to tip.

"I don't know whether I want to go over there or not." Ned stood up and started to pack pads of paper into his stenotype case. "I'll have to talk to George some more and think about it. The only advantage," he said with pointed sarcasm, "is that they're shifting to Xeroxing, and we won't be using that god-awful purple ditto."

"Christ!" Tom got up and peered into the corridor. "He could have rented another office. He didn't have to merge."

"You know what motivated the whole thing," gripped Ned. "Not the leaky roof or the electrical fire; his own damn laziness."

Tom nodded. "I figured something would happen when Theresa told him her father was ill and she was moving back to South Carolina."

"He doesn't want to handle the assignment book himself. It means hanging around 'til six, and he wants to leave at four." Ned crushed out his cigarette and started to cough.

"The trouble is Teresa isn't so easy to replace. Training somebody to handle that book takes time," said Tom.

"It's his business; he can do as he pleases." Ned struggled for breath as he talked. "But I'm not exactly overwhelmed with joy at this merger."

I turned back to my work. I knew Ned would rage for a short time before he returned to his typing.

Still thinking about the merger when I entered my apartment building, I caught my breath when the switchboard operator offered me a letter.

At last, when I had about given up and allowed myself to descend into sadness, a letter mailed from Front Royal, Virginia, arrived.

February 12, 1960.

Dear Arabella: Long time no see, long time no talk. The body is doing just fine. The head? Spending too much time with the head shrinkers.

Gee, I didn't know what to think. Psychiatrists? What did that mean? My brilliant darling.

If you have a moment, write to me c/o General Delivery, Pinehurst, North Carolina. I'll be there for one day, February 23rd.

As ever, Hank.

Say hello to your Mother and Dad for me.

Immediately, I sat down and wrote a long letter, telling him about the office move, Ned's outrage, the new people, how much I liked the work and added that my folks were fine. Then I launched into how much I loved him, how much I missed him and how I pictured him coming home to me in our small apartment.

Even though he wouldn't be in Pinehurst until February 23rd, I mailed the letter the next day. By morning, I had decided to send a telegram also just in case he didn't receive the letter.

He must have sat down the minute he got my letter because the next one I received carried the date February 23, 1960.

My dear Arabella. So sweet of you to write. And lass it was sure good to hear from you, you are so faithful, bless your heart. I'm coming up to Bethesda in March so I promise to see you. Boy will that ever be wonderful.

Just remember one thing. I love you dearly. When I get my arms around you again, I doubt if I'll ever let go. So beware.

"I love you, too," I whispered. "And I don't want you to let go of me ever."

As ever, Hank. Say hello to your Mother and Dad.

I shed tears of happiness, a relieved happiness, an all enfolding happiness. He loved me.

The new office turned out to be in the old Texaco building on the corner of Pennsylvania and Louisiana Avenue, the second floor, above all the gas pumps in the large station. Irene was thrown into a big room with the five note readers. Tom, Ned and I occupied the room rented specifically for us. We lined up the desks the way they had been in the old office—Ned in front of the window, my desk in front of his, Tom across from Ned on the other side of the room.

Other than the three old green desks and a wall phone, the gray-painted room was empty. The room next door contained the coat rack/umbrella stand along with five Superb note reading typists. That meant that each time we three reporters hurried in or went out, we had to pass through that room to hang up our coats and confront five sets of hostile eyes.

The administrative staff and Superb's reporters occupied a large room across the hall. Two small offices had been built at the far end of that room for Henry, the owner/reporter, George, and a man named Frank. Collating occupied another room down the hall. Other than three tiny business offices at the very end of the wide corridor, the whole floor was taken up in the merger by Superb's reporters and typists.

Frank handled the book in the new office, though true to his word, George made sure that his three reporters received excellent assignments. As it turned out, we continued to follow our usual routine because Frank never assigned any of the NIH meetings or other scientific work to Superb's crew.

The only thing we three really disliked was the

continuing hostility in the typists' room next to us. I nearly dropped my jacket the day the white-haired note reader with exquisite clear skin, but a discontented, sour face, asked, "Are you busy?"

"I'm swamped," I answered.

Sarcastically, the woman said, "It's too bad you won't let us help you."

I smiled, elevated my left shoulder, and opened the connecting door to my own room. Both men looked up.

"You know that sixtyish woman who sits by the window over there?" I pointed to the door behind me.

"I know who you mean," said Ned. "Why?"

"She was at me just now because we don't have our notes read."

"I hear the powers that be got a complaint on their star reporter," said Tom. "It would be interesting to know whether he was at fault or the notereaders. Apparently, the client said he didn't want--"

The door opened. In the silence, Frank's astute glance encompassed the three of us.

"Office gossip?" He sounded curt and businesslike. "Tom, can you go over to the Labor Department right away? They forgot to call in a hearing. All the information is on this piece of paper."

Tom rammed the piece of paper into his pants' pocket, snatched his stenotype and left.

"Arabella," Frank said, "come to my office. I want to talk to you."

From the doorway, I sent Ned a what-do-you-suppose-he-wants look.

Both feet planted firmly in front of Frank's desk, I watched him search through the mass of papers. The top papers seemed to aimlessly revolve counterclockwise. Those underneath followed. I had watched this before, always wondering how he kept track of anything and mentally reorganized them.

"Here it is." He pulled out a three-by-five pad. "You know medicine pretty well. What's a CPC?"

"Clinicopathological conference."

"Lovely. Now tell me what that means."

"It's a game they play. 'These are the presenting symptoms, this is what we found on physical examination, what's the diagnosis? What caused the death?' They pick the most difficult cases they can find. Then they show the autopsy results. It's terribly, terribly technical."

"I had a call from George Washington Hospital." He motioned me to the only available chair. "Put the papers on the floor and sit down."

"The medical school," he continued, "wants us to cover eight CPCs, four starting this month, November, through the middle of December and four in January. They'll be Thursday afternoons at three. About an hour. Can you handle them? I said I'd call them back."

"I will if you want me to. I'd be tied down on Thursdays, our busiest day."

"That's unimportant. I can still use you on a morning job." He shifted his papers. "I'll try to negotiate a decent page rate."

Sensing that I had been dismissed, I inched to the chair edge.

"Now," he said, giving a forward push to the paper mass, "I have to call the guy back."

Ten minutes after four that afternoon, Frank found me

alone. "Hasn't Tom come back yet?" Dumbfounded, he kneaded his jawbone between his thumb and forefinger.

"No. And Ned has gone home."

"Tom'll be loaded." He hesitated. "I guess I can leave him off the book tomorrow."

His shoulders sagged, deep circles surrounded his eyes. "What a day I've had." He slumped into Tom's chair.

I spun my typing chair halfway around to face him. "I heard the feet running up and down the corridor all afternoon. You must have had emergency on top of emergency."

"At one point, it seemed as if I couldn't get anything else done."

Having discovered that the stress of operating the business as well as restraining the president's spending sprees fell on Frank, I waited for him to talk.

The top button of his shirt lay open, his tie loosened, the knot having worked its way around almost under his ear. His heavy black beard showed a pronounced five o'clock shadow on his drooping fleshy jaws. Perspiration mixed with excessive oil clung in the crevices of his forehead. Only the intelligence and kindliness shining from his eyes saved him from being markedly homely.

"To redeem the entire afternoon, I had a stroke of luck. I had sent Billy out to Wisconsin, driving the station wagon loaded with equipment for an administrative hearing, a daily-copy job, that was supposed to start tomorrow and run five days. The judge's office called. The judge had a heart attack and the hearing was postponed." He rubbed his forehead. "A whole crew had left for the airport, two reporters and three transcribers. I had them paged in the nick of time. When I reached Billy, I said, 'How long did it take you to drive out there?' He said, 'Twelve hours.' I told him to get a good night's sleep and start back. What a day," he repeated, shaking his head.

"In between everything else, I talked to that doctor. He agreed to a fifty-dollar appearance fee plus an extra fifty cents on the regular page rate. Next Thursday will be the first one."

Frank heaved himself out of the chair, moving like an old man rather than one in his middle forties. "When this is all over, Arabella, I'll give you a nice trip." With that, he flung wide the door in a grandiose gesture and hurtled his corpulent frame through it.

Seventeen

I returned from the Hill hearing, snuggled into my brown wool coat with the collar pulled up tightly around me against the cold, blustery wind of late February. Walking down the office corridor, I saw Frank standing in front of the door to my room. He waved at me.

"Frank." I said when I reached him, "You'll never guess what happened today." Throwing my free hand up, I started to giggle, unable to control myself.

"Why don't you tell me?"

"You know that senator from Mississippi who gives me fits? I never can understand his southern accent. He was holding forth today. At one point I thought he said 'shitting in the dark.' I almost fell off the chair."

Frank started to laugh.

"It wasn't until one of the other senators referred to shooting in the dark that I tumbled. Wouldn't that have been some transcript?"

Frank let out a belly laugh. "Come to my office after you hang up your coat."

I went into the transcribers' room, hung up my coat, and stopped to speak to Irene. "I got about seventy-five pages today, Irene. I'll start to dictate as soon as I've seen Frank. He asked me to come to his office."

Seated beside Frank's desk, I watched him push the papers around.

"I want you to leave next Sunday for Puerto Rico." He looked at me. "Nice trip. Right?"

My eyes widened in delight. I nodded.

"It's a week long multilingual conference."

"What do you mean, 'multilingual'?"

"Translators; a fifty-seven nation conference on the Peace Corps. The chairman is President Kennedy's brother-in-law, and I think Vice President Johnson will be there. You'll have to deal with translators repeating in English what the speaker is saying in his own language. And," he hesitated, "it's daily copy."

"My God, daily copy!" I yelled. "What are we going to do?" I leaned towards him.

My face must have looked wild, appalled, because he said, "Calm down, Arabella. Don't worry. I've hired three outside reporters, plus you, Tom and Ned. Ned is in charge. He'll arrange everything. I have just finished talking to him and Tom. Ned has already told me what you will need, and I have to get back to the people running the show. So run along now. It'll be a nice change from this cold."

"If we get outside the conference room," I quipped as I left him.

Tom stood at the side of Ned's desk looking down at Ned's smiling face when I entered. They both turned their heads in my direction.

In a gleeful mood, Tom cracked, "You notice Frank

sends the three of us, not his people who do the easy stuff, the regular contract stuff."

More sanguine, Ned said, "Most of the time, these things are not all fun and games. We're numbers one, two and three in the company, so why not send us? The object is to give the client a good product."

I took in what he said. Inordinately pleased, I made a note to tell Hank that I was number two in the new company.

We were scheduled to leave from Dulles Airport on Sunday morning. A light snow started to fall as my cab crossed the Potomac River becoming large wet sticky flakes by the time the cab reached Reston.

I found Tom waiting inside the terminal. My eyes followed the outward-soaring glass wall of Eero Saarinen's beautiful building to where the snowflakes tumbled from the roof into the floodlights. "How lovely," I exclaimed. "It's like being inside a paperweight."

"God! What an apt description—that high sweep of glass, lights and swirling snow. It makes me feel as small as the figures in the paperweights."

"Here comes Ned," I broke in. "Those three women with him must be the other reporters." I waved.

"The older, skinny one in the red suit is Harriet," said Tom. "I don't know the other two,"

"What awful taste." My practiced eye ran over the plaid wool suit of a fat, thirtyish woman mincing on spike-heeled pumps that made her walk as if her feet hurt. "The bargain-basement-style short one is probably my age. Pleasant face; she'll be good company."

"Don't be catty," said Tom.

"Isn't it exciting?" said plump Grace as soon as the two groups merged. "I've never been to Puerto Rico."

"Neither have I," I said.

"Here, we have all this icky snow, and in three and a half hours, we'll land in summertime. I have difficulty believing it," said Eleanor, flipping her shoulder-length, darkening blond hair back.

En mass, chattering, we boarded the Washington jitney that shuttled us to the plane.

Warm, moist air enfolded us as we stepped off the plane in San Juan. "How queer," I said while we waited at the taxi stand. "There isn't any entrance door in this terminal. It's all open."

"Why do they need a door," said Ned, "when this temperature today is as cold as it ever gets? Wait until you see the hotel."

"Doesn't that have a door either?"

"A long ramp leads in from the street between sunken flower beds. And your room will have a louvered wooden door as well as the regular door. If the night is hot, you use the louvered door, and the ocean breezes blow through."

"How marvelous. I can't wait."

A cab drew up to us.

"You're like a little kid." Tom held the cab door open for me.

"When it comes to travel, you're right." I wiggled into the middle of the back seat in the cab. Tom tucked himself in after me. "I don't want to miss a thing," I informed him.

Ned put the other three women into a cab and stuffed his bulk into the space on the other side of me. "Has Tom told you about the bar in our hotel yet?"

"No. You tell me."

"The hotel's in the San Turce area and the bar curves along a rocky point, right on the ocean. You sit there and watch turquoise and blue water pound against the rocks, sending spray higher than the window glass. It cascades down and is sucked out to sea again, leaving little pools of sun-warmed water where tadpoles play."

"Ned, you make it sound stupendous."

"You'll love it."

"Can we go there later?"

"If you weren't wedged in so tightly, you'd float through the roof," chuckled Tom.

"As soon as we get our workroom located and the typewriters set up," Ned promised. "It'll probably be six by that time anyway."

I gazed out the window, thinking Hank would love this.

On orders from Ned, Tom led me into the hotel. I kept straying off to look at the flowers, peek at the sandy beach, or gaze at the palm trees.

After he had registered all of us, Ned said, "Be back here in fifteen minutes so we can catch the courtesy bus for the conference area. I'm told it circulates continuously."

We were the only ones on the bus for the ride along Ashford Avenue, but from the clamorous babble, the bus could have been full.

First off the bus, Ned watched us disembark. "You girls in your bright sundresses don't look like the same crew who shivered in snowy Washington. Now," he said in his most professional manner, "I'll go find the manager and see where we're supposed to work."

He left us grouped beside masses of blooming

bougainvillea, the great blossoms trembling in the fresh breeze. Eleanor stretched her small frame up to a flamboyant red cluster and sniffed.

"Do they smell?" I asked.

"Faintly."

"Frank said something about the conference being held in a theater," said overly plump Grace. "This is a huge hotel."

"The theater's inside the hotel," said Tom. "This is one of the classier new hotels along the tourist strip."

"The delegates are probably staying here," said Harriet.

"And we get shoved off to an old hotel," huffed Grace.

"Don't knock it," said Harriet. "Ours is a nifty hotel."

"An elegant old one," remarked Tom.

"Ned's motioning us to come," I said.

"The typewriters," said Ned when we reached him, "came directly from the airport and have been put in our workroom. We'll go there first, get set up, then have a look at the auditorium. I've got two porters to help us."

"Lead the way," he said to the porters waiting in the lobby. "We don't know where we're going."

We proceeded along an inlayed stone floor corridor, polished stone like the lobby, like our hotel lobby and our bedrooms, cool in the hot climate. The corridor led into a room containing six desks placed at random. In one corner, the large typewriter carrying cases lay side by side.

"What a mess," growled Ned. "Get these desks," he addressed the porters, "out of the middle of the room and up against the wall so they face the door. Do you understand? This end up against that wall." He slapped one of the desks with his left hand and pointed with the other hand.

Tom and the two porters heaved the desks, we women wheeled the typing chairs, and Ned indicated where everything should go. Anxiously, he hung over each IBM electric typewriter as it was unpacked, explaining over and over the damage airplane travel can do to the mechanism.

"Here's a typewriter on the floor behind our junk. It looks like a Spanish typewriter," said Grace from her position by the carrying cases.

"Leave it right where it is," said Ned.

With the room rearranged to suit him, Ned said, "Okay, let's go look at the auditorium. I understand it's nearby. We take the first right turn off the corridor."

In the auditorium, we found a round table between the front-row seats and the stage. A large "Court Reporters" sign plus six pairs of earphones lay on the table.

"Oh, that's for the simultaneous translation," said Harriet, as she tried on a pair of earphones.

"English is number two," Ned said as he pointed to the black sign hanging on the window of the translators' booth in the back on the second floor level. The booth also showed black signs with numbers for French, Spanish, German, and Italian.

A portly blond man with a bushy beard hurried down the main aisle towards us. "I'm in charge of the earphones. I tried to pick out the six best sets for you, but you won't be able to test them until morning when the whole system is in operation. If you have any trouble, I can change them at that time."

"Thanks," said Ned. "We'll be here early to be sure everything is working, although by the look of the program, I don't think we'll need earphones until afternoon."

"I'll be around." The fellow stooped to fix some wires on the floor before walking back up the center aisle.

"Why don't we decide which earphones to use," suggested Harriet.

"This pair seems to be comfortable on my head," I said. "I'll use these." I laid them on the table's edge.

Tom removed a pair from his head. "Harriet, you're so tiny, these will probably fit you perfectly."

Harriet, five feet two and one hundred pounds, ran around the table, hooked the thin band over her head, threw her arms wide, and said, "Voila."

We put little name tags on our chosen earphones and laid them back on the table.

Ned arranged two chairs beside the earphone table. "For the person taking and the person relieving."

"Okay, gang, let's head for our hotel bar." Tom rubbed his hands together in exhilaration. "Who's going to be first on the courtesy bus?"

When I walked into the hotel dining room at seven fifteen the next morning, I spotted Ned, Grace, and Eleanor. Grace was sipping coffee, both hands carefully undergirding the cup.

"Have you ordered?" I asked, but really wanted to know how Grace's head felt.

"Yes," said Eleanor. "We're having rolls and coffee; Ned's having eggs."

"I'll join you with rolls," I said.

The waiter appeared with coffee.

"Thank you." I addressed Ned. "Harriet said she and Tom were coming over later because somebody had to do the last takes."

"That's a bit cheeky." Ned looked askance at Grace.

"Are you going in first?" I asked.

"Yes. Then you, Eleanor, and Grace. Okay, Eleanor?"

"Sure. That's fine with me. See that Grace takes me out on time."

"I will be on time. Don't worry about me," said Grace before biting into a heavily buttered croissant.

"Tom can follow Grace," Ned continued, "Harriet last. We'll alternate each day. So you go first tomorrow, Arabella. Ten-minute takes. Nobody should have difficulty typing their take in the fifty minutes before another turn. That way, the day's transcript will be completed an hour after adjournment."

"Then we can nightclub." Grace brightened.

A knife could have slashed through the silence.

"Don't get your hopes up," Ned said. "I have a gut feeling we'll have to report the evening speeches. I'll try to arrange things so we get a decent break and dinner while the participants are banqueting, but I think we better have sandwiches brought in at noon so everybody'll be caught up before the afternoon session starts."

"Well, let's get over there so we can check any changes in the agenda and find out what accents we have to cope with." Eleanor drained her coffee cup and set it down with finality.

Mid-morning, in our workroom, Eleanor and I hung over her desk perusing the agenda. "I almost wish," said Eleanor, "these people would stick to their own language and not try to show off their English."

"That way," said Grace, who was typing, but listening, "we would get to use the translators, and they're usually good."

"I simply can't grapple with Frenchmen trying to speak English," I said.

"Yeah," said Eleanor. "They accent the wrong syllables and you don't have time to figure out what they're saying when they talk so fast, or even slowly for that matter."

Tom stopped typing to give his interpretation of a Frenchman reading the Gettysburg Address, which effectively halted any progress on the transcript for the next five minutes.

"Just as I thought." Ned stalked in after his morning conference with the staff. "They want us to report the after-dinner speeches, which will last until ten-thirty or eleven. We won't get away from here before midnight."

"And be back by eight-thirty every morning." Tom whistled. "It'll be a rough week."

"The banquet each night will last two, two and a half hours, so we'll get a rest," said Ned.

"Goodbye any fun this trip." Grace kissed her fingers and flicked them.

"Maybe the last night." Ned's eyes swept Heavenward. I could just hear him giving silent thanks that Grace would not find the bars. "Here's the final agenda, one for each, so guard it. There are some changes." Ned passed them out. "I better get in there and relieve Harriet."

"The whole morning is welcoming speeches in English," said Grace.

"An Indian from New Delhi is scheduled right after lunch," Eleanor observed. "They can be pure hell. They speak beautiful, impeccable English, but like a choochoo train, they get going faster and faster until you're hanging on for dear life and praying you won't blow it."

My turn after lunch caught the Indian gentleman well

on the way towards his full potential. Ned signaled me to start a few seconds early so that when he stopped, I was moving right along with the speaker. By the time Eleanor arrived, the man had roared into high gear. I did for her what Ned had done for me. The last thing I did before walking up the aisle was look at Eleanor. A glaze had passed over her green eyes, but her fingers were flying.

On my way to the workroom, I saw Vice President Johnson sprawled on the big couch in the corridor talking to two men. So he had arrived.

As I reached our room door, I heard Ned's scream of rage. He stormed out, almost knocking me over, and rushed towards the hotel manager's office. Open mouthed, I watched him until he disappeared. For a grown man, a personable man, at the pinnacle of his profession, a man whose judgment I respected, to constantly indulge in violent temper tantrums disturbed me.

Inside the room, except for the typewriters, all was quiet. I stopped beside Harriet and whispered, "What happened?"

"His typewriter broke down," Harriet whispered.

"You don't have to whisper," said Tom.

"It's scary," said Grace.

"It must have broken in transit," Harriet said, "and didn't show up until he started really pounding it. He immediately switched to that Spanish typewriter that had been left in the corner and started getting those curlicues the Spanish write above some letters all over his transcript."

I concentrated on my own work, but was aware that Ned had returned, still fuming and jumping from typewriter to typewriter as the reporters came and went, trying to finish his take. As usual, he finished before I did and stomped out. I found him in the lobby outside the auditorium, smoking cigarette after cigarette, alternately coughing and choking.

"I never saw such an outfit in my life," he announced, his voice broke with irritation. "You'd think somebody around here would have an English typewriter. They not only don't, but God forbid they'd know where I could get one."

He dropped his cigarette on the stone floor, twisting his heel on it as he gagged from coughing.

I decided not to ask if he didn't think his coughing would stop and his breathing improve if he gave up smoking. "There must be someplace in Old San Juan where you could rent a typewriter. Isn't there a U.S. Government Courthouse here? They would use English and the standard government twenty-five-line page. So the ratchet on the typewriter would be geared to reporting needs."

Dumbstruck, Ned cried, "I was so furious that I forgot the courthouse. Of course. You're right. There is one here. I'll telephone. I can taxi down as soon as we have the dinner break."

Tom passed us, carrying his notes. "Harriet just took me out. You're up next, Ned."

Ned checked the time. "I'll telephone and be right back. The French and German speakers should be coming up. I hope to God the earphones work."

Seating myself at the back of the auditorium, I listened until my turn. On my way past Ned's desk afterwards, he said, low enough so as not to disturb the others, "I reached one of the reporters. He sounds a gracious chap. He's going to Ponce on a case and will let me borrow his typewriter, but I can't have it 'til morning. I should be here in time for my take as I'm up last."

"If not, I'm sure Tom will split your turn with me."

The first speaker after the dinner break happened to be Pablo Casals. Ned told us that the staff had asked him to play for them. "It would be nice. We'll see."

Mr. Casals started speaking by thanking everybody for inviting him and telling them what a wonderful thing they were doing by organizing the Peace Corps. He also said that he had just returned from a concert tour and had not had time to practice. So after apologizing for not entertaining them by playing his cello, he sat down.

"That's the way it goes," I said as I handed the transcript of my last take to Ned.

Tom had started towards the door for his first take the following morning when Ned swept in, followed by a wiry porter in his late teens carrying a typewriter.

"By the way," Tom said casually, "Arabella and I decided not to have lunch brought in today."

Ned bristled. "What did you do that for? We don't have time to run all over this hotel."

"We're going to the sandwich bar by the pool. It'll be the only time we see the sun or the sea."

"You saw the sun this morning on the way over," I teased. "In fact, you complained about it being so bright."

Tom smirked. "I was too tired to look at it." He winked at me on his way out.

"Come with us, Ned. You'll have time to get your typing finished. We can get a table and come and go as our work permits," I said.

"We'll see. It would be fun." He fussed with the

papers on his desk. "If there's any problem, we'll go back to having lunch brought in tomorrow."

Eleanor and Grace were the first to leave for the sandwich bar. They told the rest of us later that they had to wheedle the headwaiter into giving us a table with a large beach umbrella, assuring him that the rest of us would be out shortly. Ned, Tom, Harriet and I went out together. The minute we reached Grace and Eleanor, Tom moved one of the chairs to the periphery of the umbrella's cast shadow. With a beatific smile and closed eyes, he turned his face towards the sun.

On her chair, Grace had hiked up her skirt to expose plump white legs as well as turning her face to the sun's rays. In the end, only Ned and I remained shaded, watching the people in the pool and the changing light on the blue-green sea beyond.

"Is that reporter going to be in Ponce the rest of the week?" I asked.

"He thinks so. He'll leave a note in my hotel mailbox if he comes back sooner. Otherwise, I'll take the typewriter to the Courthouse when we finish Friday. At least there won't be any night speeches Friday. The exodus will probably start right after lunch."

"Let's come out here and have a drink tonight when they go to dinner," Grace broke in.

"We don't have time for that," Ned said, exuding disapproval. "I better get back to our work room. It's a good thing my wife didn't come. With all these night sessions, she'd have a fit."

I nodded agreement. Hank wouldn't have been happy about the dinners and night sessions either, though he would lie on the beach all day and soak up the sun.

The dinner break, like the night before, was scheduled for two and a half hours so everybody had time to finish typing their last take before going to dinner.

When Eleanor placed her completed take on the day's transcript, Grace said, "Wait for me; I'm almost through."

The four of us remaining in the room watched them leave. Ned was frowning. I knew he thought, as I did, that they would head straight for the pool bar. As soon as the rest of us finished, Ned sent Tom and Harriet to the dining room to make a reservation and took me with him to the bar.

Grace was perched on a stool, aggressively flirting with the bartender. We heard Eleanor say, "Grace, I think we better go."

A quick two-step that ended in waltz time brought Ned to Grace's side.

"Yes," he said, taking her elbow. "We have a table in the dining room."

If she had objected, the firm grip would have assisted her off the stool anyway. Because she willingly abandoned her spot, the hand only served to steady her.

Once seated at the table, Grace giggled and started telling amusing stories.

"How many drinks do you think she had, Harriet?" Sitting together across the table from Grace, Harriet and I had no fear of being heard.

"I don't know, but too many," said Harriet.

"Do you think she can report? Using those earphones as we have all day, she'll have to pay strict attention."

"And she has to go in second, right after Eleanor."

"You two stop talking." Grace slapped the table edge. "This story is hilarious, and I want your undivided attention." She wigwagged her head mischievously.

Tom, on the other side of me, said under his breath, "We better take some black coffee back with us."

In the workroom, Grace demurred. "If I drink that coffee, I'll be awake all night."

"Oh, come on! We'll be here five more hours. It'll wear off," urged Tom at his most gallant.

"All right, but if I'm awake all night, I'll bang on your door." She batted her eyes.

"What'll my wife say?" He batted back.

Grace drank the coffee, but refused to switch to a later take.

Four reporters watched her departure. "If any of you are given to prayer," said Ned, "pray now."

Fifteen minutes later, Grace returned, notes in hand, and sat down without looking at anybody. Tom, who had taken her out, was late coming back. He arrived carrying another cup of black coffee. With great solemnity, he placed the coffee in front of Grace. She ignored it, making a big show of reading her notes.

Ned circled the room, stopping at each desk as if he had something to impart, his ploy to see Grace's notes without appearing obvious.

"Arabella," he said, moving past my desk like a battleship, "Take me out in fifteen minutes this time."

He passed Tom. "Will you stay fifteen minutes on your next take?"

"Right."

"We'll keep Grace off this round and try to get her sobered up so she can go in on the last round."

The moment Ned left, Tom signaled Eleanor to join him by my desk.

"What happened?" Eleanor kept her voice down to a

whisper, but Grace was working too hard to pay attention or care.

"She got the earphones tangled up so she had trouble getting them off her head. When she got up, she knocked her stenotype over. I thought the chairman was going to stop the meeting, but he only glared at her. She walked out straight as a ramrod."

"Arabella, when you come back, bring some more coffee. She'll be awake all night, but tough," Eleanor hissed.

At the end, the other five of us split up Grace's seven pages, reconstructed them for sense, and retyped them. Even so, an hour after the session's conclusion, the day's transcript was placed in the hands of the Conference Secretary.

Feeling tired in the morning, I thanked the Lord that the week was most over. My second wind had already been spent. To pamper myself, I chose to breakfast leisurely on the conference hotel patio and didn't see Grace until the day had well begun. Looking yellow-gray and worn, Grace was working slowly, but steadily. All of us were working slower. The hours and the tension had taken their toll. Stress appeared in a snapped response, a complaint about the earphones, an angry glance at talkers who had finished.

I complained to Ned that while the translators were good, the other languages came through the earphones as background noise. Harriet complained that she was getting a stiff neck from holding her head in one position to keep the earphones functioning at their maximum. Tom continued to complain about no sun. Everybody complained about no rest.

When the chairman drew the conference to a close at four-thirty Friday afternoon, five reporters, including me, stood in the back of the auditorium to listen and join in the applause, although we admitted to ourselves that the applause was for Grace, who sat alone at the reporters' table.

The minute he finished typing, Ned went to call the Courthouse. When he came back, he announced, "The local reporters have just returned from Ponce. I invited them to have dinner with us."

"Did you say they were men?" asked Grace.

"Both," came his grave answer. "I don't know their marital status so you're on your own."

"Oh, pooh," Grace said, the only thing she could think of to say.

"I'm going to cab down to the Courthouse with the typewriter," Ned said as he packed his personal belongings. "When you leave, take with you anything you want to carry on the plane. I'll tend to getting the typewriters sent to the airport in the morning."

"Does that mean we can go back to the hotel and freshen up?" Eleanor sounded weary.

"Of course. I'm sure the two locals will want to go home first. What time shall we meet in the lobby?" Ned indicated the Courthouse-bound typewriter to the porter in the doorway.

"Eight o'clock?" suggested Harriet.

"Good enough," Ned answered after quick calculation. "Tom, will you see that the Secretary gets the transcript in his office?"

"Roger."

"Eight o'clock in our hotel lobby." Ned hurried after the porter.

"I'm to tell you," Tom said, "no matter how big a night you have or what you do in the morning, like the beach or shopping—"

"Or sleeping," stuck in Harriet.

"—or sleeping, the plane leaves at two. It's your responsibility to be there." After which comment, we applied ourselves to our typing.

Eighteen

March flew by. We all worked at the usual steady pace, but I stewed. Hank didn't come in March as he had promised in his letter. He had had another setback, I just knew. How bad was it this time? Did he know what was going on or was his normal life a blank and he lived in another world unbeknownst to the doctors? Was he kept in bed? Was he kept in constraints? In coming out of these setbacks, did his mind move in and out of normalcy? Was any pain involved? My mind went round and round wildly. I dragged through the days, murmuring, "Oh, my darling, this uncertainty is destroying me, too."

April came and went. I was frantic. No word. Why? Couldn't he write? Didn't he sense how I needed something, anything from him? Better or worse, dead or alive. I stopped short. Dead, I would be told by that telephone man. I pulled myself together.

On May 19th, a letter greeted me as I walked in the front door of the apartment building and picked up my mail. At last! I could hardly wait to reach the apartment. I dropped my handbag and groceries on the floor by the door and plopped onto the nearby bed/couch. As I slit open the envelope, I made happy little gurgling sounds.

I read: *May 17, 1960.* It seemed longer than that. So much had happened to change my life. Work, which took most of my time, was definitely better. However, the sadness and worry about Hank was pervasive. It never left me. What had happened to the little mirror-written comment, "Six months to go?"

Been a crazy two years, hasn't it?

Unless you hear to the contrary, I'll be at The Homestead, Hot Springs, Va. on Saturday, May 21st and Sunday, May 22nd.

I almost shrieked in my excitement.

Happy Anniversary. Hank.

Don't lose sight of this.

An arrow pointed towards the small clipping stapled to the letter. The clipping read: "Revive in your own home the lost art of romance and take a bath with your husband... Step daintily into the bubble-filed tub. Mon Dieu, this is no time to bend over... Don't offer to his horrified eye the ungainly sight of a bare bottom that will only remind him of a blimp struggling through a storm... Lower yourself gradually into the water. Don't just plop in like a baby whale."

As the letter said, "Mon Dieu." I laughed, delighted. So he thought of me as his wife, not just engaged to marry. Saturday, May 21st. I danced around the room. We were going to celebrate our anniversary at The Homestead.

"Oh." I grabbed the phone, flipped through the list of phone numbers on my desk, and excitedly dialed The Homestead.

"Yes," the desk clerk told me, "we can let you have a room for Saturday, the 21st."

"I'll be arriving mid-morning." I hung up. Clothes. I rushed to my closet to examine my formal dresses. Humm. Hank hadn't seen the ankle length aquamarine silk dress. I had to look glamorous. He liked me to look smart. Tomorrow, Friday, I had a Senate Banking and Currency hearing scheduled for an hour, meaning it could run one and a half hours, and Irene was loaded. I had to type it myself, but I could manage that much by five o'clock.

I woke early on Saturday, instantly alert and eager, feeling happy. I jumped from the bed and headed for the kitchen to plug in the coffee pot before whipping into my dressing and bath area. I had already laid out the Ben Rigg dusty rose silk linen dress I intended to wear and had partially packed the small overnight case.

By nine o'clock, I backed my car out of the parking space behind the building. Three hours later, I drew up to the entrance of The Homestead.

When I checked in at the Registration Desk, the clerk told me that Mr. Martz was playing golf. I groaned. But, of course, he didn't know that I was definitely coming. How stupid of me. I hadn't left a message when I called the hotel. I could kick myself. I constantly did things halfway.

At twelve fifteen, I reached him in his room. Two minutes later, he rapped on my door. "If I had known you were here, I could have seen you fifteen minutes earlier," Hank moaned.

"What a loss," I pretended to grieve.

He grinned.

"Let me hold you in my arms a few minutes, then we'll go to lunch."

After lunch, we sunned by the pool. Lying next to each other in deck chairs, we somehow found ourselves talking about jewelry. I commented that I had always wanted a medium colored topaz ring and would buy myself one some day. In the same breath, I said, "It's hot here."

Hank laughed. "Let's get dressed, walk around the grounds, and take some pictures of each other."

Among other shots, while standing in front of the hotel, we asked one of the porters to take our picture together.

On the way to the dining room for dinner, Hank admired my aquamarine silk dress. I said, "I saw a gorgeous light brown and white linen suit on sale in Garfinckle's for one hundred dollars."

"Why didn't you buy it, honey?"

"I thought about buying it, but didn't really need it." I cogitated, not only is he the world's most wonderful man, he's generous to boot. He won't object to what money I spend. I cast an adoring glance his way as we entered the dining room.

During dinner, we danced. He held me close. To my everlasting delight, he danced superbly.

Sunday morning, we attended the Episcopal Church, Hank being a member of that particular faith. Though I belonged to the Presbyterian Church, if he wanted us in the Episcopal Church, I wouldn't object. Together, we knelt at the altar for communion, knelt together as if we were really man and wife. I thought myself in paradise.

By mid-afternoon, Hank asked me when I planned to leave. I mentioned a late hour. He said, "I think you should go earlier, honey." He laid out his reasons, the main one being crossing the mountains along the winding roads after dark. I listened carefully. Much as I wanted to stay with him as long as possible, I agreed with his reasoning. "Okay, four o'clock."

As my car climbed the twisting, already shadowed road to the summit, I realized that he had been right. Interesting. First, he stated his thinking about why I should leave early, then let me make my own decision. He knew just how to handle me. And I wasn't sure I knew how to handle him. Actually, I reasoned, there had been no occasion for me to assert myself. And now with his physical problems, I couldn't control anything anyway. Plus, knowing that he wouldn't answer specific questions and not wanting to bring up his problems when he was obviously relaxed and enjoying himself, I had remained silent. The last thing I wanted was to sound like a shrewish wife. He needed joy between us, the joy of being together, to savor during the hard times. All I wanted was what was best for him.

Back at the work grind Monday morning, my thoughts kept returning to the weekend with Hank. As far as I could tell, he seemed to be fine. His mind worked at its normal brilliance and his body was doing well. Did this backsliding come on him suddenly? Was that improving or not? How long did these episodes last? Did he have any premonitions about its happening? So many questions remained unanswered. I had trouble concentrating on typing.

By noon, after Ned and Tom had returned from morning takes, Frank walked into our room.

"Arabella, how about a week in California starting Sunday afternoon, the thirty-first, for a medical conference at Stanford University?"

"Lovely," I said.

"The subject is brain function."

He added, "I'll make a Saturday night hotel reservation for you at the airport. That way, you can rent a car Sunday morning and drive down to Palo Alto."

"Fine."

Frank walked out.

"Boy, do you ever rate," said Tom.

"Would you rather go, Tom?"

"No way. I'm happy staying home. But I'll bet a lot of Frank's other people would like to go."

I shrugged. "They can't do medical." I sat down at the small table where I kept the dictating equipment to dictate a short deposition for Irene.

At nine o'clock Sunday morning, May 31st, in the San Francisco airport, I picked up the reserved rental car to drive down to Palo Alto. Following Frank's explicit directions, I sped down the new expressway, passing green hills, a sun-spangled lake, and Daly City houses. In leaving Daly City behind, guesses as to what the motel would be like began to intrude my mind. What Susan Murphy, my contact, would look like, how big a meeting. All of a sudden, I saw the motel sign on the left-hand side of the road.

After registering and freshening up in my room, I started in search of the pool. Frank had suggested I bring my bathing suit. Along with the one-story blocks of rooms, the pool nestled among tall green hedges, blossoming hibiscus, tiny secluded gardens, and pervasive flower fragrance. White lounge chairs in an even row formed a rectangle around the pool's cement apron. No ripple disturbed the tranquility of the blue water, nobody lay in the lounge chairs, nobody was around at all. The emptiness made me change my mind. I went hunting for Susan Murphy instead.

I crossed another blossom-surrounded patio, and entered an oblong wood-frame building. A table covered with piles of folders, neat rows of name tags, and stacks of back-up material extended three quarters of the width of the large, rectangular room. At the opposite end of the table, a gray-haired woman in a pearl gray suit sat, separating papers.

"You must be Susan Murphy. I'm Arabella."

"Arabella! We're delighted you could come." The wide slash of thick red lipstick separated, exposing yellow teeth with gold fillings. In my usual instant judgement of the people I had to work with, I noted the managerial aura and decided Susan would understand reporting problems, make quick decisions, and be a pleasant companion.

"Your stenotype pads came in the mail this morning, along with a letter and dictating equipment. The box is under the table."

I lifted the table's dark green felt skirt and peered underneath.

"You can leave them there," Susan said.

"It's as good a place as any." I extracted the letter and readjusted the folds of the skirt.

"Enjoy the pool now if you want to. You're going to work hard for the rest of the week. The Planning Committee is talking about a night session on Wednesday if they get behind."

"They always do get behind." I pursed my lips.

"The overall chairman is pretty strong. They're shooting for a mid-afternoon adjournment on Friday so he'll try to keep them on schedule."

"How many people are you expecting?"

"One hundred signed up, and I think most of them are coming."

"The room will be pretty full." My eyes plunged over the row upon row of folding chairs set in formation between the central and side aisles.

"Here's a folder for you. It contains the revised agenda, some abstracts, and the list of participants. The session chairman and the panel will sit at that table in front on the left. They will present from the podium on the right."

"Will there be questions after each paper? It will be difficult if they start hopping up all over the room. What about names? Do you want the questioners identified?"

"We're having microphones set up in the aisles. They will be asked to go to a microphone and state their names. Twenty minutes at the end of each group of five papers has been set aside for questions."

I wanted to say, but restrained myself, that unless the session chairman enforced the rule, as soon as the subject became controversial, participants would neither go to the microphone nor say their name. I decided to wait and see how the meeting went.

"What are those?" I asked, indicating two large, box-like structures, a TV screen in the upper section, that were standing against the right side wall.

"Those are the brain wave machines which will be used to demonstrate the subject of the papers. I doubt anything will be said about them until Thursday morning."

I opened my folder to look at the new agenda. "Is this right?" I put my finger on one agenda item and raised my eyes to meet Susan's "Wednesday afternoon is free?"

"For you and me. All the participants want to go through the research labs over at Stanford. That's Wednesday afternoon, making the night session almost mandatory, but that decision will be announced Wednesday morning. Thursday afternoon will be the demonstration of those machines. I don't know how you're going to manage that." Over the rim of her half-glasses, Susan directed a penetrating glance at me, still immersed in the agenda.

"I'll grapple with that when the time comes," I said, continuing to study the agenda.

"You might want to look at some of the vocabulary in those papers I gave you."

Susan resumed her work at the table. "We can have lunch when I get through here. The opening session starts at two. I want to be back before anybody shows up."

"Fine. That would give me a chance to look over the abstracts."

Half an hour before the starting time, I carried my equipment to the front of the room. I set the stenotype down before the first center aisle front row seat, having made sure that the seat gave me a good view of anyone sitting at the table or standing at the podium. I laid some papers on the seat next to mine to prevent anybody from sitting there, locked the machine into place, and sat down to run through the vocabulary again. Central nervous system, evoked potential, both visual and cortical—it didn't seem so difficult. I added the papers and agenda to those on the seat beside me and began to watch the men and women roaming about the room. Some drifted in, greeted friends, acted uncertain; others hustled up to the panelists' table, back to the slide projector, over to the podium to test the microphone.

The chairman, of medium height, wavy gray hair and sharp blue eyes seen through thick-lensed glasses, moved with aplomb through his opening remarks, then held each speaker to his allotted thirty minutes. During the question period, the few who had questions raised their hands, waited to be called on by name, and went to the microphone. I packed up with the secure feeling that I would have a good transcript.

On the way out, I said to Susan, "This afternoon was duck soup."

"Don't bank on it continuing. I told you this session was preparatory."

Susan was right. By Wednesday, they were way behind on the agenda. All control vanished with a weak session chairman who neither made people say their name nor stuck to the time limit. When they broke at twelve-thirty, the overall chairman announced an evening session from seven to eleven.

"Let's go lie by the swimming pool," Susan said when I reached her station at the rear of the room.

"I was hoping you'd want to do that."

We staked out two chairs partially shaded by hibiscus, then swam, sunned, swam, read, and swam. "What a lovely afternoon," I said as we prepared to leave. "I think I can survive the night session."

By twenty minutes before seven, I paced back and forth between panel table and podium, waiting for the sedate, quiet, Nobel-Prize-winning chairman.

"All ready for a long evening?" He placed his writing tablet on the table.

"I need your help."

"How so?"

"To keep the participants under control. They get tired, they get restless, they all talk at once. It's just that if you want a decent transcript, there has to be order. I get tired, too," I ended apologetically.

"Of course, you do. I've been watching you. I'll do my best. Give me a signal if I forget."

He didn't forget. Twice when multiple voices objected, when an argument loomed, he made everybody stand, stretch, and sit down again.

"Okay?" he asked at eleven while others merged in a reasonable jumble through the door.

"Okay. Thanks," I said.

"See you in the morning."

Sleep turned out to be only a good idea. Overtired and wound-up I switched the light on at least once an hour to check the time. In the morning, Susan and I sat listlessly drinking coffee.

"I feel as if I hadn't slept at all," I said as we walked across the parking lot behind the administration building.

"It'll be interesting to see how many show up for the first presentation this morning."

The audience was spotty when the chairman called the meeting to order. They wandered in throughout the morning, showed no spark, and nothing was controversial. Even the mid-morning break was subdued. Before lunch, the chairman explained the afternoon demonstration. The brain-wave machines would be used on two volunteers from the audience.

Right after he adjourned the morning session, the chairman walked over to me. "You're on your own this afternoon," he said. "There won't be much I can do about it."

The two volunteers were hooked up to the machines immediately after lunch. Then the afternoon session chairman made a few remarks, the lights were turned off, and the switches for the two machines flipped on. Tension simmered through the room, excitement alongside it. Anticipating silence hung over everything. Nobody moved, nobody spoke, all waited. The screens, which looked like television screens, blazed with light. Jagged white lines started to snake across the surfaces.

For several minutes, the audience maintained the silence. Then excited yelling started.

"Did you see that peak delay?"

Someone else yelled, "There's another."

I could tell from the quiet movement behind me that people were standing.

"Was that a spike?" someone shouted.

"No, a slow wave," another voice yelled.

They fought over the spikes, the fast waves, the slow waves, the peak delays. I pivoted in my seat, trying to distinguish the different remarks, if not the speakers.

At last, it was over. The participants streamed outside to erupt in excited talk. I slid in slow motion against the hard chair back, my hands limp and listless in my lap.

Friday morning, on the verge of tears from fatigue, I pulled the box of stenotype paper from under the table, opened it, and let out a gargled sound between a squeak and a squeal. The few doctors around stopped all motion, a pipe halfway to a mouth, the page of a book unturned, a sentence unfinished. Everybody looked at me.

"A bug," I gasped.

Nobody laughed. A heavily built man wearing horn-rimmed glassed asked as though an everyday question, "A big bug or a little bug?"

"A big bug."

With scientific care, he reopened the box, cornered and killed the bug. The unflappable efficiency quieted me, allowing my sense of humor to assert itself. I giggled. The man beamed brightly back at me. "Anytime," he said.

That broke my depressed mood. I tripped down the aisle to my seat, worked as though it were Monday morning after a restful weekend, and felt delighted when the session ended an hour ahead of the rescheduled one P.M.

In starting the ignition of the rental car for the drive to the airport, I remembered that Susan had said Route One, unlike the new expressway I had driven down, was neon-walled, motels, shopping areas, car dealers, all the way to the airport. In other words, interesting things to look at, not a boring express way. I took Route One. Traffic flowed in a constant stream.

Unhurried, I stayed in the right-hand, slower lane, glancing from side to side. I lingered over some dress shops a fraction of a second too long and had to ram on the brakes to avoid hitting a car stopped in front of me. I came to a halt a foot or so behind it then jolted forward as I was struck from the rear.

Mashing my eyelids together, I clenched my teeth and waited for the expected sound of shattering glass as my automobile was bumped forward.

A man's infuriated howl made me open my eyes and

confront reality without broken glass. Pot bellied, a great bulge over a low-slung belt, florid complexion, suggesting too much alcohol, the man from the first car strode towards me.

"Jesus Christ," he swore. "You almost shoved me over that guy lying in the road."

My eyes widened. I started to speak, but the man had already turned to the car behind me.

"Why the hell don'tcha watch what you're doing? You almost killed a guy." In the rear-view mirror, I observed the second man get out of his car. Unusually tall and gangly, he towered above his attacker. I figured there must be twenty-five years' difference in their ages.

"A guy in the road?" The man sounded incredulous.

"He 's drunk. He staggered at the curb. Before I could say Jack Robinson, he fell flat, right in front of me. If I'd been going any faster, I couldn't have stopped."

The two men passed me without looking at me. "Then, damn your hide, you almost pushed me over him."

Getting out of my car, I followed them, watchful of the traffic, drivers in the left lanes slowing to look. Already people had gathered on the curb.

"He's pretty drunk," one bystander offered.

"No he's not," another said. "I followed him down the street. He acted very peculiar, but not drunk. Maybe he's on drugs." The woman speaker sized up the form lying on the street, eager to prove her theory.

I, too, looked at the body. The front wheels of the automobile had come within inches of where he lay, face down. The hair was oily, the face, what I could see of it, covered by a scruffy beard. He had mud on his ill-fitting clothing and one torn pant leg. Something I couldn't identify made me uneasy.

"What's going on here?" One of California's finest, a policeman, walked up to the two men and me. Flashing red lights from his patrol car backstopped the three accordioned vehicles.

"A drunk playing Russian roulette," said the curbstander holding the "drunk" opinion.

"Was he struck?" asked the officer.

"Fell right straight down in front of my car," said the red-faced driver. "Nothing but a miracle I didn't hit him when these jokers hit me from the rear."

The policeman knelt down beside the motionless man. "This is fresh mud." The officer crumbled a bit. "He must have fallen before and torn his pant leg."

"Probably lying in somebody's bushes," said the 'drunk' theorist.

The officer felt the man's forehead, seized the body, and laid his hand on any exposed skin he could reach, cheek, neck, wrist. "This man is burning up with fever. He needs an ambulance, not a drunk tank."

I bet the big Irish policeman with the hard face had seen plenty of violence in his years on the force, but when he rolled the prone man over, his hands were gentle as a baby's.

As if slapped, I tottered backward then riveted every eye by gasping, "Charlie."

Nineteen

In the hospital lobby, I picked up a scientific magazine and leafed through it as I waited for the nurses to finish making Charlie presentable. My eye suddenly caught an item that said cosmic rays could cause brain damage. I uncrossed my legs, sat up straight and focused on the article. The gist of it informed me that if people weren't shielded from the dangerous radiation in cosmic rays, their brains could be damaged as well as their bodies.

My mind screamed. These lapses Hank suffers. His comment that the body was doing fine; the head wasn't madly rang bells. Radiation? Chemicals? Again, I didn't know what his symptoms were. But articles like this made me uneasy, set me wondering. I was sure in my own mind that his work involved outer space. And that could mean radiation.

I flung the magazine aside and stared out the window. Had Hank been in some lab, unshielded, working with cosmic rays? The government let brilliant men do this and didn't protect them. Anger surged through me. I could feel my face reddening.

"You may go up to Mr. Steven's room now, Miss Robbins."

The soft, cultured female voice of the Red Cross volunteer brought me back to earth. I looked at her.

"You may go to Mr. Steven's room now." She repeated, smiling at me.

"Thank you," I managed, still under the influence of that article.

"Room 209." She turned and walked towards the reception desk.

Still seething, I took the elevator to the second floor. How dare the government allow men to be exposed that way! I stood in front of Charlie's door, trying to compose myself. It would never do to talk to him, feeling this intense anger. He would sense it and question me.

Charlie's hands kneaded the sheet of the lone hospital bed in the small white-washed room. A supply stand with the usual glass and water bottle on the top stood at the right of the bed. I sat in the only chair.

His hair had been washed and the facial stubble shaved off. Charlie spoke lucidly, though emaciated and weak.

"What did she say?" he asked.

"Who?" I had been three thousand miles away in thought.

"Mrs. Henderson, of course. Who'd you think?"

"I've made so many phone calls since admitting you to this hospital two days ago, between your affairs and the banged-up rental car, I forgot the man I love most in the whole world."

With an effort, Charlie pulled the sheet over his head.

"You had to find out sometime, so pull the sheet down and let's talk like two adults."

He clutched at the sheet with a helpless-looking pale hand and managed to get it off his face. "You sound snappy as a mongrel stray with a bone."

"What do you expect? These last days after finding you on the street, out of your head with fever haven't exactly been restful."

Charlie was silent, gathering strength to pursue his questions.

"You called Mrs. Henderson because you didn't know how to reach my parents. What did she say?"

"She was very concerned, most gracious. She said she would tell them you were in the hospital, but much improved, and if there was anything else she could do to let her know. When she couldn't reach them, she called back to say she would keep trying."

I consulted the page of closely written notes I held in my hand. "I hope you don't mind my involving her. I thought your family should be informed. You're pretty sick, you know. The doctor said it was one of the worst cases of flu he had seen this season."

"When do you think they'll let me out of here?"

"Not for a couple more days, anyhow. You'll have to take it easy for a bit, and I can't stay to look after you. I've got to get back tomorrow."

"What about the rental car?"

"I talked to Jack, Mrs. Henderson's attorney. He called the insurance company's lawyer. Jack and the other lawyer are handling it. I gave a statement this morning." Then I asked offhandedly, "How do you like the work here, the living, et cetera?"

"The work's lousy. At least in New York you can work without passing the Certified Shorthand Reporters exam. Out here, there's little you can do without it. They don't give it every day. And with my luck I just missed one session and had to wait three months. Since passing the test, I've been busy enough, but the work isn't that interesting. I wouldn't mind going back east."

"That would be heresy to a lot of Californians."

"They don't know what an Eastern spring is like." His eyes moved past me towards the window where the palm fronds swayed back and forth in the dainty breeze, creating a changing pattern of light and dark as the long, spindly leaves spent their momentum. "It's sunny like today all the time."

From where I sat, I could see the black shadow cast by the wing of the building, sharp, like a Corot painting.

"Well, they do have a rainy season," Charlie added.

"Come to Washington. The work's neat, better than New York. And there's so much bad reporting around, Frank would welcome you with wild hosannas."

"How come? Washington, of all places, should have first-rate reporters."

"There isn't a CSR exam for one."

"Nor in New York for free-lancers, which means only in the courts."

"True, except, overall, while stimulating, the work's harder in Washington."

"So I should come because the work's hard? And your boyfriend would be real pleased," Charlie said as he carefully smoothed the already smooth sheet.

"Listen and get this straight. I respect you as a reporter and like you as a friend. Nothing and nobody is going to come between Hank and me. I'm going to marry him as soon as he gets well."

Charlie lowered his eyelids and lay still for what seemed forever to me.

Finally, he said, "You really want me to come to Washington, don't you?"

"I wouldn't coax otherwise, silly."

"We'll see." He managed a wan and tired smile.

Rising, I patted the bed sheets. "Get some sleep." I stuffed the page of notes in my pocketbook. "Tell me in the morning what you decide. I'll see you before I leave town."

Twenty

Though I felt exhausted and jet lagged, Frank sent me to Senate Commerce the day after I returned from San Francisco. I dragged in from the Hill like a sleepwalker and started tinkering absently with my notes the minute I sat down at my desk, unable to move to the table holding the dictating equipment.

Irene appeared in the doorway. "Oh, Arabella, you're back. Frank asked me to type for you. How many pages do you think you have? I'll have to work it in somehow."

"Not much, thank God. Something like sixty."

"I was petrified it might be a hundred." Irene advanced to the desk hesitantly. Cocking her head to one side, she said, "You look like death warmed over."

"Gee, thanks. I'm tired. I'm going home as soon as this is dictated and the hell with everything else." With considerable effort, I attempted to zero in on Irene.

"You need a couple of toothpicks for those eyelids. It's time you took a little care of yourself instead of being a workhorse. Bluntly, Hank wouldn't like it."

"Please, Irene, don't." I felt ready to cry and must have looked that way. My long fingers rose automatically to cover my face. My chest rose and fell in deep sighs.

"I didn't even discuss with Frank the reporter from California that I hope he will hire." I ruffled the ends of the notes back and forth. "I'm in such a muddle."

From behind me, Irene slid her hands under my armpits and attempted to lift me from the chair. "Up you go," she urged as though to an infant, her voice loving and sympathetic. "Right over to the dictating machine."

When I reached for the notes, Irene seized them. "Oh, no. I'll carry those." I imagined her mind's eye picturing the inch-and-a-half thick pack slipping from my grasp and unwinding all over the floor. She watched while I sat down at the table and switched on the machine and inserted the cassette. "Now, tell me the starting time," she said, "and who was there. I'll make the title page. You do the dictation."

"Eleven-thirty, and Senator Unger, the chairman, was the only one there."

"Okay. You get started. I'll drop by in a bit to see how you're doing." She snatched a piece of paper, wrote "Do not disturb," on it, tore off a piece of Scotch tape, and taped the paper to the door as she left.

Once started, I dictated rapidly and automatically. Steady, subtle pressure from Irene moving in and out of the room encouraged me not to let down, not to slacken my pace. In a couple of hours, I finished.

Picking up the notes and the last cassette, I walked into the typists' room and straight to Irene's desk. "If anybody asks for me," I said, handing the cassette to her, "I've gone home. I'll talk to Frank about Charlie Stevens in the morning."

"Right," answered Irene without the slightest idea who Charlie Stevens was.

I spent part of the night awake, my sleep-wake cycle upside down with jet lag. After finally getting up later than usual and drinking coffee, I carefully applied makeup to hide bloodshot, dark-circled eyes before going to the office. Any hope of slipping unseen into my own workroom evaporated when I saw two of the typists, Sonia and Marie, standing in the hall in private conversation. Like Mutt and Jeff, they were always together, tall and buxom Sonia with her round, pleasant face, next to small boned and olive skinned Marie.

"Did you hear about Jim?" they asked in unison.

"No," I said warily, apprehensive of what was coming and concerned for the new typist/reporter hired the previous month.

"He was mugged last night in the parking lot, kicked in the face and his ankle broken," said Sonia.

"At one in the morning," announced Marie. "We don't know what he was doing here unless he and his boyfriend had been out on the town and left their car here."

"Was his roommate hurt, too?"

"No. He got away. He's the one who called Frank," said Sonia.

"Where's Jim?"

"In George Washington University Hospital." Marie answered.

"Poor Jim." I gripped my throat to still my pounding heart.

"Frank's probably looking for you," said Marie. "The schedule's all balled up."

"Oh, hell," I spat out and ran toward the door of my room.

Tom was talking on the phone and Ned was packing paper into his stenotype case.

"You look upset," Ned said quietly in deference to Tom.

"Marie and Sonia were gossiping in the hall. They told me about Jim's mugging," I said, glad to lay the blame for my wretched looks on Jim's misfortune.

"I suppose he didn't have much money on him, hence the deliberate physical injury."

"Hearing about that kind of thing scares me," I wailed.

Ned snapped his case shut. "What's the matter with you, Arabella?"

Tom kicked the wall. Ned dropped his voice. "Frank told the fellows in collating to walk the women to their cars. Get one of them to go with you if you're afraid. I can't tell you what else to do. Right now, I have to go over to House Judiciary."

"Tom," he said when Tom clapped the phone on the hook, "take Arabella for coffee. She needs some, and I don't have time."

Tom looked me up and down. "Come on. I have until ten-thirty."

The minute we entered the kitchen, Sonia and Marie, who were sitting at the large, round table in the center of the room, stopped talking.

"Were you gossiping about us?" Tom asked lightly with bantering, careless indifference.

The note-read reporter, in a tight leather skirt, stood near the sink, pouring coffee for herself. "We were discussing all the fags in this office and wanted to see who was coming in."

I liked Isobel, but I thought she wore her clothes too short.

"He's the only one," said Sonia.

"No. There are others who only type," retorted Isobel.

"Oh, you're right. I forgot." Sonia rolled her eyes. "How could I forget? If they'd only do their work and not get the whole office stirred up with their bickering, the work would run smoother."

"Jim stayed out of that," said Marie

Sonia said. "If the others aren't fighting among themselves, they're needling us about which one has the best work." She turned to Tom. "You should have seen the tantrum Don pulled on Friday. He screamed at Frank for the way the work is handed out and accused him of playing favorites."

"That's one thing you can't accuse Frank of," said Tom.

"Frank screamed right back. They were so loud, George told them both off in his bashful way. Don announced he didn't want to work in such a place; they could give him his retirement money because he was leaving. He stalked out of the room. I thought he'd blow a gasket, he turned so red."

"That won't last long—unfortunately," said Isobel. "There's something unsavory in the way he paws the other fellows."

"Isn't he the one who transcribed APL, which is supposed to be 'apple,' as 'American'?" said Tom. "The transcript went to the client reading 'Rotten Americans in a barrel'."

Marie doubled up with laughter. "I never heard that. How dumb."

"Even though some reporters use that as a short form for 'American,' you can tell the difference from the context," said Sonia. "I'll remind him of that the next time he gets on me." She squealed in glee.

"Maybe he'll really quit this time," said Marie.

"He won't. He has threatened to do that too many times already," said Sonia.

"Before the merger," Isobel said, "we had a kid in collating who was sent over to the Senate Office Building with a package. Instead of delivering it, he stuffed it in the mailbox. The Committee members sat biting their nails, waiting for the transcript. After a while, somebody called up, wanting to know where it was. The office had to run off a whole new set and rush it over."

Exhausted and unable to control myself, I erupted into hysterical laughter, which started the others. Marie was wiping the tears from her eyes when Frank walked in.

"Well," he said caustically, "it's nice to know you all find everything so funny considering the tragedy we've had this morning."

His back to Frank, Tom rolled his eyes at Isobel and me. I fained coughing and Isobel pretended to drink coffee. Sonia and Marie slipped from their chairs, past Frank, and out the door.

"Arabella, I need you to take a Senate hearing at eleven."

"I'm loaded, Frank. I can't."

"You have to. I have no alternative. I had Jim on the book for a short hearing on an emergency basis. As a result, I'm in a jam. Somehow, I'll get it typed for you so you won't have to do it, but that's the best I can offer."

"Where?" I'm sure I sounded weary enough to drop.

"Don't pull that on me," he said, catching my inflection. "I can't take any more today."

Meekly, I followed him from the kitchen.

Twenty-One

July disappeared in heavy work. August petered out to nothing. Some of the typists didn't even bother to come in. The reporters went off on holiday. Irene was offered an outside typing job from ten a.m. to four in the afternoon every day for three weeks of the month. In her free time, she busied herself fixing up the small apartment she had just rented.

I fumbled along with the few meetings where I was requested and stretched out the typing. Fortunately, nothing required fast delivery because with worrying about Hank during sleepless nights, I couldn't work fast. His letters now came so spasmodically. Long since, I had forgotten about cute little nurses trying to marry him. His mind seemed to be disintegrating. Was he going crazy? That idea sent me crazy. It meant the end of the road. I couldn't face it. I had to hang onto hope.

Frank watched me. I knew he was concerned and talked to George about me. George came into my room every few days just to sit and talk. Neither of them could do anything to help. As I fretted about Hank, they worried about me.

The first week of September, the weather became perfect—warm sunny days and cool nights. The leaves on the trees turned gold and red. The book picked up. I left the apartment early on Thursday of that week to walk around the parks and the Tidal Basin before going to the office. All explosive in exuberant fall color, the trees hovered over beds of red and yellow flowers. I loitered, I drank in the color, gloried in the flower beds, before retrieving my car from the parking area and drove to the office.

Ned was away. I expected quiet to finish a small transcript before my Hill assignment at eleven o'clock.

To my astonishment, Tom was typing when I arrived.

"Well, if you aren't the early bird," I remarked.

"Something's cooking; Ned called me last night."

"You mean he's home? I thought that hearing was scheduled for two more days."

"Home and madder than a hatter. He must have called Frank, too, because he's already been in here twice looking for Ned."

Tom and I were absorbed in our own work when Ned arrived. His "Good morning" was bearish and required no response, but two heads revolved with each step he took towards his desk. "You two don't have to stare at me," he hissed.

The door cracked. "I thought I saw the back of you." Frank sounded affable, pleasant, tranquil.

"I don't ever want to work with that woman again." The high-pitched scream slashed across Frank.

"At least let me say good morning before you light

into me," said Frank in dulcet tones. "Now, what woman is this you're referring to?"

"You know perfectly well what woman. Who do you think I've been in St. Louis with this week? Molly Barnes."

"She's one of the best typists we have." The stance, the movement of his body, the backward snap of his head, indicated real surprise. "That's why I sent her with you. I can't believe she didn't do a good job."

"It wasn't her work." Ned was getting purple. Tom and I exchanged a wary glance. "She showed up in the hearing room in her nightgown."

Frank's eyes went round and got perceptibly brighter. His mouth became a delighted Mephistophelean leer. "Was it thin?"

"Of course it was thin," shouted Ned, looking first at me then at the foolish set of Tom's face. "You two may think it's funny, but I was mortified. I asked the judge for a recess and bundled her out of there. Later, one of the young attorneys asked me if that was a nightgown she had on."

Tom joined me in bellowing laughter. Ned surveyed us. His angry blue eyes began to twinkle.

"She's pretty spaced out at times," said Frank. "But what brought that on?"

"It was cold on Monday, then turned warm. The heat in the room where we had to work became unbearable—no ventilation, no window, heat pouring full blast from the register. Tuesday night, she announced if it were that hot the next day, she was going to wear her nightgown. I never expected to see her in the hearing room. As casual as can be, she walked in and sat down. You know what a tyrant that Administrative Judge is. He stuttered through a full sentence before I could ask for a recess."

Ned stopped talking because Tom and I were making so much noise. His glance leapt to Frank. He, too, was obviously fighting to keep his cool.

"From a distance, I can appreciate the comic in reporting, but not at the time," Ned said. Eyes cast down, he pushed some papers around on his desk. "Something always happens when I work with that judge. Like the time he stacked his exhibits on the wastebasket for easy reference and the trash man threw them out."

At that, Frank lost his fight. "I'll see you later," he roared.

"I hate to leave now when the conversation's so sprightly, but Senate Foreign Relations isn't going to wait for me," said Tom. "Are you going over to the Hill, Arabella?"

A squawk came from the next room.

"Frank was so exuberant about Molly's nightgown, he probably pinched one of the typists." I snickered.

"Someday, he's going to get slapped for doing that," said Ned.

"My hearing isn't until eleven," I said.

"Keep a stiff upper lip, Ned." Tom grinned and let the door bang behind him.

I didn't leave the office until seven o'clock that night. As I walked into my apartment building, the face of the desk clerk brightened. "You have a letter," she said.

I beamed. But my joy turned to shock as I looked at the envelope. Everything was printed, not Hank's usual nice writing. "A. ROBBINS 1220 Mass. Ave N.E.

Washington, D.C." In brackets, he had printed "c/o Winthrop House." Somebody, presumably in the Post Office, had written, "Try 1727 Mass. Ave."

Once reaching my apartment, I stood in the middle of the room, hardly breathing, and slowly ripped open the envelope.

Sept 21, 1960.

Dear Arabella: Everything went blank a long time ago.

Everything went blank! Again, the same thing. He remembered nothing, like amnesia. But people got well after amnesia, or did they? That put me in such a fret that for a few minutes I couldn't finish reading his letter.

But now I remember you. And a topaz ring. I do not remember the color but it may soon come back to me. In any event you will soon receive it.

Hope this letter finds you just fine.

As it goes, Hank.

That farewell didn't sound good either. And again, I knew nothing and could do nothing. For long minutes, I stood there unable to move, blinking back tears, my chest heaving. The tears came, coursing gently down my cheeks. Slowly, I sank to the floor. Even though I became depressed at not hearing from him, never before had I realized that possibly, he might not come back to me. Suddenly, life had no meaning. How could I possibly go on without him? My mind shut down. There was nothing and more nothing. Nothing to do, nothing to look forward to, nothing to live for.

I had no notion of how long I stayed on the floor. When my legs began to hurt, I got up.

Realizing that I hadn't taken my coat off yet, I went out, and aimlessly walked the streets in my neighborhood until the traffic disappeared, the streets emptied out. I became chilled. Still, I walked, watching the sidewalk, my mind numb. Occasionally, I agonized over Hank and the emptiness that loomed ahead. Finally, reaching my apartment building, I went in. Four hours more and I would normally get up, being an early riser. I lay down, but didn't sleep.

As I ambled slowly down the corridor of the office building the next morning, I saw Frank start to enter the room where I worked. He saw me, shook his head, pressed his lips together, turned, and reentered his office. I had reached my desk and was standing there indecisively when he came in.

"Arabella, I don't think you're particularly backed up, will you take a daily House Food and Drug meeting this morning? It will be held in room two hundred three of the House and probably go from ten until noon. If they decide to go longer, let me know. I'll free up Irene to help you, otherwise do it yourself."

"Okay," I said flatly.

He watched me for a minute then left the room.

I stored the transcript I had been working on in the desk drawer, laid the notes on top of the transcript, and shut the drawer.

Tom walked in as I was putting a fresh pad of stenotype paper into my machine.

"Where are you off to?" he burbled.

"A House Food and Drug hearing," I said in a flat tone.

He looked me over and noted, I felt sure, my ashen, tired face and sat down at his own desk.

The hearing ended at 12:30. I returned to the office and immediately started to type, forgetting lunch. Ned and Tom, working away at their desks, said nothing. In silence, we typed. At three o'clock, Tom left the room and came back with a cup of coffee and a chocolate bar. He set both of them on my desk and returned to his own work.

I turned to him. "Thank you, Tom."

I thought I was going to cry.

At four o'clock, Frank entered and gave each of us an assignment for the next day. After that, he stopped by me. "How much did you get?"

"About eighty pages. I'll finish a bit after five."

"Good girl." He left us.

Tom left at 5. I finished at quarter of six. When I left, Ned was still typing like the wind.

The minute I walked into Winthrop House, the switchboard operator hailed me. "You have a package." The woman handed me a small, two-by-two package.

Upstairs, sitting on the bed/sofa, I carefully ripped off the heavy brown wrapping paper. A ring box. My heavens. Slowly, I lifted the cover. Tears sprang to my eyes, and I smiled. There lay a beautiful large, oblong topaz set in gold, one small diamond on either side. I slipped it on my ring finger, spread my fingers and stood looking at it. I smiled. My hand really looked beautiful with that ring on it. The yellowish tones of my skin blended perfectly. Twisting my hand this way and that to see the yellow color change, I thought, though we act like man and wife every time we're together, now I have a ring to prove it.

Oh! I pulled the ring off. Then, holding it poised before my ring finger, I whispered, "With this ring, I thee wed," and gently replaced it on my finger, "to love and to honor as long as I shall live."

Twenty-Two

On top of everything else, Charlie Stevens, having made his peace with Mrs. Henderson, showed up the last day of September. The book was full to overflowing. In dire straits for reporters, Frank assigned him to an afternoon hearing and ordered one of the old green Colonial desks moved into our room for him. To the fellows pushing the desk through the door, Charlie said, "Put it against the wall in front of Tom and across the room from Arabella." Staff introductions, some kind of orientation on the dos and don'ts of the office, even where to find supplies, were pigeonholed in the swamp of work.

Caught in my own workload, I forgot about Charlie until the day Irene shoved the office door with such vigor that it crashed against the wall, causing me to jump two inches off the chair.

"Oh!" Irene shrank within herself. "I didn't mean to do that."

She retrieved the handle and with great care soundlessly shut the door.

"Arabella," she said, her eyes starry, her face sparkling with demur charm, "Is that new reporter your friend from California?"

"If you mean the one with the dark hair and the velvety blue eyes—"

"They really are velvety," Irene mused. "When did he come?"

"Last week."

"He came to my desk, introduced himself, and gave me some work. He's so handsome. I've never seen another man like him."

I laughed. "Irene, you're radiant. You should always blush like that. The pink tones make you glow. Love at first sight," I teased.

"Is that the way it hits—one minute nothing, and the next minute you're all shivery?" The radiance faded. "He would never look at me that way. What am I going to do, Arabella?" Irene clamped both elbows hard against her abdomen and seemed to fall apart.

Instantly, I sprang up and threw an arm around her waist. "Give him a chance. Let him discover what a good transcriber you are, get him coming to you. We'll plan a strategy. But let's talk later." I returned to the typewriter. "I have to do this."

When Irene left, instead of typing, I went to the window and looked out. Leaves blew along the street ahead of a gusty wind. People pitched into the blow, coat collars pulled tight against the chill. I thought about Charlie. Could he take an interest in Irene? He wanted to get married. He needed a wife—one who would hover over him and meet his every wish. Could Irene be that girl?

The door opened and Charlie Steven's voice made me turn around.

"Frank let me dictate some of my daily and give it to a girl named Irene. I hope her work is better than her looks."

"That's unfair. She can't help her looks." Immediately defensive, I slapped my black leather-covered foot on the floor.

"All I said was she's ugly, which is the truth. Why are you so riled up? What's she to you?" he asked, nonplussed.

"I asked Frank to hire her. I feel kind of responsible."

"So I'll say good morning." He acted indifferent to the whole subject.

By mid-October, I had mostly recovered my natural happy disposition. The 18th was my birthday. At noon, I walked into the kitchen with Tom and found both reporters and typists ranged around the table drinking coffee and talking shop. Isobel turned from the large metal coffee pot, cautiously balancing her brimming cup of hot coffee, and set it on the table in disgust. The tight bleached ringlets over her ears bobbed, and the long earrings danced as she wagged her head.

"I finished checking the transcript from the meeting I took yesterday. The big technical word in the whole transcript was 'urine analysis.' And what do you think those typists did with it?" She looked furious and yelled, "You're in analysis."

All the others in the room screamed with laughter.

Trying to pour coffee, Tom had to temper his laughter. "Did it make sense?" he asked when he was able to just snicker.

"Of course not," she sneered. "Which typist except Irene transcribes for sense?"

Huffily, Marie suggested that some tried, to which Isobel replied that present company wasn't included or she wouldn't have said what she did.

"You should have seen the performance this morning," said Tom. He placed his coffee cup between Marie and Linda and sat down. "I was at Senate Commerce. Some mush-mouthed guy was reading a statement when our fat redhead walks in and slips me a note to go over to the Dirksen Building and take Ken out. I was supposed to tell him to come and take her out. A bloody ring-around-the-rosy. I didn't get the point and still don't. Frank was uncommunicative."

"Probably because he was aggravated." Irene had walked in during Tom's comments. "I was in his office when Ken called, panic stricken. They were threatening to go technical with engineering. Tina was the only reporter around, and she was dictating a daily."

"How stupid," Tom said scornfully. "Their technical session consisted of two words which were repeated over and over. Ken may not be a real heavyweight, but he's a better reporter than that."

"He was partying most of the night," said Isobel.

"I wish he'd party with me," said Marie.

"Don't make it so obvious, dear," advised Isobel.

"I had a short deposition this morning at the NOW offices," I said. "Some of what they do is kind of nutty."

"Don't you agree with their aims?" Isobel asked, ready for an argument.

"Equal pay for equal work, naturally. But that wasn't my point," I said, evading any altercation with her. "This morning, they had the opposing attorney so mixed up, he wrinkled his brow, scowled, hemmed and hawed until he didn't know what to do next. He kept asking one woman if she were Chairman of the Membership Committee. Those babes, six or seven of them, sat in a row with poker faces while the witness said 'No.' The attorney said, 'You weren't?' Then he fussed through his papers. He looked at her perplexed and said, 'Are you sure you weren't chairman?' 'No.' When he finally asked the judge for a recess, the attorney for the women took him out in the hall and told him to say, 'chairperson,' not 'chairman.' It was killing, all those beady eyes glued on that poor baffled attorney."

"How dumb," said Marie.

"Why?" asked Tom. "Wouldn't you like to be called a chairperson?"

"Those are generic terms having nothing to do with sex," said Marie.

"Don't you think we should have equal opportunity?" asked Irene.

"Natch. Women are every bit as bright as men—maybe more so," said Marie.

Tom whistled. We women whirled on him. He tilted his chair back on its hind legs and scoffed at us.

"One good thing about this business," I said, "is that race, color, creed, and sex have nothing to do with it."

"It's all that other junk they're trying to push that I find objectionable," said Marie.

When the conversation became heated, Tom stood up, you-don't-know-what-you're-talking-about written across his malleable face, and shouted, "Vive la difference."

Before he had to defend himself, Charlie walked in,

spotted Irene, and did a U-turn. Irene reddened and looked at her lap.

Livid, I knocked over my chair in my haste to follow Charlie. I found him at his desk. "How can you be so crude? That wasn't even common courtesy."

"What wasn't? I don't know what you're talking about." Non-comprehension, open ignorance, as to the meaning of my attack chased themselves over his thinning, pleasantly aging features.

"You know perfectly well. You looked at Irene, turned on your heel, and walked out."

"Because I was reminded that I had work to give her," he said with gravity. "I meant no offense."

"She took it that way."

"Christ, she's too sensitive. Walking on eggs with her gets tiresome. On the other hand, she's the best typist in the pool." He rolled some pencils around on his desk. "Actually, she's a pretty nice girl."

I almost huzzahed my approval. Instead, I became very genteel and solicitous. "I see you had a deposition today. Did you get much?"

"No. The witness was too drunk to testify."

"You're kidding."

Charlie 's laugh was brief and pejorative. "In a switch, his attorney offered to pay my fee."

"Wait until Frank hears that."

"I just told him. He seemed rankled. I think he was planning on my getting some pages."

"Unexpectedly, next week is slow. He can't figure out why. But that's always the way. When we don't have any backlog, every hearing fizzles. If you were loaded, when you went over there this morning, you'd get two hundred pages. Some of the typists are already grumbling about no work."

"They've been complaining about page rates. They say they can't make any money."

"Two of them got reprimanded last week for leaving at five-thirty when the dailies weren't finished. They don't do the work when work's there. They don't belong in this business if they expect to keep regular-hours. Even some of the new reporters around don't have any concept of what reporting is like. They come in with dollar signs for eyeballs. When they find out that reporting is hard work, they want the page rates raised."

"You 're talking to a convert, Arabella; remember? So get off the soapbox."

"Okay," I laughed. "But I do wish the schools would stop using making a lot of money as a selling point."

"They probably never will, so—" he dismissed the subject. "This is the extent of my backlog." He waved the notes in his hand. "And it's what I came to get for Irene. So I better go track her down."

"I should replenish my supplies."

Complaints about no work and nothing on the book changed overnight. Frank met me in the corridor at 8:30 the next morning.

"Oh, Arabella, the nursing group out at the National Institutes of Health wants you to come out there and do an all-day meeting. They forgot to call it in. Get there as soon as you can. They'll wait for you."

"Okay." I looked at my watch. "It's 8:40 now. With luck, I should be able to make it by 9:15."

"Be careful. The work isn't worth an accident."

The day turned out to be full, long and tiring. I called Frank from the conference room.

"I can leave you off tomorrow morning," he said, "but the book is jammed."

From famine to feast. By the end of the week, every reporter had more than could be handled easily and a solid week ahead. By November, everybody was complaining about no rest. I felt almost too tired to open the letter I received on November 4th. Again, it was addressed to 1220 Mass Ave N.E., though this time in Hank's handwriting, rather than print. Did that mean a little improvement? Obviously, not a lot. From the end of September to November 1, and he still didn't remember the address. Oh, my dearest. I slowly shook my head back and forth and sagged at my shoulders. I could do nothing.

I wondered what made him keep writing 1220 Mass Ave, N.E. We had never gone over to the northeast. By any chance was that his office? I'd drive by one day and see if that address was a government building.

Whycocomagh, Nova Scotia, Nov 1, 1960.

Dear Arabella, Looks like they're trying to hide us forever. Certainly this is the place to do it. There's just nothing and more nothing.

I wondered where this nothing and more nothing was in Nova Scotia. Was he still there or had he been moved again during the time it took for his letter to be delivered to me? Was he maybe in the southwest in the desert? Or north in bitter cold? He didn't say anything about a cold climate as he usually did when he was staying in a cold place. Did he actually know where he was? And what was this temperature change supposed to do for him?

For the first time, I thought about the other men who were with him in the accident. Were they suffering in the same way? Were any of them with him in New York City? Did they progress at the same rate? Were some of them better than he was; some worse? I knew that some recovered, that some went to a place in the western part of the country and never returned.

For a long time, I just sat there holding the letter and thinking about the cold, then turned back to the letter.

I seem to be improving. As ever, Hank.

"As ever, Hank" sounded better than "As it goes." But was he improving? I wondered if I would ever see him again. His infrequent letters came across to me so poignantly. I bled for him. I shed no tears. Sadness continually surrounded me. Only during the night when I wakened did I cry.

Twenty-Three

December came and went. I spent the week between Christmas and New Year's with my family. Not one word did I hear from Hank, not even a Christmas card. In January, the book picked up again. I worked, worked, worked, dropped into bed too exhausted to think. That kept my worry about Hank at bay as much as possible.

In early February, my favorite Air Force Association took me to Orlando, Florida, for their winter board meeting. Working their meetings became one of the plums of court reporting for me. I knew all the famous World War II pilots, now generals, who flew in Europe, Asia, and the hump into Burma. I found it exciting and the meetings interesting, particularly when they fought. I would sit alert and grin broadly. I loved it. And the staff always included me in their evening hangouts.

Of course, I came back to Washington loaded with transcription after three days. But I didn't care. Regular delivery meant I didn't have to work late nights.

Finally on April 13th, I received a letter, correctly

addressed, in Hank's handwriting. I read it over and over. Even after laying it down on the little delicate looking desk I had bought for my apartment, I kept returning to the desk to read the letter again. He had written a sad letter. Reading it hurt. Again, I read through it:

April 10th, 1961

Dear Arabella: I have written to you on a few occasions. However, I doubt you ever received the mail, because if I remember correctly the address was never right.

The hand holding the letter drifted onto my lap as I stared into space. I had received two letters. Had there been more? A totally unknown quantity? I shrugged and with a sigh glanced back at the letter.

Anyway, I hope you remember a human being named Hank. If you do you are the only one.

Oh, my darling. How awful. Internally, I collapsed. And there's nothing I can do for him, I thought, steadying my trembling hand.

I'll be in Washington pretty soon now. I'll call you. Hope you can find a minute to see me. Sure would be good to see you.

My God, I'd turn myself inside out to see him, hug him, kiss him.

Hope you and yours are well and happy. As ever, Hank.

PS: This time, I'm sure of the address.

Dear Hank, if only I could comfort you in your depression. I closed my eyes tightly and studied his face. Never have I forgotten you. If only you could know how much time I spend thinking about you every day and every night. Will I see you this time or won't I? So many times, I have been disappointed. Do you know the time lapses? In a way, I hope you don't because then you wouldn't suffer the disappointment I suffer.

I sighed and laid down the letter.

The rest of April passed. By the end of May, I found myself in tears many evenings as I prepared for bed. I ached for him. As a result, I threw myself deeper into work.

Hoping to cheer me up, Frank sent me to Atlanta to report a day-long scientific session. The following morning, I appeared before him, eyes down, mouth down, shoulders down, hangdog gait.

"What the hell's wrong with you?" he demanded.

"I blew it," I said.

"I can't believe that." He motioned me to the only available chair.

"Pride goeth before a fall," I said plaintively.

Frank leaned back in his chair and folded his hands over his stomach. "Okay."

"At lunch, I sat next to some guy who was charming until he discovered that I was the court reporter. Then he made some pretty nasty remarks about reporters and their incompetence. I told him that not every reporter could operate with medical vocabulary, confident that I could." I stopped and looked at Frank.

"Okay, that's the pride."

"He turned out to be the first speaker after lunch. He commented on the meeting and how pleased he was to be there. You know, the usual stuff. I had the best notes of the day and was ready to sail through the afternoon without a flaw when he put his head down and started to read, or mumble, I should say, as fast as he could. I couldn't understand three words out of five; I couldn't get any thread of meaning. I faked it, intending to ask our contact person at the break to get me the manuscript."

"And did you?"

"I almost tripped over the stenotype in my haste to reach her. Fortunately for me, she couldn't understand him either. But the upshot was, he refused to give her the manuscript and made some more nasty comments."

"Well," said Frank, "in that case, I would simply write a parenthetical statement that he read a prepared paper. He himself is the problem with reporters. Your contact person knows it. I wouldn't fool with him."

After a fierce battle fought and won to shed no tears, I said, "I feel like quitting reporting."

"Listen, these things happen to everybody. I'll stand behind you if anything's said. Which I doubt." He selected a piece of paper from the stack on his desk. "Here's a new page-rate sheet that came out yesterday and is effective the fifteenth of this month. Go look at it and don't scourge yourself over that doctor."

I did as he told me to do with the rate sheet, but the doctor haunted me for the rest of the week.

On Friday, I ran into Irene in the corridor.

She said, "Can I interest you in the movies tonight, Arabella?"

"Sure can. Any ideas?"

"No. We'll look at the paper in my place after work."

Directly from work, we drove to Irene's apartment. I plopped on the sofa to peruse the entertainment section while she looked at the international news. For some reason unbeknownst to me, I started to tell her the difficulty I'd had in Atlanta. It began to seep out, slowly at first like ointment from a split tube then a geyser that wouldn't stop. I began to feel embarrassed. I hadn't intended to burden Irene with the affront to my ability. She laid the newspaper in her lap and listened, her face sympathetic. The doctor, the pressures, and the overwork gushed forth. When I reached Hank in the litany, Irene broke down.

She started to talk. At first, my head pulled back in amazement, my eyelids fluttering. I listened. Desire for Charlie, the stress of hiding her love, anger at her distorted features, rolled in gigantic, measured waves from the depths of Irene's winsome, unpresuming soul.

Astonished at the unrepresentational display of emotion, the searing misery of her physical disfigurement, I cast aside my own unhappiness and tried to comfort Irene.

"I didn't mean to carry on like this," sobbed Irene.

"What are friends for?" I said. "Get it off your chest." After obtaining a cold, wet facecloth from the bathroom, I passed it over Irene's hot forehead.

"Men! The oceans of tears we shed over them, and they're not worth it."

"But Hank loves you." Irene appropriated the washcloth.

"But I don't know how he is or what's happening." When self-pity again threatened to overwhelm me, I shook myself. "Anyway, we're talking about Charlie Stevens."

"I love him so much." Irene cursorily wiped her right eye.

"There's no reason why he shouldn't love you." I jumped to my feet, maneuvering through the small room. "I know. I'll have a dinner party and invite you both."

"No. I couldn't face it." The already saturated cloth began to leak water, which dribbled along her uplifted wrists and arms in a wavering, slow-moving pattern. Irene brushed one wrist dry with an annoyed flick of her arm. She lowered the facecloth to test its usability then dropped it into an empty candy dish, swept the damp hair from her forehead, and forced back the remaining tears.

"Now," I said, "next week might be a good time. The three of us can have an elegant, candle-lit dinner party—I know, to celebrate Hank's birthday in absentia."

"Is it his birthday?"

"Of course not. But Charlie wouldn't know that."

"Arabella, you're too much." With an effort, Irene stood up. " I need a drink—a strong drink," she emphasized.

"Good idea. What should we drink? Martinis or Manhattans?"

"Gin," said Irene with punch.

"Okay, Martinis."

"I know how to make good ones."

The two of us proceeded to the kitchen where we mixed double-strength Martinis.

"Um-m-m, terrific," I observed after a tentative taste.

"Luckily tomorrow is Saturday."

"Why? Do you think we'll have a hangover?"

"Probably."

"Tonight, somehow I don't care. Let's have another drink."

"Let's whoop it up," cried Irene.

Sometime later, the doorbell rang. I staggered to the door and managed to open it. "Charlie Stevens! What're you doing here?" I said thickly, toppling by infinitesimal degrees in his direction.

"You called and asked me to come. You said you needed help with Irene." I saw his eyes shift over my head, as he spotted Irene on the floor. "Christ, what've the two of you been doing?"

"She passed out."

"It's a wonder you didn't, too. This place reeks of gin," he said, looking around the homey room with its good reproductions of master painters on the walls and color repeats from them in the upholstery and carpet. He steered me to the easy chair and pushed me into it.

"For the love of Mike, keep your hands off the table," he commanded, gathering up the larger pieces of broken cocktail glass with cautious thumb and forefinger. "I'll get you home, but first let's take care of Irene. Is there a bedroom?" His glance rested on the bathroom door.

"The sofa opens into a bed." I hunched up my shoulders to push myself from the chair.

"No you don't." He placed a restraining hand on my arm. "You stay right where you are while I get Irene to bed."

He piled the sofa pillows on the floor and pulled open the bed then dropped onto one knee beside Irene. "At least, she doesn't have to worry about anybody taking advantage of her."

"That wasn't necessary, Sir Galahad," I said, defensive even in my stupor.

"Touche. Uncalled for and actually surprising. I haven't given her looks a thought in months."

He bent over and, like a bulldozer, scooped up Irene.

Her eyelids flickered open and gently closed. "Oh, Charlie," she breathed, slipped an arm around his neck, and nestled close.

Watching him through half-closed lids, I noticed a very peculiar expression cross his face and the gentleness with which he braced her on a chair while he threw the bedcovers back. He may not know it yet, I thought, but he likes her. Cold-blooded, fiendish glee invaded me moments before I felt my head fall forward.

By the time Charlie returned to me, I had almost gone to sleep. My head rested where the bits of broken glass lay. Using both hands, he picked up my head, turning it from side to side, obviously looking for cuts. With a grunt, he laid my head back down. I guess I had no cuts.

"Well," he said—he must have been talking to himself; I didn't think he was addressing me—"Irene is asleep in the bed, you're half out of it with drink, I feel totally helpless." I heard him slap his hands against his thighs.

After some silence, he said, "It's going to be two girls in the bed and a man stretched out on the floor."

He jostled me to make sure I was sufficiently awake so as not to be deadweight then pulled me to my feet. "Come on," he said, shifting his arm to my waist, "walk over to the bed."

We walked slowly. He had to keep tightening his hold on me or I would have collapsed. "Get in beside Irene, Arabella." He pushed me onto the bed, swung my feet up, took off my shoes, and drew the blanket over me. Before I passed out, I heard him say, "It wouldn't surprise me if both of you were sick before morning."

When dawn climbed over the horizon, black, leafy tree limbs crisscrossing against the fire-red streak in the sky, we three occupants of Irene's apartment were up. Two of us were spending an inordinate amount of time in the bathroom.

Alone with Charlie, looking at the sofa cushions in a row on the floor where he had slept, the chair cushion and Irene's shawl tumbled over the sofa cushions, I wheedled,

"Please don't tell the office that we got drunk, Charlie. George doesn't like people to get drunk."

"So what? He isn't going to throw you over for that."

"Sometimes, I wonder."

"That's the morning after talking. Anyway, I won't tell." He looked at the bathroom door. "What's Irene doing in there so long? Go see if she's all right."

"That's a new tack from you."

"Never mind the cracks; go see."

Slowly, I unwound from my curled position, seized my head, and moved in crablike fashion towards the bathroom.

"Are you all right, Irene?" I asked into the vertical thread of light.

"I don't know," came the weak response.

I disappeared inside, leaving the worried man crossing and uncrossing his legs.

Twenty-Four

Late Monday afternoon, the last week of November, Frank handed me the assignment slip for the next day. I studied it. An all-day hearing on business economics. I scowled and looked up at Frank.

He shrugged. "It's government and business, a rules session."

"Oh, lovely." I bristled with sarcasm. "Probably all uncontrollable attorneys."

"I'm told some well-known CEOs will be there."

"A bunch of prima donnas. Thanks."

"Enjoy." He grinned at me.

By eight-fifteen the following morning, I hustled into the hearing room, chose a seat at the head of the elliptical table, and set up my equipment.

Promptly at eight-thirty, the chairman banged the gavel. "As you know, this is a working session. We need your thoughts and ideas before new legislation is drafted."

Half a dozen people immediately tried to talk. The

chairman looked at me. My eyebrows went up, and I shook my head at him.

"Gentlemen," he said, "you have to observe the rule of one speaker at a time if you want a decent transcript. I will stop you if you do otherwise."

The meeting proceeded. They held to the "one at a time" rule, but there was no breath between speakers. I had to stop them once to change my tape, but they started right in again without letup. Lunch was brought in. They tried to continue the discussion while they ate their sandwiches, but the chairman nixed that. All in all, I had fifteen minutes to eat and pull myself together for the afternoon onslaught.

By four o'clock, I was working almost unconsciously. Why, I thought, don't these attorneys ever shut up? They just want to hear themselves talk. My mind emphasized, I hate attorneys. Finally, the chairman said, "Okay. I guess we have enough information to start drafting a report. I'll send each of you a copy of the transcript for you to correct and add any other thoughts."

I looked at the wall clock. Five-thirty.

For a few minutes, I just sat and watched the men gather up their papers, talk to each other, and edge toward the door. A man named John Parkinson started around the table towards me. "Oh, no," I groaned. "If he wants any of this stuff delivered by tomorrow morning, I'll die."

He came to my side. "You've had a grueling day. Come along and we'll get a cup of coffee in the corner take-out shop."

Surprised, I glanced up at him. Slightly wavey, dirty blond hair and smiling blue eyes. I hadn't really looked at him before, only at his mouth when he talked.

"Thanks," I said. "I could use some coffee."

Once seated in the café, he ordered two coffees, hesitated, looked at me and back at the waitress. "Two of those Danish pastries."

I flashed smiling eyes at him and ducked my head. Along with the coffee and pastries, we discussed the current National Theater production, the local symphony's less than adequate conductor, and the movies. For a change, work wasn't mentioned.

Finally, I said, "I better go home. It's been fun talking to you."

"May I call you, Arabella? I'd really like to do that, but I must tell you that I'm in the midst of a rather nasty divorce."

Looking down at the table, I said, "That's all right, John. I'm engaged to a man I may never see again."

He gave me a startled look.

I picked up my purse and stenotype without further comment. As we parted, he said, "You're with Colonial Reporters, right?"

"Yes, I am."

"I'll call you." He turned and walked down the street, a medium height, broad shouldered man, soon lost in the evening work crowd.

I returned to the office to leave my notes and pick up my car. Driving home, I thought, what a pleasant interlude. God, I missed dates and male company.

A week later, towards the end of the day, he called. "How about dinner tomorrow night? I know enough about reporting to know that you can't make dates way ahead."

I laughed. "A great idea."

"Seven o'clock. Where do I pick you up?"

I gave him my apartment house address.

The dinner date was sheer joy, even though at least a quarter of the time we were together, we spent discussing our personal problems. I told him about Hank, what I knew of his problems, my love for him and my agony, the highs and lows. He told me about his divorce, and that he refused to give up his children, that he feared the unpleasantness might get worse, and that that would involve the children. Of his two boys, the younger one was the still unmentioned problem. "I love him, naturally, having cuddled him since the day he was born. But I don't think he's mine."

I gasped. "How awful."

"More and more, he's starting to resemble one of my closest friends." He examined his fingernails. "That isn't what brought on the divorce. I think she plays fast and lose with a lot of men. But actually, she's the one who started the proceedings when I accused her of bring men to the house when I wasn't there. As you can imagine, if some of that gets opened up in court, the newspapers will have a ball. So I wait. The lawyers are still circulating." He shrugged and changed the subject.

Home in bed alone that night, I thought about his children and the effect on them, particularly the younger one, to find out that his father, the man he loved and looked up to, wasn't his father. My thoughts then passed to our possible relationship. Actually, I was pleased. My sadness had lifted somewhat. John had suggested another date. If they continued, I could look forward to some happy times with him. I figured that his knowledge of my love for Hank and his divorce proceedings would keep him from becoming too involved with me. Nothing suited me better. I snuggled down and went to sleep.

Twenty-Five

Work went on as usual. John and I began to see more and more of each other. He would pick me up at the office, and we cooked dinner, either at his two bedroom, very male apartment or in my efficiency. One week, John invited me to attend a Saturday ice hockey game along with his two children. Even though I accepted his invitation, I thought that over. As far as I knew, there was nothing new on the subject of his divorce. That hadn't come up in our conversations recently. Introducing me to his children had a personal undercurrent I didn't like.

The children were darling. In the seating arrangement at the game nine-year old, Jaime, sat next to John and Timmy, aged seven, next to me. Light brown eyes sparkled up at me out of an impish face, light brown hair falling over his forehead. He hopped up and down constantly and yelled each time a player made a score. At intermission, while Jaime and John went for sodas and potato chips, Timmy nestled against me. I put my arm around him and held him close. He said, "I like you."

Naturally, I said, "I like you too," but thought I was having bad vibes. I could easily love this little boy, and he wasn't even John's child.

After the game, we ate dinner in a little family restaurant John knew about before he dropped me at my apartment house. Timmy flung himself on me to say goodbye. Jaime was a little more reserved, but friendly.

John called later that night to tell me how much his children had liked me. "Timmy announced that he wished you could live with him," John said, laughing. I laughed, too, but hoped he wasn't getting ideas about my being their mother. He had no right to do that. He was still a married man, and I was engaged to a man I loved dearly. I didn't like it. Unhappily facing a problem I might have, I realized that I should probably stop seeing him so constantly, but didn't know how to do that without hurting him and maybe putting a stop to our relationship. I pondered that. I couldn't do it.

Then a letter finally arrived from Hank, dated February 20, 1962, from Stuart, Florida. I looked at the neatly written address and wondered if good or bad news awaited me. Sitting on the sofa/bed closest to the door in my apartment, my heavy coat still on, I studied the envelope, almost afraid to open it. When I finally did open and read it, I yipped for joy.

Hello Arabella. I'll be in Washington, D.C. in March. And will be in touch with you at that time. Fact is, expect to see you. As ever, Hank.

The next evening, I waited until we had reached his

apartment after work to tell him about the letter and that I would see Hank in March. I knew I glowed.

"And all is well?" he said, not looking at me, but continuing to mix us Manhattans, which he was doing in the kitchen with me standing beside him.

"He didn't say anything about that. His letters aren't usually much more than notes. All he said was that he would be here in March and expected to see me."

John didn't say anything more, but I instinctively knew that he was upset. I had difficulty trying to act naturally, as if there had been no letter, though I knew my joy showed all over me.

John went to California on a case and then to visit his sister, so I didn't see him for the next three weeks. I worked. At first it seemed strange to again devote myself entirely to the office and my assignments.

With the arrival of March, I greeted each day joyously. Would this be the day that Hank comes back into my life? Even when John returned and we picked up our usual thing of dinner at his or my place, a night out, the movies or a concert, Hank was always in the back of my mind. And I knew John guessed that. I just wasn't totally with him.

March slid by. The evening of the first of April, we were in my apartment. John was mixing the Manhattans. Finished, he carried them to the living room coffee table. I sat on the sofa watching him. Suddenly, I crumpled. "He didn't come," I said through the spread fingers of my hands and started to cry.

Instantly, he was beside me, gathering me into his arms. "Darling, darling," he whispered, his lips against my forehead.

"It's another bad time. He does well, and then these

times happen. Actually, I'm not sure what happens. But from a few of his comments about time passing, I think he is unconscious of time flitting by."

I fished around in my jacket pocket for a handkerchief. John shook out his and handed it to me. I mopped my face, sniffled, and sipped my drink.

"If I get drunk, will you take advantage of me?" I quipped.

He noisily sniffed, closed his eyes, and shook his head.

"I won't get drunk, John," I said gently, "but I think I'd like another Manhattan, if my master mixer would be so kind."

He rose and pulled me along with him into the kitchen. While he mixed, I drew some little crab cakes and small Greek spinach pastries that I had made from the freezer. "We need something a little more substantial with the extra drinks," I said, shoving them into my toaster oven and turning it to high. Then, I pricked two baking potatoes before placing them in the oven.

"I'll do the salad while you tend the lamb chops," John said, trying to act like nothing different had happened while we carried our drinks and food back to the living room.

Twenty-Six

By May, after a glorious cherry blossom season, tulips bloomed all over the city in massive bunches, the dogwood still lifted pinkish flowers above the sidewalks, making an archway of small petals. Rhododendrons and azaleas competed in vibrant color. The air caressed my skin. I reveled in the beauty of Washington's spring. The whole city seemed to be wallowing in glorious color with the pale green of buds and new leaves.

Charlie walked into the workroom where I was typing. "It's beautiful out," he said. "I just came from the Hill. It's so lovely. Spring makes the whole city one big fragrant blossom. The day is absolutely perfect, the sky a gorgeous blue, the beds of tulips about. There's still a lot of color. This evening's going to have that balmy feeling when you want to be outside, sauntering around.

"Yes, this year is one of the better ones; no heavy late storms to shed all the blossoms." I smiled at him and returned to typing.

After fifteen minutes at his desk, he said, "Maybe

I'll ask Irene to have dinner with me tomorrow night. Afterwards, if the weather remains like this, we could walk around the flood-lit Tidal Basin."

I blinked. That comment put a new twist on things. That drunken night in Irene's apartment did have an effect. He rose. I watched him stick his head through the door of the transcribers' room to see if Irene was there.

He turned back to me, irritation on his face. "Frank's there, too. Nuts. Having any personal conversation with Irene when others are sticking around is impossible." He scowled. "Particularly with Frank standing near her desk."

I kept on typing, but inwardly tingling, mentally pushing him into action.

Fifteen minutes later, he again poked his nose into the typing room. His head swiveled around, then he closed the door and walked back to his desk. Apparently having made up his mind to date Irene, he couldn't do anything constructive until the thing had been accomplished. Perfect. I continued to watch him.

Tom hustled in from the Hill and started to type. Noticing Charlie's actions, he walked passed my desk, poked me, and nodded towards Charlie.

I put my left index finger to my lips.

We both watched Charlie.

Again, he got up and opened the door to the typists' room. After a quick glance around, one eyebrow shot up and he nodded. I heard a door slam. Somebody must have left the room. Charlie again surveyed the situation. I could hear the typewriters clacking steadily. Sonia and Marie must be deep in work. Obviously, Charlie considered them safe because he flipped the notes he carried as an excuse and disappeared into the other room.

He didn't come right back. I checked the clock. Ten minutes since he went in there. They must be having quite a conversation. I hoped Irene was keeping her head and didn't blubber. Finally, Charlie came back looking kind of pink and with a silly grin on his face. He sat down at his desk and proceeded to do a lot of purposeful deep breathing. That surprised me. The guy must be in love to take her acceptance--I assumed she had accepted--this way. A sense of euphoria, unexpected anticipation enveloped him. He smiled as he unpacked his day's notes.

Tom's eye caught mine. He grinned and made a surreptitious mission-accomplished thumb gesture. Irene must be ecstatic. I was truly happy for her.

Later, I saw her in the kitchen looking vibrantly alive, but didn't say one word about Charlie, didn't mention anything about their conversation. I couldn't fathom that. Dying of curiosity, I had to bite my tongue to keep from asking her what he said and what she said. I thought she would instantly tell me everything that went on. Why was she being so mum about it? She couldn't possibly have refused him. I simply brushed that aside as unacceptable.

That was on Tuesday. On Thursday, she came to me and suggested we take sandwiches out to one of the little parks.

We sat down on a bench in a small park with a splashing fountain over towards the Capitol. Halfway through her sandwich, she told me what happened. Her face glowed and her eyes sparkled happiness.

Charlie had walked over to her desk slowly, constantly glancing at Sonia and Marie. That puzzled her. He extended the thin pack of notes he carried in one hand, the cassette in the other, and said, "I know you like to try to read the notes as you listen to dictation."

"I asked him the deadline," Irene said. "It was a whole week later."

She continued. "Without saying anything, he examined my desk. I think he was trying to see my stenoprompter and figure out whose work I was doing. Then, looking a bit awkward, he said, 'I just came back from the Hill. The blossoms make the sidewalk a romantic bower.'

"I said, 'I must go see the trees around the Tidal Basin.'

"To my utter amazement, he said, 'Good thought. Why don't we do it together tomorrow night?'

"I know I blushed, but told him I thought that would be nice. Then, I couldn't believe my ears." Irene stopped talking to shake her head in amazement.

"He said, 'We could stop in one of the restaurants around here first, if you like.' Imagine!" Irene laid the remainder of her sandwich in her lap then turned to me and said, "I didn't tell you right away because I wanted to see how things went first."

"And I gather all went well," I said when she hesitated.

She nodded happily. "We went to that nice French restaurant on the corner and had a lovely time. Walking around the Tidal Basin, he held my hand. And"—Irene dropped her eyes—"he even kissed me goodnight, a little peck on my cheek."

She smiled at me, absolutely glowing. "I'm going to see him this weekend."

I hugged her. I couldn't refrain. She was so happy. And I thought her the exact type of girl Charlie needed.

Twenty-Seven

Standing beside his desk, Ned was arranging pads of stenotype note paper when I arrived at the office on Monday morning.

"What are you doing here?" I blurted out. "I didn't know you were back from Florida."

"I came back last night." He turned towards me and leaned against his desk. "When I called, Frank said that he would be in early, and I want to talk to him about Tom."

"What's wrong with Tom?"

"We're supposed to go to Tokyo in August for the East-West Conference. Everybody in the office knows that. Here it is the end of June, and Tom is threatening not to go."

"Whatever for?" I asked, taken aback.

"Nobody has asked him. He's being sensitive as only Tom can be when he puts his mind to it. Discussion on the subject has been going on for two months; he has known he's going with me." Ned rapped the desk he was braced against with a felt pen. "When it comes right down to it, nobody has asked me either, but I intend to go."

He started for the door. "I thought I'd tell Frank to ask him casually someday. Frank does that kind of thing well."

"Good idea. While you were gone, he informed me he hadn't been asked. I didn't know what to say to him. He's very prickly."

"Jeez." Ned shook his head and opened the door. "I'll see you later."

During the first week of June, Frank sauntered casually into the room, George behind him. I was standing by the side of my desk hunting through the stacked papers when they opened the door. Immediately, I sat down. Tom and Ned, each at his own desk, stopped talking.

"Well, gang," said Frank, "we received the final word from the East-West crowd so I'll get your acceptance." He looked at Ned. "Ned, will you go to Tokyo?"

"Yes."

Frank turned his head to look at Tom. "Tom, will you go to Tokyo?"

"Yes."

"Good." Frank let out a long, relieved breath. "That's settled."

George sympathized with me. "They decided to take only two, Arabella. You don't get to go. Sorry."

"That's okay. I really didn't expect they would take three reporters."

Frank strolled out, head up, a smile on his lips, mission accomplished. In his unpretentious way, George smiled, waved goodbye, and followed Frank.

Nobody in our room moved initially. Then Tom swung his chair around to face Ned. "You told him to do that."

I clutched my stomach, swayed back then started to type. My fingers flew as if one hundred pages had to be delivered in ten minutes.

"Don't be an idiot. Why would I do a thing like that?" Ned's typewriter started at a fast speed.

Tom began to type, reluctantly at first, then increasing in speed. The usual camaraderie settled over the room.

Tom and Ned left for Tokyo the last week of July. I hated the emptiness their absence created because Charlie spent most of his time working out of town. Other than Frank and George, nobody dropped in. Frank started coming in late in the day to discuss his scheduling problems. With Tom and Ned away, he found it necessary, unusual for August, to bring in two reporters from Pennsylvania to cover the heavy book. But, as it turned out, he had to be careful where he sent them because they couldn't keep pace with Washington-type hearings--hearings with anywhere from three or four to one hundred people, all vying for a chance to talk.

"Reporters come to Washington from all over the country," he remarked one day, "thinking they're real hotshots. Like they're going to take over the city. They blow the first hearing I send them on."

When he rushed past my desk the next morning, pale and disheveled, I cringed, expecting to be asked to jump in and save some fiasco. In a tragic manner, Frank let all his weight sink into Tom's chair, his hands and face dropping onto the typewriter.

Rigid with sudden fear, I cried, "What is it, Frank?"

Through his fingers, the sound muffled, he said, "Tom called. Ned's in a Tokyo hospital with pneumonia. He didn't feel well yesterday, but was determined to finish the meeting."

I cascaded forward, caught myself before striking the typewriter and swiveled my chair around to face Frank.

He lifted his head. We sat numbly, looking at each other without speech, imagining the worst. The buzzer sounded summoning Frank.

"George went to tell his wife," said Frank. He rose with the same tragic motion. "She'll want to go right to Tokyo. I'll have one of the fellows in collating take her 'round for a visa."

"What are we going to do?"

"I don't know. He's the best reporter this city has ever had. It's not good; it's not good," he kept repeating.

The buzzer became insistent.

"I better get back. Tom'll keep us posted."

An aged, shriveled man left. Like an automaton, I packed my case to go to Senate Banking, an ache in my chest that was real. Frank was so tender-hearted, so caring, so involved with all the office personnel. While my spirit grieved for him, it was woebegone over Ned. All during the hearing, Ned's innate kindness, overpowering ability, his help to me as a beginner in Washington, inviting me to go to Africa with him on the Dag Hammarskjold trip, and other things, percolated through my mind, distracting me. Nothing flustered him. Every office, every organization, every attorney in town, knew Ned's name and applauded him.

Instinct forced my footsteps towards Frank's door when I returned. He sat scribbling on a pad, a hand over his eyes, blocking the light, unaware of me.

"Frank." The name was a whiffet, a soundless puff.

Frank looked up. "Jill is heading for Tokyo tonight. Tom will come back the minute she arrives. Apparently he's on life support. His emphysema doesn't take well to pneumonia."

Two days later, wakeful, thinking about my backlog, I got up early and went to the office. Nobody else had come in yet. The main office door remained locked. Looking worn out and jet lagged, Tom hauled himself in at 7:30. I let out a little scream. He greeted me perfunctorily and scribbled a note to Frank saying he was in his room.

"I'll Scotch-tape this to the office door," he said. "Have you made any coffee?"

"Yes." I jumped up. "Sit down. I'll get you some."

"Thanks." He slumped into his chair.

I rushed to the kitchen, poured the coffee, picked up a muffin left over from last night and returned to Tom.

He was unloading unused stenotype pads onto his desk when I got back.

"Boy, do I ever need this," he said, taking the coffee from me. "I'll even eat the stale muffin."

The door opened. With a nod to me, Frank headed straight for Charlie's chair. He turned the chair around so he could face Tom at his desk and planted himself in it. "Now, tell me what happened, how he is, and what you think about getting him back here."

Tom detailed how Ned had thought he had a fever. He felt weak, but kept pounding the typewriter until they finished. Then he stood up and collapsed. The staff who always hung around rushed him to the hospital where he was diagnosed with pneumonia. "That's when I called you," said Tom.

"You stayed with him?"

"As much as I could. Because of his emphysema, the doctors had him hitched up to an oxygen tank most of the time."

"And Jill? I told her to check into the hotel where you were staying. In fact, I made her a reservation."

"She did as you told her, though she can be pretty ditzy. The minute she got to Ned's room, she threw herself on him, crying. The nurses rushed in and made her sit in a chair. I left them. And, of course, I left Tokyo yesterday." Tom looked down at his hands, raised his eyes, and said, "If I read the doctors right, Frank, Ned'll never be able to report again."

The two men stared at each other in silence. I felt devastated. I couldn't work.

Then Frank said, "We'll manage, but I don't know how." He rose. "The office won't be the same without him." He turned and left us.

"Neither will those of us in this room be the same without him," said Tom.

There was nothing I could say. That's the way it was.

The two of us talked quietly until nine thirty when I said, "Well, I better go to the Hill. I'll report, but don't know how much typing I'll get done today."

"I guess I'll go home. I don't feel up to working yet." Tom rose slowly.

"Take care, Tom. I couldn't lose you, too." I hurried out of the room.

Two weeks later, an ambulance took Ned directly to

Sibley Hospital from Dulles Airport. As soon as he could have any visitors, Frank went to the hospital.

Tom, Charlie and I waited impatiently in our room for his return.

Serious faced, reflective, Frank entered. He sat down at Ned's desk. "He's weak, but smiling, gave me thumbs up." Frank grimaced sadly. "During our short conversation, he said he planned to retire and maybe go to Hawaii to live. He and Jill have a little place on the big island of Hawaii."

"Gee." My fist went to my mouth and I shook my head.

Elbows on his desk, Tom put his face in his hands.

Charlie sat eyes down, looking at nothing.

"That's it, folks." Frank hurried out of the room.

The three of us who remained in the room went silently and sadly back to work.

As the day's passed, Tom and I separately visited Ned as often as we could and as he felt like company. Those of us in the workroom returned to our normal chatter. The day the paper announced Dag Hammarshold's death in a plane crash over Africa, I announced, "If George hadn't pulled Ned and me off that earlier trip, we could have been on that plane with Dag Hammarshold."

Tom nodded. Charlie stared at me, not believing what he was realizing.

On a beautiful, bright morning at the very end of September, Irene wafted into the reporter's room looking for me, her feet barely touching the ground. Busily packing stenotype pads into a satchel, I stood alone in the room.

"Arabella," purred Irene, a happy sparkle in her eyes, "Last night, Charlie asked me to marry him. I wanted you to be the first to know."

"How wonderful." The words floated out on such a wispy stream of air that they were almost not there. Then, as realization sank in, I cried, "How marvelous," and flew towards Irene. We came together in rapture on the part of one, sincere delight on the part of the other, tinged with a fleeting painful wrench.

"I keep pinching myself. It's real; it's me. It's hard to believe," said Irene.

"Have you set a date?"

"Christmas time. I want you to be a bridesmaid."

"I'd love to, Irene."

Touching fingertips in joy, we parted.

Twenty-Eight

Life flowed on with John and his two darling children, but no word from Hank. I tried to keep my spirits up, particularly when I saw John. If he said anything about my feelings, I laid it on overwork.

A letter finally arrived, dated September 18, 1962. Standing in the hall, waiting for the elevator, I examined the writing. His usual neat, beautiful handwriting. In my apartment, I plumped onto the sofa/bed, put my thumb under the envelope flap and ripped it open.

Dear Arabella: I have no idea how long it's been. Time, time, time. I just don't know about time any more.

If massive radiation had struck him, was it burning his mind rather than his body? If it wasn't radiation, what was it? My mind drew a blank.

Beginning to feel human again.

Beginning to feel human! That upset me. Was he in pain? Did he know what was happening? I had had visions of him simply losing his memory, which wouldn't hurt. He would just be wandering around blankly. How terrible if he were in agony. I hunched over as the tears dribbled down, wetting the letter. With an annoyed motion, I brushed off the tears and finished reading Hank's letter.

If it keeps up, I'll be up Washington way in the near future, but don't plan in it. As ever, Hank.

Sure hope you're well and happy.

In slow motion, I folded the letter and laid it with the others. No, I wouldn't plan on it. I had planned too often and been disappointed. All I could do was bleed for him. True, he sounded better. The letter was up-beat. The address was correct. He almost sounded like his old self. But would it last? Would I see him? Unusual for me, I could put no faith in what he said. The ups and downs of his letters were starting to get to me emotionally. I just had to steel myself and not live towards any possibility he threw out. And luckily, John was the perfect man to spend time with.

I decided not to tell him about that letter. Actually, I hadn't seen as much of him lately. His divorce was coming to a head. He was tied up and not very happy. We talked on the phone every other day, and I tried to encourage him. He let off steam like a wild cougar and said he didn't dare come to see me in his current mood.

Also, his friend Jack had come to town, was staying with him, and had caught sight of Timmy. John said Jack drew back in shock and swiveled his eyes to his.

John said (so he told me), "Spitting image, isn't it?" and turned away.

Jack asked him what he was going to do about it.

John said, "I don't have to do anything. He's mine legally."

That was all John told me on the phone, but they must have had a lot more to say after the children went to bed.

Then on November 20, I had a heartrending shock: A note typed by the office secretary with a little inked date and time down in the right-hand corner. "11-20-62, 2:55 p.m." The note was simple, to the point. "Arabella Robbins message: Hank called. Will drop a note—I missed you."

The next day, a government postcard arrived in my mail slot. I read it on the way upstairs in the elevator.

Dear Arabella. Sorry I missed you, would have liked to hear your voice again. On the way back from Boston. I'll try to get hold of you again. As ever, Hank.

In the apartment, I sat down and cried. I cried a long time, letting off deep sorrow, frustration, tension, longing. Finally, I simply crumpled over and slept.

I plunged back into work, the usual daily on the Hill, an occasional deposition, a government conference, nothing exciting.

A Christmas card came, addressed to my Washington apartment, with a Baltimore postmark. When I opened it, a little note fell out.

Hi Girl: Merry Christmas to you and yours. Be talking with you right soon now. Remember Hank.

Dear Hank. I remember. I have never forgotten. But I just don't know any more. I've lived with sadness for so long. This insecurity must be awful for you, too. What do you do all day? Do those others with you have the same problems? Are they better or worse?

I pulled myself up short. I couldn't dwell on it this way. I had to continue getting out with John, occasionally with others, and doing the other things I enjoyed, like the theater and concerts.

He did sound as if he were improving. I hoped so. But would it last? I didn't feel comfortable depending on it. I ached to have him with me. I loved him to distraction. All this being better and not better was tearing me apart. But I couldn't let go. I belonged to him, and he belonged to me.

The three o'clock wedding of Irene and Charlie took place in a small, old stone church in Westbury, Long Island. The other bridesmaid and I wore a lovely shade of brownish green, lighter than the darker tones of the blending green worn by the maid-of-honor. I loved the dress, the style, the way it fit. All three of us carried mistletoe. Irene carried deep red roses with a touch of mistletoe green. Her white brocade down reached within two inches of the floor, long sleeved, and a fingertip veil. She looked radiant.

At the nearby clubhouse, we danced until eleven after the three-course dinner. I danced and laughed, talked to everybody, seemed to be lark happy. Inside, I ached. I went to parties and to an occasional dinner with some man other than John whom I met through work, but didn't encourage the relationship. Occasionally, after one of those dates, I mentioned it to John. He didn't say anything, but I knew he didn't like it. I was afraid he was getting ideas, and I was incapable of doing anything about it until matters were settled with Hank.

Three days after the New Year, Charlie and I sat at our desks laughing at Tom mimicking Senator Broadbench when Frank burst in.

"Don't anybody go through the main office until I let you know otherwise." He sounded edgy.

"Tom, you get on the intercom. That man who was in here two days ago, demanding a copy of his transcript, is back. He thinks you left some quotes out."

"I did not," said Tom.

"Don't tell me," Frank barked. "He never put them in. Everybody does that, but they don't rampage around. You get on the intercom and say whatever is sensible to get him out of here. He's in the main office walking around the desks with that spooky look on his face. Nobody can do any work; they're scared. They know the judge said he was dangerous. If he goes near my secretary, she'll let out a scream that could set him off."

All the time he was talking, Frank had been jouncing up and down on one jittery foot then the other. Now, he popped out of the room. Tom made a face and started towards the wall phone. Frank popped back in.

"Why leave me the dirty work?" Tom drawled.

"Just do as I say," snapped Frank.

"Arabella, this has me so upset, I forgot that I want you and Ken to split Senate Banking tomorrow morning. When that ends, the FBI will take you to a top-secret clearance hearing then bring you back here and sit with you while you type."

"Why do they have to sit with me?" I objected. "That'll make me nervous."

"They won't pay any attention to you. We'll move you into the windowless room next to my office."

"Why can't I type here?"

"Tom isn't cleared, plus no windows allowed on top secret." He hustled out, letting the door slam.

Tom lifted the phone. Charlie and I watched him alternately attempt to speak and back away from the receiver. When he spoke, he said, "Yes, I'll make all the changes... No, I can't do it today... Yes, the transcript will be available next week... All right, Monday."

He hung up. "I never heard such an erratic, unrelated conversation in my life."

We were all typing when Frank reappeared. "He's gone. The attorneys on both sides of the case have assured me that he won't be back."

Frank pointedly addressed Tom. "You won't change the transcript, naturally."

"Naturally."

On Thursday evening, the last week of January, 1963, I circulated among the many guests at one of the usual mixed office crowd cocktail parties when an attractive middle-aged woman dressed in fashionable black approached me.

"I'm Mary Jane Booth."

"Arabella Robbins."

"The court reporter?"

"Yes."

Mary Jane smiled an amazed little smile. "How nice to meet you. Your reputation goes before you like a flame."

I almost stepped backward in my surprise.

"Oh, my! Thank you." I blushed

Mary Jane laughed gently. "I didn't mean to bowl you over. It just came out in my surprise at meeting you. You're very well thought of, you know."

"How nice of you to tell me. I appreciate it," I said, giving an unbelieving laugh.

"Most of the time, we just get complaints."

"Isn't that the truth about all our work?"

A young couple rushed up to us. "Mary Jane," bubbled the girl. "I have something exciting to tell you."

I moved off. The party had taken on a glow. I had a wonderful time. As I crawled into bed much later, I smiled. What a neat thing to say. My spirits could use something like that. "Your reputation goes before you like a flame."

Twenty-Nine

Hank's next letter, dated February 14, 1963, staggered me.

Dear Arabella: Since I haven't been able to contact you after several tries, comes the strange feeling that you would rather not see me again—

"Contact me—rather not see you," I sputtered, continuing to read aloud. "—and I can hardly blame you."

I clutched my throat and gasped.

However, it would be nice to really know. If you so desire, I'll be in Hallendale, Florida, one day, Feb. 20th, 1963, then on to Joleta.

Write me at Hallendale, care of General Delivery.

As ever, Hank.

Once I recovered from the initial shock, I rushed to my desk to write to him. After grabbing a piece of stationery, the pen in my hand poised to write, I stopped. Today was the 16th. My letter might not get there in time. I better send a telegram immediately before writing the letter.

I reached for the desk phone and called Western Union. After a few alterations, satisfied with the telegram as the operator read it back to me, I returned to writing the letter.

That letter became a long epistle, saying how much I loved him, waited for him, wanted to be his wife, how I longed for him to come home to our little apartment, adding some newsy items, then posted it in the building's mail chute.

Hank's reply arrived eight days later, dated February 22, 1963. My arms being full of notes and read speeches, I tucked the letter into my coat pocket until I reached my apartment. Once inside, I walked quickly to my desk, laid down the work stacked on my arm and sat down. Only then did I rescue Hank's letter from my coat pocked and read it.

Dearest Arabella: My humble thanks for the telegram and letter. Bless you. Because you're you, I have someone in this world to come home to.

"Someone in this world to come home to." My God, how awful. He must be very depressed. Though I don't wonder. The way he has had to live would make anybody depressed. No family, no friends. I doubt he had contact with anybody beside me and his sister. Or maybe, just me.

You have my solemn promise that I'll see you real soon. Plan on it.

I shook my head. No, I wouldn't plan on it.

Take care of yourself, and I'm sure glad there is still someone like you left in this universe.

Sure will be good to see you and hold you again.

As ever Hank.

I shed tears of thankfulness. Somehow, that letter lifted

the sadness I had lived with for so long, at least until the postcard dated April 25, 1963, arrived. On the elevator, I read the postcard and ground my teeth.

Dear Arabella: Just missed you by minutes according to Colonial. Should have called you from Bethesda, wanted to surprise you.

I clapped a hand over my mouth, and rapidly finished reading the letter.

In the District just for the evening. I'll be gone for a short spell. Next time I'll see you get more notice.

As ever, Hank.

Upside down on the bottom right, he had written: "(Cannot wait to see you. Bless you.)"

Such frustration. I gave the desk leg a little kick, not enough to damage it, and shook my head in helplessness. I just couldn't spend my time sitting at home waiting for a phone call. And none would come. I'd go stark, raving mad.

Three days later, late in the afternoon, John called. "Arabella, by chance are you free tonight? I hope you are; it's important."

"Yes, I'm free." When am I not free, other than seeing you, I thought savagely.

"I'll be at your place at 6:30."

"Okay." I hung up nonplused. What on earth should be that important? I drew my eyebrows together and flutter my eyes, unable to make sense of this important meeting this late in the day. Well, I thought as I walked over to my desk, I'll do as much typing as I can of this meeting in my stenoprompter and leave at six. Thank goodness it wasn't daily copy.

I sat down and continued to work.

At 6:20 in my apartment, I combed my hair, hurriedly straightened the mess on the coffee table, put on some lipstick, and surveyed the room just as the bell rang. I opened the door to a grinning John, long-stemmed red roses in one hand and a bottle of champagne in the other.

Taken aback, I stepped aside. "What's with you?" I managed.

He walked to the coffee table, laid down the roses and placed the bottle beside them. Turning to me, he held out his left hand, pulled off the wedding ring and threw it on the floor.

"John," I squealed, throwing my arms around his neck.

He grabbed me around the waist, lifted me off the floor and twirled me around.

"The judge approved the divorce and awarded the children to me about 2:30 this afternoon. The commotion in the courthouse among my friends was tantamount to a party, and they dragged me out for a drink. I had to fake a need of the restroom to put in a phone call to you."

"I'm delighted, John." I picked up the bottle. "Is this cold enough or should we use one of those in my refrigerator?"

"It should be cold enough." He headed for the kitchen. I followed to hand down glasses.

Seated in the living room, he went through the day's proceedings. The near panic at one point when he thought the judge was about to award the younger boy to the so-called mother. But in the end, he awarded both boys to John.

He refilled our glasses. "Now," he said, looking me in the face, "we have to come to another important decision tonight, Arabella. And this is your decision. My mind was made up months ago and so were the minds of my two boys. I want a yes or no answer from you tonight."

I wiggled down in my corner of the sofa, knowing what was coming, and didn't answer. I had to think about how to answer him.

"I'm asking you to marry me, Arabella."

Silence stood stormily, threatening, electric, between us. I couldn't find my tongue and John looked at his hands. I could feel the tension. Finally, he said, "If your answer is no, I walk out of that door for the last time." He raised his head. Our eyes met. In his, I saw the longing and the worry.

I tore my eyes away and seemed to crumple in my corner of the sofa. "John, if I weren't committed to Hank, yes, I would marry you. But with his sickness, his feeling that he has nobody else in the world, and most importantly, my love for him, I can't send him a 'Dear John' letter, even if I knew where to send it."

John stood up. "Then, this is good-bye, Arabella. If the situation changes, you know where to find me. But don't expect me to wait forever." He pulled me up, gave me a passionate kiss and noiselessly closed the door behind him.

I sat down with a thump and stayed there a long time, sad, but relieved. What had to be done had been done.

The next morning, baggy-eyed, not having slept very well, I showed up in the office as usual. Frank announced a full staff meeting at five thirty that afternoon in the main office.

Along with Tom, Irene and Charlie, I sat down on a chair towards the back of the room. Frank stood in the front. George and Henry, the two owners, sat in chairs on either side of Frank.

The gist of the meeting was that the Texaco building we occupied was scheduled for demolition. George and Henry had rented the second and third floors of a house on the other side of Union Station. The two men considered it an ideal location for their work on the Hill and easy access to transportation for any other place in the city. The move would occur in June. It would be done conveniently over the weekend so all the work would go on normally.

That was all.

We three went back to our room along with Irene and sat down. Charlie and I made indifferent comments about the move.

"However, I suppose we'll be stuffed in with their note reading reporters," I said.

"I won't go," said Tom.

My head swirled around, and I stared at him. "What do you mean by that?" I demanded.

"I think this will give me the chance to retire."

"Oh, Tom. No."

"I've been thinking about it ever since Ned moved to Hawaii. And this is the perfect time to do it."

"Well, as I like the work, I'm going to stick around."

"You really have great contacts, Arabella," said Irene. "The Air Force Association takes you all over the country, as does the State Governors Association. The people at NIH always ask for you." She smiled at me.

I smiled back. "It is fun, in spite of the hard work. I guess it's true, no reporter would suggest to someone else that he or she become a reporter, but not one reporter would get out of the business."

Tom told Frank the next day that he intended to retire. Frank fussed and fussed at him, but couldn't change his mind. He put up a notice that there would be an office farewell party for Tom on the last Friday of May.

On the designated Friday, the men in the main office pushed two desks together for the table. The women decorated their table with fresh flowers, a carnation button holer for Tom, and fancy paper napkins. They set out the punch bowl and left space for the cake. Jim from collating picked up the enormous chocolate cake Frank had ordered, and Henry made punch.

After the party, Tom picked up his personal belongings, gave me a smacking kiss, and walked out the door.

Thirty

The end of May, just before the move to the new building, another letter dated May 21, 1963 came from Hank.

Dear Arabella. Sure looks like we are not destined to see one another.

Oh, Hank, Hank. Tears sprang up.

However, this will change.

Will it? I'm beginning to wonder.

I plan to let you know in advance the next time I'll be in or near the District.

Really won't know how to act if I ever get to hold you in my arms again. It's been so long.

Take care of yourself. As ever, Hank.

Sadly, almost shrugging off the letter, I stored it with the others. It had been too long. Also, I didn't put any faith in his comments about seeing me. Too many times, I had been disappointed. And time went on. In the beginning, he had said six months and he would be well. Four years had passed, and he only seemed to be getting worse. And I had to admit, I missed John, though

I did what had to be done. I was one being with Hank for all eternity.

By July, the new office was running smoothly. The boss's office had been placed in the front of the building, the secretary in an open area next to it. The remaining space consisted of a huge room with various small rooms horseshoed around it. The windows of the two medium sized rooms looked out onto the entrance to the parking garage in the rear of the building. Two small rooms faced the center room from the right as did the kitchen from the left. Charlie and I occupied one of the small rooms on the right.

I had just settled down to type one morning when the secretary buzzed the room. I got up and answered the wall phone. Hank's voice came over the wire. "Arabella, at last."

"Oh, Hank," I cried and almost dropped the phone.

"How about dinner tonight?"

"Heavenly. I can hardly wait."

"You and me both. I'll pick you up around 4:30. Is that okay?"

"I'll be home waiting."

He rang off.

I had trouble paying attention to my work. I skipped along, giving a little hop in between some of the skips, up to the Hill for a short top-secret meeting. I marveled at the beautiful trees along the walkway, the way the water splashed in a small fountain. What a glorious day. Going back to the office, an FBI man walked in front of me, another FBI man behind me. In the office, Charlie had been sent to a desk in the big room and thick black fabric covered the window in my little room. The FBI man ushered me into the room and closed the door behind me. He said he would sit down in front of the door and work on papers in the folder he carried.

Happily finished in two hours, I knocked on the door, handed the FBI man the notes and transcript, and bounced out of the room. Half dancing and hopping I proceeded down the hall to the front office and announced to Frank that I was going home.

He looked me up and down. "Good idea. See you tomorrow."

Meeting Hank turned traumatic for both of us. Standing in the middle of the efficiency apartment, we clung together.

When I came up for breath once, I said, "You look the same as you always have, the way I remember you."

"Yes, the body is doing well; it's the head that isn't."

Eventually, we taxied to the George Fifth bar on Wisconsin Avenue. There, sitting side-by-side on red velvet covered chairs behind a small table, we caught up on our lives. Hank couldn't say much about what was happening to him, but I chatted away almost without end. Among other things, I told him that I was leaving in two weeks, a Saturday, sailing on the Queen Elizabeth with a friend called Muriel, to spend a month in the British Isles. "I met Muriel at church," I said. "She sings in the choir."

He thought that fabulous. He wished he could travel with us to London rather than the kind of traveling he was doing.

Finally, Hank said, "How about O'Donnell's on Eleventh Street for dinner?"

"Great."

"We'll have the taxi drop us at the Manger-Annapolis so we can walk over to the restaurant. Okay? It's just nostalgia for me."

"Darling, walking with you would be perfect." I tucked my arm in his as we stood waiting for a taxi.

Walking along Eleventh Street, Hank said, "I constantly replay the times we've been together. Do you remember walking down the main street in Newark, New Jersey? You said, 'Kiss me.' And I did. Nobody seemed to pay any attention to us. Nobody cared."

"Yes, I remember. Shrubbery bordered the sidewalk and trees shaded it. I had looked around. Nobody walked behind us or in front of us, only the traffic kept rushing by. And I wanted you to kiss me so badly." I smiled at him.

After dinner, back in my apartment, Hank unwound some about his situation. He sat on the second bed/sofa, the one perpendicular to the one near the door, his shoulders hunched over, his hands dangling between his knees. I stood in front of him in the middle of the room.

Then, without looking at me, he said, "They're experimenting on me."

I gasped, in agony. "How do you know?"

"You wake up one morning and you know."

"Do you think it's LSD? Could that be what's affecting your mind?"

He shrugged. "It happens at night. Maybe an injection."

"What can I do?" I begged, my brow wrinkled in anxiety.

"Nothing. There's nothing that can be done. Even if you broadcast it, it would be hushed up politically plus flat denials."

I knew he was right. The great secrecy of his work would keep anything I tried to do cloaked. Beyond that, I had only his word for it. I couldn't prove anything. Lawyers would make an imbecile of me.

Then, he added, "Under President Eisenhower, the men got well."

For a long time, we were silent. That sentence kept running through my mind. The idea that surfaced, that President Kennedy allowed it, was shocking and agonizing. Then, sounding forlorn, Hank said, "I should release you, but I can't do it. I love you as much as you love me." After a second, he added, "Maybe more."

I doubted that, but refrained from saying anything. All I could do was love him, whatever happened.

When he left me that night, I saw desolation in his eyes. Somehow, instinctively, I knew that this was the last time I would ever see him. He had said that he should release me from our marriage contract though I didn't want him to. I knew he would try; I hoped unsuccessfully. He had seen the future; he knew it was no use pretending that he would get well. His correspondence might drift on a bit, but then drop off. My world fell apart.

With all he had said on my mind and the worry about him, I struggled through the days and agonized the nights, making a zombie of myself for the next two weeks, until even Frank yelled at me. Finally, early in the morning, Muriel and I taxied to Union station, kind of twittery, our trip had begun, and boarded the train headed for New York City. In New York, we had to find a porter to help us with our extraordinarily heavy luggage. Grinning at our excitement, he placed us and our luggage in a taxi. The chatty driver swerved in and out of traffic and finally deposited us on the dock beside the Queen Elizabeth, the enormous ocean-going ship that would take us to England.

We discovered that President Eisenhower and his wife were traveling with us, but in first class accommodations. We decided that we would invite them to tea, mentioning that we had been in the group of singers who entertained them at the White House one evening when the Governor of Canada was visiting. They responded with delight, but were unable to join us. However, they did invite us to their cabin for about ten minutes as the ship docked at Le Havre to let them off. We went on to South Hampton, the ship's terminus.

In London, we rented a car and drove all the way up to Inverness in Scotland. Driving along Loch Ness, we poked, probably to the annoyance of all the drivers behind us, looking for the Loch Ness Monster. Needless to say, we didn't catch a glimpse of him, not a splash or even a ripple of the bright lake water.

We spent three days sightseeing in Inverness on the east coast then started back down through the western half of the country. Wherever we felt like looking further at some small town, we simply stopped, or just found a charming little B&B for the night. Again London, the end of our adventure. A connecting train took us and many other passengers to the dock where we boarded the Queen Mary for the voyage home.

About three days out, the ship ran into the tail-end of a hurricane. Muriel and I ate dinner that night in a nearly empty dining room then rushed out on the deck to watch the storm. We clung, really clung hard, to the rail and watched that great ship plow into violent, thunderous mountains of waves then turn the bow up and slowly churn out of huge troughs of water only to plunge into another trough after reaching the top. We felt so small and our ship seemed so small out there with all that raging water. We didn't stay on deck long, but sought our stateroom.

I carried home with me an antique beer stein along with the red leather bound Episcopal Book of Common Prayer that I had bought in Westminster Abbey. I intended to give them to Hank the next time I saw him, along with the letter I wrote while staying at the North British Hotel in Edinburgh, Scotland. Relaxed and happy, my mind kept hoping I would see him and be able to give them to him personally, and not have to leave them somewhere or mail them to him. At every place we stopped, I imagined him with me, looked at the things in the shops that I thought he might like, and picked out clothes in the windows that would look good on him. I couldn't resist buying him something. Obviously, I had seen the future, but couldn't accept it.

Then, in December I received another letter.

Dec 2 '63. Dear Arabella. I know you got home from Europe safely. I feel sure you had fun and saw just about everything you wanted to.

More proof that he kept track of me through the S.S. boys.

They're trying to freeze us to death again, at least that's the way we feel. Temp 12 degrees F and snowing like H.

So, cold weather again. Why keep up the farce if they were experimenting on him? I shuddered. To keep him well enough to experiment on?

I clapped a hand over my face. "Just stop it," I said.

Have a nice holiday, Christmas that is. And take care. Cannot forecast when I'll see you.

As ever, Hank.

Too bad about J.F.K.

Yes. I had been out with a friend that night. Walking along the street, we became aware of the silence in the whole city.

Sitting on the desk chair, I continued to hold the letter in my hand and looked at it. It didn't strike me as depressing or upbeat, just a nice chatty letter.

However, after that, months went by with no word from Hank. In the spring, Frank sent me to Alaska with a Congressman who had sponsored a bill on environmental issues. "Go up a day early," he said. "You know, to get over the jet lag."

I spent a day of easy sightseeing, plus an hour's plane ride over the wildlife area out of Anchorage. To my squealing delight, I saw nesting trumpet swans.

After that excitement and a good night's sleep in Anchorage, I wandered around a small area of the Anchorage Hotel lobby at eight A.M. The transport bus to the hearing site, scheduled to leave at eight, hadn't arrived. A rotund six-footer with a broad smile and an outstretched hand hastened towards me.

In a booming voice, he said, "Have you joined our little group? I'm Bob Franklin, Congressman from Maine."

"Arabella Robbins. I'm your court reporter."

"Nice to have you aboard." He flashed his big smile at me then turned away to speak to others.

A warm feeling flooded through me, a feeling brought on by the just acquired knowledge that somebody was aware of my presence and probably would be approachable with my reporting problems. I smiled to myself, thinking, how nice not to be considered part of the machinery.

At the elementary school building in the suburbs where the bus dropped us, I inched around the edge of the densely packed crowd in the high-ceilinged, terrazzo-floored, glass-enclosed lobby then used my stenotype case as a forward wedge. I found myself in a non-descript, artificially lit, auditorium full of people, though the session would not be gaveled to order for another half hour.

How long would my cool-looking green and white cotton dress remain crisp? Once the crowd moved in, the room under the strobe arc lights could become unbearably hot. I wished I hadn't brought a sweater.

In the front of the auditorium, I set up my stenotype and looked around for the best place to sit. The Congressmen had appropriated a long table on the stage, and the usual tall floor microphone had been placed in the center aisle between the front row of seats.

"Why don't you sit on the stage at the end of the table?" a good-looking man in a tailor-fitted pin-stripped suit suggested.

Seeing me hesitate, he said, "I'm on Congressman Franklin's staff. He's chairing the committee. Come around this way." He pointed to the staircase on his right. "The first hour is going to be welcoming speeches by the state governor, Anchorage's mayor, and some important local people. They'll sit in the front row and use the floor mike. After that, we'll have a break and go into the individual statements."

In true political style, the governor praised the chairman. The chairman returned the compliments in flowery language and created a short I-can-out-flatter-you repartee. After that, the governor launched into his speech, taking a full hour. Then the mayor and the local dignitaries had to be allowed time to say more or less the same thing.

Soon after eleven o'clock, in need of a recess and aware that the audience was streaming in and out the rear exits, my gaze searched the hall for the staff man. I located him in the back with a group of glowering, gesticulating, restless people. A sixth sense told me that the irascibility involved the extended political speeches and meant no break. I shifted the machine to my left side, stretched as much as I could, and brought my full attention back to the speaker.

By the time the chairman had elaborately thanked the last politician, the clock high on the rear wall showed twelve o'clock, noon. Bending forward, his attitude one of sympathetic concern, he said, "Unfortunately, this has taken longer than expected. We are going to recess now, have a quick bite of lunch, and reconvene at twelve-thirty. We'll start right in with the individual statements. Check the lists posted in the lobby for the order in which you will speak. This includes only those who have made written requests. If there are others who wish to be heard, we'll see how much time is left after we complete the list."

In an attempt to forestall more vociferous objection, he added, "Unfortunately, we have to stop by six so we can catch our plane for Nome."

A discontented murmur swept the hall.

"We are going to hold another hearing in Nome tomorrow. We want to hear from as many Alaskans as possible on this legislation before we decide how to vote. What we do here affects all the American people." He banged the gavel. "Adjourned until twelve-thirty."

I watched him walk across the stage then shifted my gaze when I heard my name. From the chairman's vacated spot, the staff man said, "Lunch is in room one hundred eight. Hurry down there so you can get back on time."

In the lunchroom, I alternately munched a cheeseburger and checked my watch, meandering slowly around the periphery of the room.

"Arabella," the Committee Clerk called, hastening towards me, "take this iced tea and for heaven's sake go sit down. The Congressmen are going to eat here, too, and they're not going to start again until they're good and ready."

"It's been a long morning." I laid my burger on a coffee table, sat tensely on the edge of one of the chairs, took a long drink of iced tea then sank against the cushions.

"It'll be a longer afternoon, so relax." The clerk turned away to help someone else.

The six Congressmen entered, accompanied by two women. I heard one of the men say, "I don't know where my wife is. She went sightseeing with some of the Governor's people, but promised to join me for lunch."

"I wanted to hear the speeches this morning, but this afternoon will be a bore," said the brown-eyed, silvery blond woman.

The youthful Congressman standing nearby took possession of the blonde's waist. "Do you want a cheeseburger, dear, or a plain hamburger?" To the man the woman had addressed, he said, "Will you join us, Joe? Those tables"—he indicated two nicely appointed round tables on the left—"have been set up for us."

"Thanks. My wife should be along any minute."

I tried to touch my right ear to my right shoulder. It did stretch the tight muscles. I tried the left ear, but couldn't reach my shoulder. I settled back. As long as the Congressmen and their wives stayed in the lunchroom, I could stay.

Again in the auditorium, a number of college-age girls swooped by to ask how the machine worked, complain about the time the politicians had taken, and state that they, the individual speakers, would now be short-changed.

"I came all the way up here from college, where I just finished my freshman year, to testify in favor of this bill," a stringy-haired girl in fringed shorts and a slept-in looking loose blouse told me.

"I thought this was only supposed to be for the people who live here."

"Don't be silly. A lot of us have come up from the lower Forty-eight. Didn't you see all those raggedy, moth-eaten old men? They're prospectors and are against this bill. We have to beat them."

"Those prospectors in their old clothes and heavy shoes, the local people in their business suits, are fighting for their livelihood. Everyone has a right to fair competition, no matter which side they're on."

The look I got excoriated me from my combed hair to my high-heeled slippers. "Who cares about them?" the girl sneered. "They only care about money."

There being no middle ground, I found nothing to discuss. Pointedly ignoring the girls, I broke the seal on a new pad of paper and replenished my machine. Momentarily, the girls watched me then drifted off. I straightened the fold in the tray. During the morning, I had time between speakers to change the paper. This afternoon, I might have to halt the proceedings, which I hated to do.

Sometimes when I interrupted to change the pack of paper, speakers looked at me blankly, uncertain what to do, though I knew it was because they had lost their train of thought. Sometimes speakers looked my way and went right on talking. Others stopped, waited for me to finish replacing the paper then restated what they had said. Having to change the paper tape always distracted everyone involved. And if the speakers spoke rapidly, the paper would probably only last one and three-quarters hours instead of two hours.

The chairman reconvened the hearing at one forty-five. In his warm, empathetic manner, he tried to put everybody at ease by apologizing for the late hour. Late hour, I thought. You don't care about being an hour and a quarter beyond the time you specified for everybody else. Twelve-thirty didn't suit your convenience.

"Please feel free to speak your minds. We want to hear you all," he reiterated.

I decided I thought him a fake.

Twice during the grueling afternoon, I had to thread a new pack of paper into the machine and the ten-minute break at four o'clock was only a teaser. The Congressmen tried so hard, without success, to hear everybody that the last word didn't come until six fifteen, followed immediately by the rush to the airport.

I didn't realize until I unpacked my nightclothes in Nome that I had left my sweater in the Anchorage auditorium. My mood plummeted to new depths. I had bought that sweater only two weeks ago. I loved it for its warm cashmere beauty. In my depressed mood, an acute need for Hank, for his voice, his nearness, his strength, surged through me. As a result, I did not rest well.

While we waited for transportation the next morning, the chairman confronted me, his hand outstretched, a broad smile across his face. "Have you joined our little group? I'm Bob Franklin, Congressman from Maine."

"Arabella Robbins," I responded politely.

"Nice to have you aboard." He flashed his smile and hurried away.

I remembered my warm, pleased reaction to his greeting in Anchorage. What a ninny I was.

Unlike the day before, the Nome session had no political speeches, plenty of time for extra comments, and a four-thirty adjournment, assuring leisurely arrival at the airport for the flight to Fairbanks.

I cringed the next morning when Congressman Franklin started towards me. "Good morning," was my response to his outstretched hand and friendly patter. As he turned away, my glance met the laughing eyes of two committee people.

"Does he think you hire a new court reporter in every city?" I asked.

"Probably," one of them said.

"He obviously never takes a good look at those working with him."

"With his own people he does; the others don't matter."

Just as in Anchorage, the Fairbanks school auditorium was jammed. I realized from snatches of corridor conversation that those unable to make statements in Anchorage had come to Fairbanks.

Right after banging the gavel to open the hearing, the chairman announced that the committee would continue the meeting as long as necessary. "There is no plane to catch," he said, "and we will keep going until everyone who wishes to speak has had an opportunity to do so."

Involuntarily, I made a face. I expected pandemonium. Instead, the morning ran at an even pace, though steadily. I had started to number and date my notes at the luncheon break when an old, weather-beaten man in heavy work boots approached me. In his browned, leathery hand, he carried my sweater.

"Oh," I said and raised my eyes to watery slits behind which no color showed. Wisps of gray hair hung from the rim of his bald dome, but his beard grew full.

"After you left in such a hurry the other day, I saw your sweater. I figured you'd be here, so I brought it along."

"Thank you so much. How thoughtful. What a kind thing for you to do." I took the sweater from him, abashed by my effusive repetition of the same sentiment.

"That's all right. Don't think nothin' of it." He wrinkled his brow. "You think this bill'll pass?"

"I don't know. From listening, it seems pretty even. Which way do you want it to go?"

"Be defeated. I've been a prospector all my life. My cabin's not big, but it's all I've got. If this passes, I'll have to leave, get out. I won't be allowed up in them mountains no more."

"Don't you have any family you could go to?"

"Nope. All dead."

"Oh, dear." Though he had aroused my sympathy,

I was at a loss for something further to say. I couldn't do anything to help him. My position had to be neutral.

"I'm gonna testify this afternoon. I don't talk too good. Can you fix it up a little for me?"

"I can fix your grammar, things like that, but that's all."

"That's what I mean."

"I always try to do that. I'll be sure to check yours."

"Thank you, ma'am."

I watched him walk up the aisle, a sturdy mountaineer's frame, and wondered if he was as old as he looked or if his hard life had prematurely aged him. A note to check the grammar of the gray-haired prospector was quickly written, and I hurried to the lunchroom where I found an excuse to sit next to the staff man.

"The score for and against this legislation seems pretty well balanced to me," I said. "How do you think the Congressmen will be able to make a decision?"

"They all knew exactly how they were going to vote before we came up here. This is just a show for the public. It won't change their ideas one iota."

I attacked my sandwich. What a farce this whole thing was. And they had hoodwinked the local people, making them think what they said made a difference. Plus, they were spending taxpayers' money to joyride themselves. What a despicable crowd. I fumed. People like that old prospector were pouring their hearts out.

The old prospector spoke among the last of the scheduled speakers to testify. He carried a scrap of paper, which he held up to his eyes when he got to the microphone. But the tremor of his hand made him drop it. I gave him a swift smile of encouragement when he looked my way. The chairman, too, tried to put him at ease. "Just tell us slowly in your own words what you have to say," he said kindly.

The old man spoke so slowly that I corrected his grammar as he talked. Listening to his tale of life in the mountains, I seethed. It was so unfair. Here he was pleading with his heart to have his living saved, and the Congressmen wouldn't even take what he said into their calculations.

I looked at them. Some hung over the table, ostensibly intent. Others sat back, but had their eyes fixed on the speaker. I wondered if they really listened behind those concerned facial expressions or thought about their personal affairs.

At five o'clock, the chairman said, "We're going to take a break now. As I told you this morning, we'll stay as long as necessary to hear everybody. And there still are a great number. When you come back from the break, those wanting to speak line up, starting at this staircase," he pointed to the right-hand staircase, "coming along the stage and down this way." He swung his arm to the left. "Give your name to the staff man—Where is he?" The Congressman twisted to glance at the people behind him.

Instantly, the staff man reached his side.

"You stand at the end of the table," said the Congressman. "Have a microphone set up by the court reporter."

He turned to the audience. "You'll each have two minutes. Just keep moving and we'll get through."

The startled exclamation from me was swallowed by the cacophony that swept the hall at the chairman's statement.

"Buck up," said the staff man as he placed the microphone near me. "I'll help you as much as I can."

"Get them to say their names at the microphone as well as giving them to you so I can match the sounds to your list."

"I'll number the speakers consecutively. If you have to change paper, stop them."

Before the Congressmen returned from the break, people were lining up at the foot of the platform stairs behind me. I paced back and forth near my chair, motion for the sake of motion. I knew that once the panel reconvened, I would be unable to change my position until the end.

A staffer's wife ran up the steps. "Here, Arabella, I brought you a Coke."

"Gee, thanks. I really appreciate that." I sipped the drink, continued to pace, then finished the Coke in a few gulps when the chairman sat down. As the gavel struck the table, I dropped onto my chair.

From that moment until quarter of eight in the evening, I worked at full speed, chewing my lower lip, the supple movement of my fingers setting up a torque with my tense shoulders, scarcely a breather between speakers. No longer able to smile, I grimaced in concentration and held on.

The murmuring of the staff man and the people over names distracted me. I seemed cut off from the world by the good-natured, ragged line of shuffling bodies on one side of me and the line of seated Congressmen on the other side.

The hot yellow light beams in the windowless auditorium softened the tired lines of the faces around me, but drew tiny pinpoints of perspiration from shiny foreheads, drops that crept along the hairline and trickled slowly down sideburns, to be mopped by a wrinkled handkerchief pulled from a pocket in mid-sentence. Beads of perspiration formed on my forehead and the backs of my hands, not heat related, but exhaustion. When the gavel finally fell, I could no longer think.

"Get yourself a good stiff drink when you get back to the hotel," said the staff man. "You need one." He handed me the list of names, three sheets of legal pad paper. "Remember the plane takes off at nine in the morning. We leave the hotel at eight-thirty."

A tired smile was all I could manage. For a moment, he stood looking at me then took the stenotype case from my hand. "Don't forget your sweater."

I straggled unsteadily after him towards the oversized, half-full bus, the sweater over my arm and the day's notes stacked on top of it. The bus took us to our hotel. After neatly arranging my notes on the desk in my room, I headed for the bar, to order a tall whiskey and soda plus a snack before going to bed.

In the morning light, the silvery jet plane sitting on the tarmac at the Airport shimmered, hit by sunbeams that cascaded through cool, fresh air, air that made the blue of the sky a deep sapphire color, that enveloped the visible world of the soaring Alaskan landscape with brightness.

Shading my eyes, I read the large letters printed on the side of the huge plane. "The United States of America." Underneath in red, white, and blue paint, the stars and stripes stood out. A lump formed in my throat. I swallowed hard, at the same time winking to stop the inevitable tears. Some people got goosebumps when powerful emotion swept across them. I cried. Why be ashamed of the thrill? The feeling had kind of snuck up on me, surprised me. On the other hand, I found the feeling neither unpleasant nor objectionable.

The minute I stepped from the boarding staircase into the plane, I was handed a glass of champagne. Carefully juggling the lovely bubbling stuff, I found my window seat in the rear of the plane. We took off. Planting my nose firmly against the window glass, I sipped and watched the rugged Elias-Wanger Mountains below, part of the territory the bill, if passed, would make wilderness preserve. Great snow-covered peaks thrust themselves upward, pink in the morning sunlight. Purple, green, and blue streaks played around the lower shadows, shooting up crevasses to pale the moment they reached the towering ice. How glorious it all was. Hank would love it. I smiled to myself and glanced behind me just as if he were there. In fascination, I followed the changing colors until the mountains disappeared as our plane headed south.

In September of 1964, I moved into a one-bedroom apartment at 2801 Quebec Street, North West. The fourth floor end apartment facing Rock Creek Park made me feel like a queen. The entrance hall with its huge closet led me into the large living room, the bath and bedroom off a tiny hall to the left of the living room. A small, square extension of the living room at the Rock Creek Park end led into the kitchen. I gloried in the new space, more space than furniture. I went shopping.

The sofa I bought to replace the two beds I had used as sofas came upholstered in cream-colored rough fabric. It centered nicely on the only long wall in the living room.

My piano fitted perfectly across from the sofa against the wall between the dinette and the tiny hall into the bedroom. For my old apartment, I had purchased the dining room table with four chairs plus the coffee table. I didn't need to buy those. And, of course, the two twin beds went into the bedroom as beds. I spent time searching for proper bedspreads. As I intended to have the walls of the bedroom painted Chinese red, all the accessories needed to be white.

Mother gave me an antique bedroom chair. I had that upholstered in white cotton.

Of course, the living room walls and hall walls were painted the usual off-white.

The only other things I purchased immediately were one chair covered in avocado green velvet and two end tables. Everything else I needed could wait until I saved some money.

For recreation, I joined the Friday night ballroom dance group on Connecticut Avenue. Anybody who wanted to dance could pay seven dollars and dance all evening along with interspersed lessons. Dancing made the work tensions fade away, and I sparkled.

The end of November, a letter came from Hank, addressed to 1727 Mass Ave, which someone in the Post Office had scratched out in pencil along with the Apt 508, and written 2801 Quebec St., N.W.

Nov. 22, 1964. Dear Arabella: It's been a long time. How long, I have no idea. Memory-wise there's a lot to be desired, amongst other things.

So he must now be having pain along with the memory loss.

I expect to be sent in the opposite direction of Washington

D.C. in a little while. Haven't any idea when I'll be in the District again.

Hope all is well with you and yours.

As ever, Hank.

So that was it. The end had come. Without really saying so, he had released me. I couldn't imagine finding another man as wonderful as Hank. Knowing I faced a lonely life, I gritted my teeth, determined to make it an interesting one.

I would never hear from him again. Whatever his problem was, it seemed to be closing in on him. I dreaded the next few days, knowing I would think only of Hank and weep internally.

Actually, when I considered it, I knew so little about him. For both of us, our love had been so instant and all consuming that we hadn't gone into even the usual detail. I knew he had a sister that he was close to. Did she have children? Were his parents still alive? He never mentioned them. I had had a feeling that they were both dead. The only thing he had ever said involving his parents was in a restaurant one day when the waiter asked him if he wanted coleslaw. He declined. As soon as the waiter left, he said, "I hate coleslaw. I had to chop too much cabbage when I was a kid."

Of course, his name, Martz, was German. How long had his family been in America? Nothing but questions. I knew he was extremely bright, and my taste in men led to extremely bright. I suspected that the government had head-hunted him. I knew he liked the theater, and liked to dance, things that I liked. We got along well, with similar interests. He respected my independence and handled me expertly. Actually, he was much more thoughtful than I. Though all he had to do was mention a subject, and I would do whatever he wished. He would be the head of house. And I wanted it that way. Both of us seemed to have easy dispositions; we would have had a happy marriage.

True, he had a jealous streak. Or was it possessive? At breakfast one morning, he had suddenly said, "That's a man's ring you have on. Where did you get it?"

I explained that it had been my father's signet ring; that he had my initials put on it for me. Nothing more was said, but I stored away the knowledge the comment gave me.

Well, I had to make a life for myself without him. Fortunately, I loved my work and would keep at it as long as possible. As I had said to others, age, sex, or race made no difference in this business. Ability was the name of the game. And I sat on the top rung.

Right now, thank goodness for the upcoming hearing in Puerto Rico. At least the work in sunny Puerto Rico with blue sky and blue sea would distract me. My mind wouldn't dwell so much on Hank. I couldn't wait for two o'clock Sunday afternoon to leave Washington.

In June of '65, in scanning the social part of the newspaper, the name of John Parkinson jumped out at me. He had married a society girl from New York City. My heart thumped a few times. I had heard nothing of him since he walked out of my apartment. I hoped she was as nice as he deserved. I really, really meant that. And those two little boys deserved a good mother. I stopped discussing John with myself and thought of the boys. The elder should be entering the teen years. With any luck, the girl could manage him through that wild time in children's lives.

Anyway, I wished them the best of everything, especially a good marriage. Maybe they'd have a baby of their own, a little girl. Then John's wife wouldn't feel the need to push her son ahead of her stepsons.

Anyway, I decided to have some champagne with dinner and raise my glass to them.

I became a frequent visitor in Puerto Rico for U.S. Federal court cases. Two women reporters I met gadded about with me. Some of the hearings took me to the other end of the island where, on an occasional evening, I wandered to the nearby restaurant and boarded their little tourist boat. The owner motored small groups out into the phosphorescent sea. Returning to the restaurant afterwards, we ate fresh fish right off the grill for dinner.

I also traveled to Alaska and Hawaii on a regular basis. In Hawaii, I saw Ned as often as my work schedule allowed. I flew all over mainland United States for scientific meetings. I dated and partied with friends as I tried to pick up my life. The months disappeared in frantic activity.

On December 23, 1965, in my packet of mail, I found a card with familiar writing addressed to A. Robbins, 1727 Mass Ave., N.W. I held it up and looked at it. All my love for him, which I had submerged in a constant whirl of activity, came flooding to the surface. This time, his S.S. boys hadn't told him that I had moved, or he could no longer remember what they told him. On the other hand, did he have to remember to ask them to check on me? I didn't know. Thoughts of how he might be mentally devastated me.

The fold-up card showed a long Christmas tree decorated with nice little wishes. On the bottom, he had written, "It's been a long time, Hank."

For days, my heart bled for him. So much of our few

months together traveled around my mind, things I had pushed down, tried not to think about. The least little thing kept them swarming back. I had to live with it, learn to love him without the sadness. True, I had started seeing other men, but Hank was and always would be the great love of my life. In fact, I told any man I saw more than three times that I had already met and lost the great love of my life.

The first few days of 1966 turned the whole east coast into a deep freeze. The birds sat on bare tree branches looking twice their size, their feathers fluffed up. Then a snowstorm blew in from the south and paralyzed the city. The small, dry flakes that descended lazily down around midnight on the eighth, turned into fat, wet flakes by morning. The weather casters were predicting a foot of snow by evening. Many struggled to work in spite of the government's liberal leave policy. By the middle of the afternoon, the city panicked, and the government shut down.

As far as I was concerned, nothing of interest happened the whole month other than that storm. The usual hearings went on in the usual monotonous repetition. Charlie Stevens bought out Mrs. Henderson's agency when she retired. So Charlie and his contentedly pregnant wife Irene moved back to New York.

The first Monday of February, Frank stormed into my typing room. "Arabella, I don't know what I'm going to do with you."

I blinked, and pulled my eyebrows together. "What have I done?"

"Every order that comes in here requests Arabella Robbins. I have no work for anybody else."

I lowered my eyelids and grinned.

"I'm partly serious, Arabella. There are times when I simply have to send somebody else because you're busy." He shrugged. "Anyway, some woman called, very insistent, very concerned that she be given the most competent reporter in the agency. And she had your name. She wants a reporter for one week in Accra, Ghana, West Africa."

My mouth opened and my chin dropped.

"Nice. Right?"

"What's the subject?"

"Population—over-population."

"Interesting. When?"

"The first week of March."

My face lit up. "I'd like to go the week before, Frank, and visit some of the game parks."

"I think I can let you do that. It is a great opportunity. Where would you like to go?"

"Fly into Nairobi and visit Tree Tops, the animal viewing place, maybe take a two-day bus trip through the Great Rift Valley."

"How do you know so much about Africa?"

"It fascinates me. I read."

"Okay. Is that all?"

"No. I'd like to travel by bus down to Johannesburg to the diamond mines and on down to Durban on the Indian Ocean. From there, I could fly to Ghana."

Frank shook his head. "You're beyond me. I'll have to find out the round-trip fare to Ghana then schedule your other flights. You'll have to pay for those."

"Right."

For days, Frank helped me map out my trip. I walked

around in a twitter. He laughed at me. He even made my reservation for one night at Tree Tops, the famous animal watering hole in Kenya. "I'm told," he said, "their bus picks you up in the early afternoon and takes you to Tree Tops. You have afternoon tea on the roof of the place where wild baboons join you."

"I don't know that I'd like that," I said.

"Later, you eat an elaborate dinner before spending the night gazing out the panoramic window at the floodlit watering hole."

"Oh my goodness."

Frank went to the airport with me. He feared I would lose my stenotype in my excitement. He didn't let me have it until I had to board the Pan Am plane.

"Now, don't leave it on the plane when you get off," he said as he turned to go back to the office.

It turned into a spectacular trip. I loved the meeting itself as well as living at the university, sleeping in a dormitory room, eating very different, but delicious, meals, even taking a trip into town to see their supreme court. I also chatted with a judge about their reporting system of tape recording, and toured the game parks at the end of the conference before going home. Really, I thought my job fabulous.

Towards the end of the year, the National Governors' Association met in Ohio. Two State Special Forces Officers met my plane, carried my equipment, and led me to the Governor's private plane for the trip to the lake-district conference site. I loved the royal treatment, but felt rather amazed at my luck, thinking somebody had made a mistake.

Thirty-One

It was a brisk morning in March 1974 when I arrived at the Dirksen Senate Office Building. Entering from the First Street side, I flashed my badge at the guard and set out in search for Hearing Room 416. The building lacked the grandeur and elegance of the Capitol Building itself, but still felt prestigious. While Senate staffers busied themselves going from office to office, an occasional senator appeared, speaking to someone in whispered tones and then departing quickly. I could not help but smile at the knowledge that I had been personally requested to transcribe a meeting of the Senate Select Committee on Health Practices and Policies. I had to admit that it sounded a bit boring, but it was scientific-based work, which I enjoyed, and I was eager to delve into something new.

Among the rows of benches reserved for the senators, a small chair and table had been set up for me at the side of the room. A few papers were waiting on the table: an agenda, a list of names, senators and witnesses, and opening remarks by the chairman, or "chairperson," as I guess we had begun calling a woman in that position. I clicked my stenotype into place on its stand and threaded the paper tape through the rollers so it would refold in the holding tray. Ordinarily I would have hummed to myself while I set up, but I focused instead on controlling my breathing and having extra materials at the ready. One pack of paper would be enough for two hours, but I opened a second pack and laid it on the table beside me within easy reach, just in case. I could not imagine interrupting a Senate hearing for something as menial as not having enough tape.

The senators and their aides began to file in and there was a sort of nervous energy as people settled in, putting their briefcases on the tables and shuffling through documents.

At precisely ten o'clock, Senator O'Malley, the Committee Chairperson and the only female member of the Senate, arrived. When they spotted her, everyone fell silent. She was portly and had a short haircut, making her look mannish. Looking back, she embodied the kind of fashion trend that women later utilized in the 1980s to show that they were capable of working beside the world's most powerful men. Only Harriet really was. Her shoulder pads seemed to confirm that she was aware of the prestige her position warranted, and that she was willing to prove she deserved it.

She had a pleasant but serious mien when she took the podium. "Hello everyone, I'm Senator Harriet O'Malley. It's nice to see so many of you here to represent the medical profession and to work with the government in relation to such a sensitive dilemma. I know this hearing was scheduled rather quickly and I appreciate my colleagues—and indeed everyone's—effort to rearrange things."

I captured every word, not sure if the hearing had officially begun.

"Before we get started I feel that it is necessary to point out a few things. Some of you may know that I have been interested in pursuing the truth about a number of events that took places years ago. I and others believe that the Army, the CIA and other military and intelligence offices were involved in a cover-up about medical procedures performed on American citizens. Since this came to my attention, I have been firm in my belief that this must not be kept from the American people.

"I tried to get my colleagues on other perhaps, more, um, relevant committees to take this up and they have refused to get involved. Even after this hearing was called, the Department of Defense refused to send a representative."

"Senator O'Malley."

The ranking member of this committee, Senator Peter Riley looked up from his papers. "Defense did not refuse, but were not prepared to attend on such short notice. I would like to add my voice to those who think that this committee is not the proper venue for a hearing of this nature."

"Well, we're having it," was Senator O'Malley's curt response.

I took a deep breath. This was certainly not what I expected.

O'Malley waited a few moments for the rumbling to die down. "Now, we will begin with testimony from Dr.

Robert Hocking, Research and Development from the National Center for Health Services."

Dr. Hocking rose from his seat in the witness line and walked calmly toward the podium. He seemed at ease even in front of this crowd.

Senator O'Malley passed him the red leather-bound Bible and asked, "Doctor Hocking, do you solemnly swear the testimony that you will give before this committee will be the truth, the whole truth, and nothing but the truth?"

"I do." Doctor Hocking place his dossier on the table before repeating his name and department for the record. I typed at a steady, even pace, taking down everything.

"Do you have a statement to make?"

"Only a brief one, Senator." Hocking read from a paper. "I have brought with me today documents about a series of government-sponsored experiments that began in 1952. My office has consulted with the Attorney General's office and they have instructed me, through our attorney here, Mr. Paxton, to make clear that I am authorized to release only materials that are not classified, or have been deemed no longer classified and that neither I nor my department can be responsible for any documents or facts that are still classified."

"Hmm. We'll see." Senator O'Malley said. "What was your part in these experiments, Doctor?"

"I joined the NCHS in 1959 and was assigned a research position sponsored by the United States military and other agencies of monitoring several subjects who had been subjected to radiation and then treated with chelating agents to determine if there was any treatment or even a cure for radiation poisoning. The first goal of these experiments was in its potential for helping combat troops in particular. Later, the scope was widened to any American who might be exposed to nuclear radiation.

"At some point, a small group who had responded well to treatment were tested with Lysergic acid diethylamide, or LSD. This was eventually dropped when we learned that the British were conducting much more extensive research."

"Where did these experiments take place, Doctor?"

"The original testing took place at our facility at Oak Ridge, Tennessee. The LSD experiments are still classified. I should make clear that I did not perform any experiments. I was only in charge of monitoring the subjects afterward."

Senator O'Malley shook her head. "Well, what do you know about the experiment that took place before you joined this research team?"

"The subjects were 147 men who presented with various symptoms to hospitals in New York City, Cincinnati, San Jose and Salt Lake City. They were asked to volunteer for experimental treatments."

The senator paused to clarify the information we'd all just heard. "Dr. Hocking, let me make sure I understand. These are *American citizens* we are taking about?"

Dr. Hocking nodded his agreement.

"Doctor?"

"I'm sorry, Senator. Yes, they were all Americans."

I typed, not sure what to make of the unexpected testimony we heard. I struggled to maintain my accuracy.

"And these men gave their consent to be part of these experiments?"

Hocking hesitated. "Yes... well, no. They had volunteered, but they had to be unaware of the specific treatments so they could not taint the findings."

"So the NCHS and the military performed experiments on these men without their knowing it, Doctor?"

"Yes, Senator," he answered, sensing that this information was not going to be well received by the committee.

There was a quiet murmur growing from the crowd. I could not stop myself from gasping. Those poor men. A doctor on my left looked over at me. I was afraid he was going to express disapproval at my unprofessional outburst, but he nodded and his wide eyes told me that he too was shocked.

"And what were your criteria for choosing these test subjects, Doctor?"

After a moment the doctor continued, "We chose men between the ages of 25 and 40 who were unmarried, traveled for work—government work where possible—and originally presented with minor flu-like symptoms. The age and independent lifestyle were important factors to mimic the life of the soldiers as well as to decrease the possibility of inquiring families."

I could feel my heart racing and I had to concentrate on hearing the testimony over the pounding. I could not fully comprehend how much thought had gone into the experiments before they even started—choosing men without families so they wouldn't have to answer to worried wives.

The senator remained calm and focused as she continued her questioning. "This certainly sounds very well thought out. Could you give us a little detail about how these experiments were conducted?"

"After the men were given penicillin to prevent opportunistic infections, the men received up to eight large, but not deadly, doses of radiation to induce radiation poisoning. Immediately following the first signs of symptoms, they began to be treated with various chelating agents and other medical compounds as well."

For the first time, Senator Romano, from New York, spoke. "This clearly constitutes a moral failure on the part of the United States. To do these things to Americans is not only unacceptable, but criminal."

Dr. Hocking became tense. "Senator, as I said, I was not involved in performing these experiments, but..."

At that moment, Mr. Paxton, the attorney next to him, touched Dr. Hocking on the arm, whispered in his ear.

"As I said, I wasn't involved in the experiments, only in monitoring their continuing treatment. But with all due respect, Senator, I believe these men to be heroes, not victims. They may not have known exactly what they were going to be subjected to, but they knew it had the potential to be dangerous..."

Then, an odd thing happened. While I focused on doing my job accurately recording the proceeding, his name popped into my head, clearly as if it had been spoken.

"Hank."

I jumped, accidentally dropping my tape and causing all eyes to look over at me. I made a motion to indicate I was having a technical problem and then fumbled to set everything right. I took a few deep breaths and gave a signal that I was ready to continue.

At that moment I realized that I had let my own thoughts interfere with my work. I paused for a second, and immediately tried to assess how much I'd missed.

"What happened to these men after receiving these treatments, Doctor?"

"By the time I joined the research team approximately two years after this test group received its first rounds of radiation, many of the test subjects were beginning to show adverse effects from the radiation. Some of the men became disoriented and were unsure of their surroundings, their immune systems were compromised so they were sick much of the time, and some had terrible bouts of nausea. They were prone to..."

Again, Hank's name came to me, but this time I could clearly see his face. How I missed him.

"If these men went on about their normal lives, and were not locked in a lab, how did you monitor them effectively?" Senator O'Malley asked.

I really couldn't tell if I'd lost focus for a few minutes or much longer. I marked the text where I'd lost track and then began frantically typing, forcing myself to concentrate on what was being said.

"With the aid of the Social Security Administration I kept track of where they were going, how their symptoms were progressing, which cognitive and physical impairments were improving or worsening and whether or not they seemed to be recovering from the radiation, however slowly.

"By the end of 1959 about 85% of the test participants were hospitalized. Due to the highly classified nature of the tests, the government had to move them often to prevent any medical staff from guessing the true cause of their symptoms. Test subjects were regularly filtered into military-run hospitals in small towns like those in Pinehurst, North Carolina and Davis, Alabama."

Pinehurst? With the mention of that place, the gnawing feeling that had been growing in my stomach since the beginning of the meeting came to a head. Sitting in this room, I was listening to Hank's story, the whole awful truth. I felt the blood rush to my face and took a deep breath, hoping to calm myself before my flushed visage attracted any attention.

I made a conscious choice to put Hank out of my mind and focus on work. My reputation as a reporter and the reputation of the agency depended on me keeping my composure at least until the group broke for lunch. As the testimony proceeded I continued typing.

"What were some of the symptoms associated with the experiments?"

"Disorientation, hot and cold flashes, internal bleeding, and of course, considerable pain."

"Of course," Senator O'Malley said mockingly.

Dr. Hocking did not acknowledge her comment. "Many subjects had back pain in particular."

What these poor men had to withstand! It all sounded positively terrible. But I could not let myself dwell on it. Instead, I concentrated on typing as accurately as I could.

"And none of these men are still alive?"

"No, Senator. I kept track of all 147 subjects until the last man died in 1965."

"And can you tell us their names?"

"I have a list of all of the subjects, but it remains classified. You and the members of the committee may review it privately."

Senator Riley spoke up. "Could we wrap this up now?" He looked at his watch. "I have another important meeting to attend right after lunch."

O'Malley looked around at the other senators, who were already beginning to gather their things. "All right."

She wrapped a gavel with a defeated sigh. "This committee is adjourned, for today."

As the senators and medical professionals hustled out, some appeared unsettled by what they had just learned. But others, many others, seemed nonchalant. I suppose years and years in the Senate would make one unaffected. After attending dozens, if not hundreds, of classified meetings, even I was often detached when it came to these hearings. But this time I was distraught, thinking about Hank volunteering for this horrible study, being subjected to these treatments—if one could call them that—all because he happened to catch the flu.

I turned off my machine and began to pack up my things. I had to think of a way to see that document. I knew in my heart that Hank had been among this group, but I had to be completely sure.

Dr. Hocking was standing with his attorney and a few others having what seem to be a jovial conversation. They seemed so casual, while I was overwhelmed thinking about the things Hank went through.

I clenched my jaw and walked over to the witness table. I waited patiently for a break and then introduced myself.

"Hello, Dr. Hocking. I'm Arabella Robbins. I'm doing the reporting."

"Ah, yes. I noticed that you were having a few problems with your equipment."

I smiled. "That's why I wanted to speak with you. I was wondering if I might be able to peruse your statement. Unfortunately with the technical difficulties, I missed some of the testimony." I showed him the markings on the text where I had lost my concentration. "I am a bit of a perfectionist, and part of the reason I'm so sought after as a reporter is my accuracy. I'd like to make sure that I have all of the testimony before I turn in my transcript."

Hocking hesitated. "Well, Ms. Robbins, I'm not sure..."

I pointed to the folder on the desk. "I could just have a look right here."

"You understand the sensitivity of the some of the information, don't you?"

"Oh yes, Doctor. I deal with classified information all the time. That's just one of the reasons I am so highly sought after for these proceedings. Don't worry; I'll be very discreet."

"I guess that would be okay," he relented. "My notes are on top."

"Thanks." I sat down with a note pad.

Within seconds, he was again engaged in conversation. I began to scribble, nonsense probably, while discreetly looking through his papers. I forced myself to remain calm.

Finally on page seven or eight, I found it. The test subjects in alphabetical order. It was stamped "classified."

I took a deep breath and scanned and there it was:

Martz, Henry. Deceased.

So now I knew. I struggled to keep my composure as I read Hank's name on that paper. At last, what I had felt all these years had finally been confirmed. Hank had been part of a government experiment and had died as a result. I felt an overwhelming sadness to think about what Hank went through. But I also felt a sense of closure that was so...freeing. I could finally stop wondering.

Still, my love for Hank was like no other love I had experienced. In that way I was, and still am, captive to him after all this time. I chose not to read the specifics of his symptoms and his part in the experiments. Instead I closed the door on that part of my life. Hank would not want me to relive that part of our past. I shifted it into the deep, hidden recesses of my mind. My life would be long; I intended to live it well. Hank would be proud of me.